THE GRAY ANGEL

BY M.C. VAUGHN

SPLINTERED INFINITY PRESS, LLC.   LOCUST GROVE, GEORGIA, USA

Acknowledgements:
First of all, many thanks to my family for continuing to allow me to pursue my true passion. Thanks also for trusting me when I decided to retire from my first career and begin my second one. I hope to repay your trust.

As always, special thanks to Danny Simanjaya for the wonderful cover art. I've been stalled completing this novel and dealing with COVID; Danny, I hope to see you again soon and start on the Next Big Thing. Danny can be found on DeviantArt as Simonjova. I cannot recommend, or praise, his work as highly as it deserves.

There have been a number of friends and relatives who have cheered me on, given good advice, and helped me keep my ship righted throughout the last three years… I haven't, and probably never can, express proper gratitude to all of you. Sheri & Steve Ruland deserve special mention for making their home available for celebrating even my minor success. Geoff Palmer, Rob & Rachel Moore, Ben Herr, Chris & Angela Seckinger, as well all of you who turned up to congratulate me for Monolith and Phoebe – thank you all. It has been deeply appreciated.

This book is dedicated to the memory of those lost in the past eighteen months to the COVID pandemic, and with thanks to every single individual who braved those conditions to keep us all alive and fed. Special thanks to those who worked with me in my career job right to the end. Gideon, Jaimie, Pat, Josh, Lashawn, Patti – you're wonderful. Thanks, all of you, and everyone else over the last 35 years.

In memory of James W. Stobie, 1984-2017. See you on the westbound.

ISBN #978-1-7334531-4-1
eBook ISBN #978-1-7334531-5-8
LOC # 2021920543

THE GRAY ANGEL

Prelude

Summer 2023

WILEY GRANT SAT ON THE EDGE of his bunk, staring at the floor of his cell, wondering – as he had for the past two months – what had actually happened in the lab.

Jason had been on the comm with his chick, and hadn't answered the IM ping; he'd waited almost fifteen minutes, but no response came. He'd finally had to get up and go before he crapped his pants.

He'd been squatting on the shitter when the rumble came, shaking dust loose from the ceiling tiles, closely followed by two explosions that sounded more like giant handclaps than anything else. Within ten seconds he had been back in the hall, panicked, a half-squeezed turd overfilling his already-strained briefs, staring at the blown-out wreckage that was all that remained of his station.

He'd known he was screwed, and had run out of there as fast as he could. He had managed to get home, clean himself up at least somewhat, and start packing when the government guys had come in. It had taken less than an hour.

They brought him in to a place he'd never known existed – a sub-basement of the building where, if he remembered correctly, the Criminal Justice department was housed – and questioned him pretty hard. He'd told them everything he knew. He knew better than to try to lie to anyone capable of tracking him down that quickly. After that, they'd put a bag on his head, driven him about two hours away, and then thrown him in this cell.

About once every week, they'd come back, questioning him about different details of the explosion, or some of the specs on the bridge. He wondered at times about that; Tinsworth, at least, could have told them anything they wanted to know. He answered as best he could. And then they threw him back in his cell.

At least, he thought, he wasn't in a typical prison; he guessed that this was a temporary facility. At first, he had hoped that he might be released after they finished questioning him, but after he'd asked a couple of times when they would be letting him go, and gotten no answer, he'd been dumb enough to start mouthing about his rights. The guy who appeared to be in charge – some military higher-up, from the look of him – had been very clear about one thing: Wiley was better off where he was than he would be if they turned him over to the police.

They had told him Anderson was killed in the explosion, and that with Wiley gone from his post without leave, he would be charged with involuntary manslaughter. It would be a slam-dunk case (they even showed him the camera feed that had caught him leaving his post, no more than two minutes before the blast), and he'd be in the regular prison system for the next five years after that. But they didn't stop there.

"Once you're in the lockup, I will make sure I find the biggest, meanest convict-fucking bastard in that entire facility to share a cell with you. You'll be the biggest prison bitch on earth," the guy had said, with a glare that only made it clearer that he meant every word.

So Anderson was dead, but something hadn't added up. He'd been racking his brains as best he could, trying to come up with any explanation that would account for what had happened, but finding none. There shouldn't have been that much energy in the wormhole, to begin with – not even close. The generators controlling the magnetic field might have been able to cause some sort of explosion, but Colonel Mangum and his assistant, Major Eier, had told him that they had been undamaged.

And that, he had since realized, was the reason they were still holding him here. They had no explanation for where the energy from the explosion had come – even Tinsworth, apparently, had not been able to account for it.

The last time he had been questioned, he had made that point, and also tried to make the case that he would never have left his station unattended if he had known that such an event was even possible. The colonel hadn't looked impressed, but after he made that observation, they had been willing to share more information on the blast. It had started in Williams Hall, instead of in his station in Hampton, and had taken out most of Anderson's lab. The connecting tunnel between the two buildings had partially collapsed from the force of the explosion in Williams, forcing the air into his lab like a tube being squeezed.

Seeing pictures of what had happened, he realized just how devastating it had been, and for the first time, he felt genuinely sorry for Anderson. He had probably died in a lot of pain, unless it had been immediate. He said little at the time, and Mangum and Eier had not been forthcoming as to his own status, but he had sensed for the first time that he might still be able to extricate himself from his situation, assuming he could prove his dereliction had not caused the disaster that had followed.

His stomach growled. The food wasn't terrible – someone was having it brought in from one of the local fast food joints – but it was never enough. Wiley was used to eating enough for two, which was a major contributing factor to his size and appearance. He had been foolish enough to complain about his meals only once; after that, for the next five days, he had been served TV dinners. Unheated TV dinners.

At least they had finally relented, after he had begged for better food at the next questioning session. That bastard Mangum had looked pretty amused. But he didn't dare act anything other than grateful, and he knew he had better try to find some way to explain what had actually happened. Prison food, he was sure, was a shit-ton worse than what he was receiving.

Still, dinner wasn't for another hour – or so he guessed; he didn't have much way of telling time. It was distracting, because once he started feeling hungry, that affected his ability to think about much else, and he really needed to focus on what had happened in the lab.

Try as he might, he still couldn't imagine anything that would have caused the explosion. Anderson had been on the comm, but that had probably been with that girlfriend of his. If something had come up – Wiley had to admit it – he would have had the sense to tell her to wait while he handled it.

Wiley had been sitting with his forehead resting on his hands; now his head jerked up. Random lines of thought were cascading through his mind, all pointing in one direction: had the girlfriend – Phoebe, her name was – been a terrorist? Had she planted a bomb in the lab?

She hadn't seemed the type to do something like that, Wiley guessed – but another voice in his head whispered that you could never tell. Someone might have gotten to her, or threatened her family, or maybe offered her money.

He'd have to ask. He was already sure that the explosion wasn't caused by the bridge itself. An outside source had to be the answer – but if that was the case, they knew he wasn't the cause. So why were they holding him here?

That one was obvious: they wanted to find out what he knew. And that meant that they didn't have her. Didn't it?

The door they used to slide his food trays in had opened. Without thinking about it, he blurted loudly, "Tell them I think the girl did it!"

There was no visible reaction; the tray slid in as it always did. He sighed. Chicken tenders and fries had once been a favorite of his, but now they comprised about half his meals, and after two months he had grown pretty tired of them.

More out of habit and hunger than through any actual desire for it, he began to eat his unsatisfactory dinner, hoping against hope that the flunky with the tray would somehow pass the word up the food chain.

PART ONE – THE FUGITIVES

Chapter One

2023

JASON ANDERSON JERKED AWAKE from a nightmare, sweat-bathed and panting as through he had just run a race. He felt Phoebe next to him on their hide-a-bed as she turned slightly, and whispered his name.

He passed his hand over his brow, willing himself to slow his gasps for breath. He sensed Phoebe listening to him; their hideout was pitch-black at night and almost as dark even during the day, at least when the lights were off.

"Was it the same dream?" she whispered.

Jason drew in a deep breath, held it as he counted to ten, and then let it out slowly before he responded. "Yeah."

She sat up in bed beside him, taking a deep breath of her own. "And you still feel like you haven't slept."

"Not at all." Jason's eyes closed, not that that made much difference to what he could see. "I feel like I've been awake for the last two months."

Phoebe did not respond immediately. Her silence could not mask the calculations he knew she was making. Seconds passed.

"You know you can't keep this up much longer. *I* can't keep this up much longer. I'm afraid you're going to have a nervous breakdown. You might even die of exhaustion, if you're not getting any real sleep."

Jason sighed, and sat up next to her. "I know. I'm beginning to think I might have to go back, but I don't think even that will cure the problem. It would just make things a lot worse. For both of us," he added after a beat. Phoebe noticed.

"Jason, you were always a bit selfish." She sighed again. "I know, whoever's after you is going to be looking for me, too. But we just can't keep going like this much longer. We're both miserable here. This isn't a life worth living. If you really saved my life, is this what you wanted for us?"

His head bowed for a moment. "No. Nothing like this. But this was the best I was ever going to be able to do, at least for now." He sighed. "Sometimes I can't believe that this is the only way you and I can ever be together – but then I remember everything else that happened. This really is our one chance."

"If this is the only way, then at least let me try to reach Al. You need something to help you sleep, and his people didn't stock sleeping pills here."

"Of course they didn't. They're preparing for an apocalypse or a war of some kind, and there won't be any room for addicts or drunks when it happens."

A brief silence ensued. Jason could almost hear the scales clinking as she weighed her next words.

"Jason, I've got to get in touch with Al, and see if he can find someone who can bring you some sleeping pills. You've barely slept since we got here. You're so agitated when you're awake that you can't do anything.

"We're five hundred miles from Atlanta. It's been two months. If they haven't found us by now, then our trail has probably gone cold," she said. "You said you were going to try to do some writing, but you haven't even been able to do that."

"I know," Jason replied miserably. "The only thing we've been able to do was to send that letter from Knoxville on our way up."

Phoebe thought. "We haven't heard anything else about that since then. The government probably squashed any investigation they might have tried."

They were silent again for a few seconds, until Jason finally blurted, "I'm going to have to call Dr. Tinsworth, sooner or later."

It was too dark for him to see it, but Phoebe paled. "What do you think he'll say?"

"I don't know." He sighed. "I knew Wiley was going to be in deep shit, but beyond that, I'm not even sure if Tinsworth knows I'm alive. DARPA probably knows – if they checked the cameras and recognized us, then they definitely know, and the ATM cameras probably tipped them off too. But I don't know if Mangum and Eier are close enough to Tinsworth to tell him." Another sigh. "I'm betting that they did, so that they could tell him what to do if I reach out to him."

"The GPS on your phone is off. They can't track you that way."

"They can trace the signal well enough. If I call him, I'll have to be away from here, far enough that they can't find me easily. I'd say at least twenty miles. I'd have to make the call, and get out of there fast." Jason thought for a moment. "If I can find a taxi service that will take cash, that could do it. I could take a taxi down to…" his voice trailed away as he thought, then resumed as he snapped his fingers. "Hamilton. That's far enough away, and it's closer to Cincinnati than it is to Dayton. Even if they trace me there, they're more likely to think we'd be hiding in the bigger city."

Phoebe hesitated. Jason had become more animated than he had been in weeks, and the change was welcome, but she worried that desperation might be goading him into acting rashly. Still, they needed to do something – anything – to break him free of the malaise that had come over him.

Even in the blackness, she realized that she wore a smile she didn't feel. "Let's wait one day, and see how you feel about it after you think it through."

He drew another deep breath. "All right, but I think this might be the best thing I can do. At the least, I can explain that Wiley didn't cause the explosion, if they haven't figured that out already."

She nodded to herself, and then asked, "do you think you'll be able to go back to sleep?"

"I hope so. I'm dead tired." Jason was oddly silent after he replied, as if he had somehow made an unintended double-entendre. Phoebe waited for him to speak again, as she knew he would; she had noticed that he often paused similarly after making mordant references that implied his death, and that also worried her. He had never before seemed even remotely suicidal to her, but that had been before they had gone on the run.

"I'm going to try to get some more sleep." She could hear him as he lay back onto their thin mattress, covering himself with the sheet and the barely-adequate blanket. Phoebe breathed a sigh of relief, and curled up beside him; he drew her close with his arm, and held her.

They had been less intimate since the accident, she reflected, even as she snuggled closer to him. He had been both more present and more distant than before; he paid her much more attention, and was much more mindful of her needs than he had ever been. Still, the trauma he had suffered – whatever it had been – had created a pool in his mind that was stocked with memories he simply would not discuss with her.

At least he was trying, Phoebe mused, and wriggled close enough to kiss his chin. Even when he was exhausted from lack of sleep, or clearly reliving some terrible memory of the lab, he would try to pull himself out of it. That, more than anything, was why she wanted him to make the call, and to change what had become an almost inert existence. Deep down, she feared that if he did not make the attempt soon, he might never be able to bring himself to do it at all.

Jason had whispered something as she thought, and she made a noise as if she had been nearly asleep, and then whispered back: "what was that, baby?"

There followed a pause of one breath, and then he answered: "Don't ever forget that I love you."

THEY WERE FORCED TO WAIT until someone entered the building the next morning before Jason made his way out of the storage unit. He had been out only twice since they had arrived, and Phoebe had been concerned that his fear of discovery might cause him to develop agoraphobia, but he had seemed fairly assured. The delay was simply to ensure that no one noticed that the first person seen on any camera in the place that day was leaving, rather than entering.

He had decided exactly where he wanted to go: half a mile north of their hiding place was an old full-service gas station that still had a working pay phone. There were others that were closer – the storage unit had actually had a map of them – but Jason was concerned that he might be caught on a parking lot or store camera. Catching a cab from the gas station would also seem less odd than some of the other options he had.

Once they knew they were no longer alone in the storage center, Jason had gone to the nightstand beside their bed, removed a false bottom that the unit's owner had shown them, and retrieved enough money to more than cover the twin cab fares. Jason had decided that he would say he was having car trouble and needed a ride back to Cincinnati, go as far as Hamilton, and then tell the cabdriver to turn around and bring him back. He would call Tinsworth right after pretending to receive a text telling him his car was repaired. If pressed, he would claim to be a student at Xavier, and that he could be dropped off on campus there.

Phoebe secretly believed he was being excessively paranoid, but she said nothing, and their kiss before he left felt almost the way their kisses had before he had been named to the bridge project. She sighed, a little sadly, and returned to the storage unit. After closing the door, and waiting until he was several minutes away, she went to retrieve her travel bag. It was unpacked, sitting atop a row of shelves, and was ostensibly empty – but it had been a gift from Al when they left, and a message inside it had told her the reason he had given it to her.

She felt along the handles until she found the telltale lump, four inches long and about half as wide, that was sewn between the wide strap and the bag itself, and squeezed it along the strap until it emerged at a gap in the seam. It was a small flip-phone, ridiculously out of date, but unused – and, she hoped, untraceable. She stared at it for a few moments until she gathered enough courage to open it and power it on.

It took her a few moments to work out how to open the contacts list on the thing, and when she finally succeeded, there was only one number listed. Al's message had been clear: she was only to call him on that phone. He had a similar phone that he kept strictly to receive calls from her. She would always initiate contact – he did not want to risk giving up her location if someone obtained his phone. If anyone called her, she was to ignore it, and after the caller hung up, erase the record of the call from the call log. The external speaker on the phone had been removed – Al had not wanted Jason to know he had given it to her.

She paused, remembering what the message had said:

"Phoebe, you say Jason is a good man, and I want to believe you – but I've heard a few things about some of the projects going on at your school, and I don't want to risk leaving you with him without anyone knowing where you are or where to find you. I've watched good people turn into the worst kind of monsters. The system sucks them in and destroys them. If that's happened to him, you could be in real danger.

"Call me if you need me. I will find you, wherever you are, and I will make sure you're safe. I love you."

The message had not been signed. Phoebe stared down at the phone, hesitating, before selecting the lone contact. Within seconds, she heard his phone ringing, and held her breath.

Al picked up on the third ring and spoke without preamble: "Are you all right? Are you hurt?"

Phoebe's eyes teared, and she took a deep breath, but then she answered, "I'm all right. We're safe, but Jason's not sleeping. I don't think he's slept more than an hour or two a night since we got here. I need to know if you know someone who might be able to get him something to help with that."

There was silence on the other end of the line for several seconds. Phoebe waited. Finally Al answered, "I don't normally deal in drugs of any kind. Too dangerous, and anyway, I need my head clear. What do you need?"

"Some kind of sleeping pill, I think. Just something to knock him out enough so that he doesn't wake up in the middle of the night from nightmares."

"Has he told you anything about them?" Al's question was just slightly probing. Phoebe sighed.

"He still hasn't said much about what happened. I can't make any sense of it. He's so worried about whoever might be chasing him that he doesn't want them after me too."

Al was quiet for a few seconds. "Has he been treating you well?"

"Yes. He's actually been much better than he was before. But I think the strain, and the lack of sleep, is going to break him if he can't get some relief." Phoebe hesitated. "I know you're worried he'll hurt me, but I really don't think he would. Not ever."

There was another brief silence, and then Al replied, "I'm going to drive up there tomorrow. I can get something that should help him sleep, but I want to talk with him. I want to be dead sure that you're right about him. If he can't tell you what's going on, maybe he can tell me." He hung up before she could answer.

Phoebe stared at the phone for a moment before remembering his warning. It took her several more minutes to figure out how to delete the call from the log. When that was done, and when the phone was safely tucked away in her bag again, she looked around the cramped unit for a few seconds, then lay face-down on the bed, her face buried in her pillow, as her tears finally overwhelmed her last efforts to control them.

Chapter Two

JASON WAITED AT THE STATION beside the pay phone, trying to be inconspicuous. He pretended to use his own phone, which was actually turned off, as he tried to kill the fifteen minutes that the cab company had told him he would have to wait for his ride. He knew that his use of the pay phone would look incongruous; he simply hoped no one was watching too closely.

It had been long enough since he had been out, and he was so worried about being followed, that he found it almost impossible to act nonchalant. He felt like a drunk trying to hide his inebriation at a traffic stop, except that everyone he saw was a potential police officer. He had no way of knowing whether he had been followed, or whether he – and Phoebe – were truly safe.

It seemed like much longer than the promised fifteen minutes, but was in fact only a little more than ten, when the yellow cab turned into the parking lot. Jason tried to wave without drawing too much attention to himself, but then realized that that would defeat the purpose of the gesture.

"Ah, shit," he grumbled, and waved more visibly; the cab had stopped next to one of the pumps, but moved toward him at his signal. As it drew near, he could see that the driver's window was down. A thin, dark-skinned, Arabic-looking man peered back at him as he brought the vehicle to a stop.

"Cincinnati, right? And paying cash?" Jason asked as genuinely as he could. The driver looked slightly nonplussed, but nodded in agreement, and a minute later, Jason was in the back of the cab, and they were making their way through the suburbs of Dayton.

Jason was momentarily concerned when he realized that instead of taking Interstate 75, the driver was heading south on Highway 4, but then he relaxed; I-75 was likely to be worse in terms of traffic, and their current route would bring them closer to Hamilton. Just to make sure, he asked the cabbie, "Traffic bad on 75?"

The cabbie didn't look back, but pointed instead toward a display in the center of his dashboard; it showed a traffic map of southeastern Ohio, with a red stretch of road plainly visible just south of Dayton, and a second stretch outside Cincinnati.

"Bad wreck in West Carrollton." The driver's speech was accented but intelligible. Jason nodded, and sat back as the cab made its way out of the city onto Germantown Pike. Jason sighed; he would have to wait at least an extra half-hour to make his call. Still, he thought, he would have less to worry about than he would on I-75.

The Dayton suburbs gave way to the relatively sparsely-populated Ohio countryside, and the road shrank to two lanes as they rode in silence. Jason looked out the cab window, fascinated despite himself at the unfamiliar landscape. Ohio was flatter than Georgia, and somehow older, and more settled than the places in the rural south that he had driven through on trips with Phoebe. That thought made him take a deep breath, closing his eyes; the momentary forgetfulness was lost, and he was back in a universe that, while nearly identical, was still not quite his own.

His eyes opened, and he looked toward the rear-view mirror; the driver was watching him, though not menacingly. After their eyes met for a second, the driver's returned to the road, and Jason looked down at his hands for several seconds before turning his gaze back out the window again. The terrain was as different as before, but the spell was broken. Jason sighed, anticipating a long, dull ride.

He was not wrong. It took them twenty minutes to reach Germantown, and another ten to reach Middletown; from there, it was another fifteen to Hamilton. The traffic had been heavy on the first leg of the trip, but after they passed south of the wreck blocking the Interstate, traffic thinned to a few vehicles each mile. Jason risked a glance back every few minutes; no one appeared to be following them.

They were an hour out on the road, which had widened to four lanes again, and the businesses had become larger and more frequent, when Jason sensed that it was time. He pretended to be checking his phone, reading a text message, before he glanced toward the mirror again. The driver was watching him, as he had before. Hoping not to look as unnerved as he felt, he motioned toward an auto-parts store on their right, and asked, "can you pull in here for a minute, please? I might have to go back. The service station says my car is fixed."

The driver nodded, still looking at him for a moment, and then slowed the cab until he could turn safely into the parking lot. They were still a mile north of Hamilton; Jason hoped that if his call was traced, it would look as though he was trying to appear to have come from the north, and that anyone pursuing him would conclude that he had come from Cincinnati. It was slightly dizzying, trying to think that many steps ahead, but he knew he couldn't afford to be careless.

When they drew to a stop, Jason glanced toward the driver and asked, "Can you wait for me here? I'll pay the extra, if I have to go back."

The driver looked annoyed – yet something in his expression didn't ring true to Jason, and he looked steadily back at him in the mirror until he answered, "Five minute. Pay same."

"Okay," Jason answered, and the cabbie released the locks on the car to let him out. He walked a little way away from the cab, nerving himself, and then turned the phone on, waiting for it to power up. He knew he had turned off all of the location services on it before leaving Atlanta, but he still had to struggle briefly with paralyzing fear as the startup routine completed. Opening his contacts, he scrolled quickly through the list to Tinsworth's name. He felt as though he stood on the edge of a cliff as he looked at the number, taking several deep breaths to compose himself, and then tapped the button to make the call.

He turned his back to the cab as he lifted the phone to his ear. His heart pounded as the phone rang once, then twice, then a third time. Just as he drew in a deep breath, there was an answering click, and a brief pause, he heard Dr. Tinsworth say, "This is Robert Tinsworth. Who is this?"

Jason waited a few seconds, trying to compose himself amid a flooding mixture of stress and deja vu, before answering in a slightly strangled voice: "Dr. Tinsworth, this is Jason Anderson. Please don't hang up."

There was a much longer pause on the other end of the line. Jason was about to speak again when Tinsworth answered, "Jason Anderson is dead. He's been dead for two months. Who are you?"

"Doc, it's me," he answered desperately. "I know you think I'm dead. I saw the body. It was burned all on one side. But I'm alive."

He knew that he should not have been able to discern anything from Tinsworth's response, but he was still certain that the professor knew it was him. As the silence stretched out, he realized that Tinsworth was trying to allow enough time for the call to be traced. Smiling despite himself, Jason said, "I know why you're not answering. It's OK. I know Mangum and Eier told you to."

"*Shit.*" Tinsworth finally answered. "I don't know if that's really you, Jason. I hope it is, but I almost hope it isn't."

"I understand. Believe me, I understand *everything.* But it really is me." Jason bit his lip, as the memory of his entire ordeal in that other world threatened to overwhelm him. "And if you know I'm supposed to be dead, then you'll understand why I left."

Another pause followed, before Tinsworth replied, "I know I saw what was left of you. There's no way you should be alive, but…" his voice trailed away, then came back more strongly. "There's also no way that the lab should have gone up like that. Not a chance. Did your girl do that?"

Jason's blood ran cold. "Oh, *shit.* You think *Phoebe* did that?"

"You're goddamn right I think she did it. Or I did, until right now. You sound scared to death. If she really did it, you wouldn't be talking to me, and you wouldn't have had to go to the lengths you obviously went to. I know you're a long way away." There had been no pause; Tinsworth was finally hearing him. "What actually happened?"

Jason closed his eyes again, took a deep breath, and replied, "Where's Wiley? Is he in jail?"

The silence that answered that query told him volumes, so he continued, "Wiley was *not* responsible for what happened. Not in any real sense. If he's in jail, he shouldn't be. There wasn't anything he could have done." Jason took another deep breath. "And the body you found really is mine. Our DNA is an exact match – I can prove that, if I ever have to. I know that they probably sent me to Bryant's lab."

A hissing intake of breath sounded from the other end of the line. Jason continued, "something happened to the bridge – it got extended, somehow. I don't know how to explain it exactly –" As he spoke, he could hear an odd, flat echo in his voice, not dissimilar to one he had heard in another, lost world, in a moment where he was speaking of something that would never happen. It was that tone that made him cut off his thought, and then he said urgently, "Professor, someone is listening. I have to go. But you have to tell them that Wiley doesn't know anything."

"Wait! – what about –" Jason cut off the call as Tinsworth tried to engage him; he knew he had little time. Smiling slightly to himself, he returned to the taxi, and looked in on the driver. "They fixed my car. I have to go back for it – I came all this way for nothing. I'll pay the full fare." He reached in his wallet and pulled out a hundred dollars. "This should cover it, with something for your trouble."

The driver didn't move, and simply stared back at him for several seconds as he held the money out. The smile left Jason's face, but he didn't move, until at last the driver took the money from him, slowly, and unlocked the rear door to let him in. Nonplussed, Jason got in; he was low on cash, and if the driver was something other than what he appeared to be, he might be in big trouble.

The driver took them east along a different route than they had taken there. After a few minutes, Jason realized that they were going toward I-75, and breathed a slight sigh of relief. The driver looked back at him again in the mirror.

"I know who you are. You think they send just anybody? You got to be more careful." The driver flashed a momentary smile that reminded him of Al's, and then turned his attention back to the road. Jason could hear him still chuckling as they continued east; some ten miles ahead lay the interchange that would take him north, and from there, it would be another thirty miles back to Dayton. He would be back with Phoebe in an hour. He sighed again, and said, very quietly, "thank you."

GENERAL HAVERHILL LOOKED OUT the window behind his desk. A little more than a mile to the northeast, the Potomac flowed lazily toward Chesapeake Bay beyond the Colonial Village section of Arlington, but every thought of geography or pleasant views had been driven from his mind.

In less than an hour, he had received two calls concerning the colossal fuck-up that had taken place in Atlanta two months before – a fuck-up that had left him with no answers for a lot of very powerful, very heavily-invested people with very serious questions.

The first call came from Colonel Mangum, and it had told him nothing he didn't already know. The grad student they were holding incognito had yielded almost no useful information, and had come to the same conclusion they had – that the girl had sabotaged the bridge, killing Anderson in the process. At that point, that had only been one more confirmation of their working hypothesis.

It was the next call, only a little while later, that had completely surprised him. Major Eier had called after an unscheduled meeting with Tinsworth, the scientist who had been in charge of the bridge project, and that one had captured his full attention.

Ever since the lab explosion, agents across the country had been looking for one person – someone who had been in the right place and at the right time to cause it, and who had disappeared less than an hour later – but not before using a bank card belonging to the one casualty from the blast. Someone in a stocking cap with a heavily covered face had withdrawn the maximum allowable amount from Jason Anderson's checking account using an ATM. They had done this over an hour after Anderson supposedly was killed; his body had already been placed in the morgue under Nesmith Hall.

The girl in question, one Phoebe Michelle Reyes – ostensibly, Anderson's girlfriend – had apparently used him to get close to the project. The indication was that she had visited him shortly before the incident, and had left a bomb in the lab on her departure. There had been a background check done on her, and it had turned up nothing. She had been clean – but someone had apparently gotten to her.

That had been the consensus until the second call came. Eier and Tinsworth had monitored a contact from a cellphone traced to a tower in Hamilton, Ohio, from someone claiming to be Jason Anderson. Evidently he had been very convincing, to the point that he acknowledged the body they had recovered, but claimed that his DNA would be an exact match for it.

Haverhill snorted to himself. He doubted that that would ever be put to the test. The major problem was that the caller – whether it was Anderson, or an impostor – knew about Bryant's project, and *still* made the claim of a DNA match. That concerned him greatly; one way or another, the other significant, clandestine project on that campus had been compromised.

And by confirming what they already knew – that Wiley Grant, the sloppy, arrogant fatass they'd held on suspicion of complicity for two months, was completely blameless for the explosion – whoever it was had implicated himself with the girl as a co-conspirator.

He thought for a few more minutes, looking out across the river toward the larger, even more fucked-up hive of corruption that lay beyond it, before reaching back over his desk and stabbing the red button that activated the intercom with his secretary.

Without waiting for her to acknowledge him, he spoke abruptly: "Get me on the next transport into Atlanta. Cancel all my appointments for the next two days." He let up on the button without waiting for a response.

He was going to have to go down there himself to oversee the cleanup, and he fully intended to roast those responsible for making it necessary.

Chapter Three

COLONEL PETE MANGUM STARED across his desk at the two men seated before him.

One was his assistant, Major Fred Eier; the other was the professor whose most recent assignment – and its spectacular failure – had turned into one of the most monumental clusterfucks he had ever had to deal with. Robert Tinsworth had been a useful and loyal civilian counterpart, and until recently they had gotten along quite well. The destruction of the bridge project – along with the death of his star pupil, and the jailing of another who, while not quite to the same level as a scientist, was still a formidable and capable researcher – had caused quite a bit of tension in his relations with DARPA.

Those tensions had only been amplified by the call Tinsworth had received only an hour earlier. The caller had claimed to be Jason Anderson – the man they all knew was dead, and whose body had been turned over to the other project on campus he was monitoring – and had still been convincing enough that Tinsworth had immediately requested this meeting. The call had been traced to a tower in a fourth-rate burg in Ohio called Hamilton, some miles north of Cincinnati.

The Anderson impostor was an interesting gambit, if their previous operating assumptions were true; all of their information pointed to one likely scenario – that Phoebe Reyes, Anderson's girlfriend, had somehow planted a bomb that had destroyed the lab and the bridge, killing him. Wiley Grant, the tech at the other end of the bridge, had been held incognito since that day. His involvement in the incident was unclear, but it was apparent that he had left his station shortly before it happened, and he had been in the men's room – probably the safest place he could have been – when the explosion occurred.

Tinsworth looked shaken; Eier was as solid as always. Mangum looked at each of them for several seconds before glancing down toward a document on his desk. The memo indicated that General Haverhill was en route to oversee the proceedings. Mangum's job was straightforward: he was to find out as much as possible about the call, and the caller, from Ohio before the general's arrival.

Mangum cleared his throat, and directed his words toward Tinsworth: "This call you received – d'you really think there's any chance it was Anderson? I mean, we all saw the body. There's even a picture of it in the initial report I filed with Haverhill."

Tinsworth was silent for a few seconds, and when he answered, his voice was more uncertain than he could ever remember hearing it: "Colonel, if this project involved just about anything else, or any*one* else, I would think this was some kind of decoy. It still might be – it's still the most likely explanation – but there's a very, very small chance that it isn't."

Mangum glanced at Eier, more to confirm their agreeing interpretations of Tinsworth's statement than anything else, and then asked, "If Anderson's body went to Bryant's lab, as we all know it did, then how could he be calling you from Asshole, Ohio?"

"I'm not sure. But after that call, there's a lot I'm not sure about." Tinsworth hesitated for a moment, then continued. "He knew Grant was in jail, for one thing, but said he had nothing to do with the blast. He even knew about the body, and said that his DNA would match it. I've looked over every possibility I can think of, and I have to think the caller – Jason, or whoever – *could* be telling the truth. In fact, there's one possible set of circumstances that would not only explain what happened, but would exonerate both Grant and Jason's girlfriend."

Tinsworth glanced from Mangum to Eier as he finished; they both wore surprised, wary expressions. He waited until Mangum asked, "Wait a minute. You say this – person – is sure he can match Anderson's DNA?"

"That's exactly what he said," Tinsworth replied. "Until that moment, I thought the whole call was a false flag. But not only did he say it, *he knew where the body is*. NO one, except the people directly connected with it and the people with enough security clearance, knows about that project. Anderson sure as hell shouldn't know, but he did – and he knew that's where the body went.

"He also said something about the bridge being extended, and as he said it, something happened that was so odd that I don't know entirely how to describe it to you." He paused again, but he could see that he had the two officers' full attention. "It sounded as though his voice was speaking through thinner atmosphere – as though he was at a very high altitude, very suddenly. He sounded normal before that, and again afterward. He was telling me that the bridge was extended, and then his voice changed." He took a deep breath. "Then he said someone was listening, and that he had to go, and that was it."

Mangum had to will himself not to react to Tinsworth's last sentence. Someone *had* been listening, obviously; that was how Haverhill had known even before he himself had. This had just gotten very, very complicated. Whoever this man was, and whatever he was up to, was possibly as great a threat to DARPA as anything he had ever encountered: he knew entirely too much about clandestine operations, and he was at large. Within a region of southern Ohio and Indiana about a hundred miles across, he could be anywhere.

"You said his story could exonerate Grant and the girl, Phoebe Reyes. How?" he asked.

Tinsworth sighed, trying to remain calm. "If he was correct, and the bridge was – extended, as he put it – there could be vast consequences. Under normal conditions, the bridge would evaporate along with the endpoints if it were destroyed, and there would be no discernible energy discharge. Remember, the endpoint singularities were subatomic. Even a fusion reaction of a single atom wouldn't generate that much of an energy release – you need a chain reaction. A big one." Tinsworth paused.

"But if you create an extension to the bridge, you create all kinds of issues, especially if the extension is four-dimensional. You create an energy difference between the fixed endpoint and the extended one, because of the difference in velocity vectors between the two endpoints. The larger the distance is, the greater the difference."

Eier looked slightly confused, and Mangum knew he himself was, but he understood what a potential difference could mean, and one term Tinsworth had used gave him a sudden chill. "Wait. You said 'four-dimensional.'" Are you saying the extension went backward in time?"

Tinsworth's relief was evident; he too obviously had feared he would not be clearly understood. "Possibly. I think it's much more likely any extension would go forward in time, not back. Someone in our future calculated where the bridge endpoint was at a given moment in *their* past, and connected to it from there." He paused. "That might explain why it happened right when Grant was in the men's room – whoever it was might have known he would be in there."

"But they would also have known that Anderson was at his station," Eier objected.

"That's right. But think for a second. The caller knew Anderson's body would be sent to Nesmith Hall. The only issue is that they seem to have forgotten that Phoebe might be blamed for the explosion." Tinsworth was looking down at the end of Mangum's desk, lost in thought. "Maybe, from a future perspective, this might have been necessary. There might have been something that required that he be dead – so that he could operate in this world as a non-entity. That would mean that he, or whoever will actually cause the bridge extension he described, knew something about our current timeframe that required alteration."

"Wait. *What?*" Mangum exclaimed in disbelief. "This is *Terminator*-type shit. How is that even possible?"

"It isn't possible – right now. But in our future, it might be." Tinsworth was speaking more confidently. "And if the bridge was extended into our future by more than a few months, there would be a significant difference in potential energy. Given a few years, it would probably be sufficient to blow up the lab." He looked at them both; their faces bore nearly identical looks of arrested awe. "I don't know if that technology was sufficient to open a passage that a human being could traverse. Jason – if that's who the caller was - might have been atomized, and then reassembled here somehow. Or the bridge might have been expanded enough to allow him to pass through directly. Or he might be some completely different construct."

There followed a few seconds' silence before Eier responded. "So we've been looking for the wrong person all this time."

Mangum had been almost spellbound by Tinsworth's idea. He still found it compelling, but he had another issue to address as well. "Maybe. My contacts tell me that Grant thinks the girl caused the explosion."

"I did, as well, before that phone call. But there's this alternate explanation for the entire sequence of events that explains everything, without a bomb, and without Grant being complicit. I think you should release him." Tinsworth met Mangum's incredulous, and slightly disgusted, gaze steadily. "It's not like you can't watch him once he's out. But I genuinely think he had nothing to do with it at all, now. A future individual would be mindful of where Grant was, and when he was there, and made sure he wasn't hurt. You might need him – *I* certainly do – and he would be more likely to want to help if he's let go."

Eier was clearly at a loss, but Mangum wasn't, and he fixed his gaze on Tinsworth with every ounce of intimidation he could muster, concealing his reaction to his theory. "Why should I believe that someone from the future did all this, with all the convenient outs for everyone involved, instead of the simple explanation?"

"You don't have to, Colonel," Tinsworth answered. "I told you what Anderson told me. There's a fucking recording of the call, if you want to hear it. You might even hear that weird shit his voice did. But he knew enough that you might want to think about it before you just go up to Ohio and grab him. If that's even possible. He might already know when and where you're going."

There was nothing else for it. "I'm going to think about it, definitely," Mangum replied. "But we all have a bigger problem than this, now, if you're right.

"I talked with General Haverhill shortly before you arrived. He's coming down here, today, and he's going to be personally involved with bringing in Phoebe Reyes, and if this man calling himself Jason Anderson is with her, then he's coming in as well."

THE JUMPSEAT WASN'T HIS favorite mode of transport, but it was the fastest way available to Atlanta, and it saved the taxpayers the cost of a plane ticket. Despite all of the stories of Pentagon profligacy, Haverhill himself had always been tight with a budget, and never spent more than he had to on his own comfort or travel.

His laptop was open, and he watched the screen intently: he had just received some camera footage from his contacts in the NSA. As soon as Jason Anderson's death had been confirmed, the cameras from the surrounding buildings had been reviewed; nearly all of them had been either knocked offline, or had their angles changed, by the shockwave of the first explosion. Only one had operated long enough to show the girl leaving the building – and how she was knocked to the ground by that blast.

For nearly two months, the working assumption was that she had left a bomb, and walked away. Almost all the pieces fit: Anderson had clearly been wrapped up in the bridge project for months. She was probably disgruntled – dating a research scientist of his caliber, but unable to entice him away from his work for any length of time. Unhappy, disappointed, maybe disillusioned – a perfect asset, ready for conversion. Grant, the sloppo at the other end of the bridge, was himself a brilliant scientist, but always in Anderson's shadow – another prime target.

But one piece was missing from the puzzle, and it was a big, scary one: there had been no bomb.

The remains of the lab – and of the lab assistant – had been very, very carefully and thoroughly searched. There had been a lot of concerned interests involved, and concerned people, and it had served everyone best to ensure that every single dust mote at the blast site was overturned, checked, measured twice, logged, and photographed. That had been done. The autopsy on Anderson had been done by Bryant in conjunction with the Army Surgeon General himself. Not a single scintilla of evidence of any explosive had been found. Whatever had blown up that lab had left absolutely no traces at all.

Haverhill had assumed, until he had seen the footage he now watched and rewatched, that the lack of telltale residues could only be explained by a new type of explosive – one that dissipated into the air, or was in fact composed entirely of atmospheric elements.

But there had been one camera, a high-definition traffic camera situated almost two blocks away on a rooftop, that had been jolted by the blast. Its field of view had dropped almost precisely onto the green outside Williams Hall, where the explosion had occurred.

Cleaned up and zoomed in – even for high-definition, the distance had left some distortion – he could clearly see the girl, looking back at the building. Then, just before the second – larger – blast knocked the view away, he saw a man hurtle into the frame, shoving her down and covering her with his body. A piece of sheet metal that would have decapitated them both sailed not a foot above them as they fell to the ground together.

The man had come from the direction of the building – and the blast. Even with the scrubbing of the image, it was difficult to be sure, but Haverhill's gut confirmed what his sources were telling him: the man who had saved Phoebe Reyes was almost certainly Jason Anderson.

And that, coupled with the call from Ohio, meant that Anderson was within reach of the wrong people, and they would certainly make use of him if they got to him first.

Chapter Four

IT WAS STILL SHORTLY BEFORE noon when Jason returned to the safe house. Phoebe had been trying to read a book, to no avail; her call to Al, and his impending visit, had scared her. Knowing that Jason's mind might break from the strain and exhaustion was just one more worry on an ever-increasing list in her head.

He gave the code knock – three soft knocks, one hard, then two more soft ones – before he entered; Phoebe relaxed slightly, thankful that he had come back safely. He locked the door behind himself, and came through the decoy box that concealed the entry to their hideaway. As he came in, his face was so grave that for a moment she was almost frozen with fear. He sat down beside her on the bed, staring at her for a long time.

"I called Tinsworth." For a few moments he said no more; she knew that the implications of that one sentence alone were fraught. Trying to control her fear, she asked, "What did you tell him?"

He sighed, and shook his head. For a moment she thought he would say nothing, and keep her in the dark again, but then he said quietly, "It's time I told you everything, Phoebe. You're in danger that I never dreamed you would be in, and it's my fault. It's time for me to tell you the whole story."

Phoebe's eyes grew tearful, and before he could say anything else, she moved next to him on the side of the bed and hugged him. For a moment he held her close, and then pulled back slightly, looking in her eyes. She returned the stare, and for a moment, she had the strange feeling that more than one person was watching her through his eyes. His breath caught, and an even stranger expression – a look that told her that somehow, he completely understood – crossed his face.

Confused, she looked down at her hands for a moment, and Jason said quietly, "The first thing you need to understand is that everyone thought I was dead until this morning."

That made her look up again in amazement. "But I thought we were hiding because the – whoever it is, the government – was looking for you, because you sabotaged the bridge."

He smiled slightly. "I did sabotage it, but not the way anyone thinks. It's a really long and confusing story. But what really happened was that the bridge I was originally working with got extended from one endpoint – Wiley's endpoint."

"Extended? What do you mean?" Phoebe asked.

"This is going to sound insane, but it really happened. Someone in our future figured out how to extend the bridge from our time into theirs. It was at least forty years, probably more. The problem was that the energy differentials between the two endpoints resulted in an explosion. A big one. Wiley's lab was blown up.

"I think I know why that happened the way it did. They had to send something through four-space that would anchor the passage until the endpoint was secure. But that thing, when it emerged in our time, was moving with a completely different direction and speed, and it blew up immediately. It was small – probably no bigger than a golf ball at most, or it would have collapsed the building. But the endpoint was stabilized, and the explosion didn't affect it once the vectors had matched."

Phoebe's face had the familiar look of engrossed confusion that he had seen so many times before, in that world that was gone. He sighed, and looked at her sadly, and said quietly, "You had just broken up with me over the intercom in my lab and left Williams Hall when the explosion happened. A chunk of something blew out of Hampton Hall – somehow – and hit you, and…" He gulped, and closed his eyes, remembering what had happened to her.

"Jason, none of that happened. Nothing hit me." Her eyes and her voice betrayed her – she was trying to soothe him, but she was terrified.

"Not in this universe, it didn't. I made sure it wouldn't. But it did – in mine." His eyes opened and he looked directly at her, and again she had the sense that more than one person was looking at her. That frightened her even more.

"It killed you, immediately. People came – the people who handle organ donations at the university, I guess – and they took you to the lab under Nesmith Hall. That's how I know what's going on there. They eventually made you into a cyborg – a Cybwoman, they called you. They made a bunch of them.

"But even with all that, we had to do something about the rift that formed in Hampton, because it wasn't stable, and we were all afraid that if it disintegrated, the explosion would be *really* huge. Wiley and I went through it, into our future, and –" he was still looking directly at her, unflinching – "we met you, and another Cybwoman named Allison. Allison killed Wiley, immediately. I went back through, and you followed me back, and brought Wiley's body back with you."

She was speechless, staring at him in fearful, fascinated horror. He told her the rest of what had happened – about the fall of civilization, and their flight first to the Covingtons' base, and then to Agnes Scott College. But when he got to the last part of the journey, and the battle among the remaining Cybwomen, he faltered for a moment. Phoebe waited as he gathered himself to tell her the worst part.

"Phoebe, you need to understand that you are the same exact girl I love, and that I'm almost exactly the same Jason you love. But I could only find one way to save you, and that was to make sure that none of that could ever happen to you. I had to change something that had happened in the past, and still get back to my own time – or someplace just like it.

"I reversed the direction that the bridge collapsed, so that the rift formed in my lab instead of Wiley's. But the problem was, it wasn't my universe. The moment I changed the rift target, it became a different one. And in that one, I was still working in the lab when the explosion came." Again Phoebe thought she saw more than one person looking at her, and she was afraid.

"That Jason was killed in the explosion, but the rift that it formed only lasted for a few minutes. My own universe began disintegrating as soon as I reprogrammed the engine that generated the rift, in my own future. I almost didn't make it back here – you said I would die if I went back, and you were tasked with protecting me. Another Cybwoman – I don't know which one – had to knock you out of the way. But when I got back, my own body – the other Jason, the one in this universe – was in the lab, and he was really torn up. I knew he was dead.

But I also knew you were going to be outside the building, so I ran after you, hoping the first explosion hadn't killed you. I got there just in time – I know you remember how close that was." Jason sighed, and looked down at his hands again. "But the thing is, this universe has two Jasons in it now. One of them died in the explosion, and is in the lab in Nesmith Hall. I'm the other one, the same man, but from another existence."

Phoebe was visibly staggered by the last thing he had said, and she shied slightly away from him. He nodded, again clearly understanding her fear and confusion. She finally whispered, "I'm not sure I can stay here with you any longer."

"But you have to, Phoebe," he said, more urgently than at any time since they had begun talking. "The thing is, they found my body. They think someone sabotaged the project with a bomb." His eyes smarted, but he continued on, bitterly: "They think the last person to visit the lab planted a bomb there. They think Wiley was in on it, and that he was taking shelter in the men's room at the time it went off. Tinsworth told me that there's people looking everywhere – for you, not me. They think you're a terrorist, and that you killed me."

"I'm not sure yet that I won't do that," she replied shakily. "What the hell have you done to me?"

"I told you, Phoebe – I saved your life. This was the only chance I had to keep us together. I had no idea they would blame you. I was afraid that if the DARPA guys found me, after they found my body in the lab, that they might put me someplace where I would never see anyone again, so I ran. It's lucky you came with me, because otherwise, they would have found you by now, and you would have had a hard time convincing them you didn't do it."

"This is crazy. I – I need you to stop, now. I can't take any more of this." She took a deep breath. He still watched her, and pain wrung his face as he sensed the wall, invisible and yet iron, that had come between them.

She was becoming angry; he could see it, but he could say no more. She glowered at him for a full minute before she finally asked, "So, you're not my Jason. Who are you, then?"

Jason's shoulders slumped. "That's the thing, Phoebe. I *am* your Jason. My timeline didn't divert from his until after you left the lab. Until that time, we were the same individual. Quantum physics is a fucked-up thing to understand even in theory. You wouldn't believe how fucked-up it got when it started messing with my reality."

Phoebe glared at him. "Well, you won't have to worry about it fucking *me* up for much longer, *Jason*. I can't leave here today, but tomorrow, I'm getting out of here." She paused. "And you're damn well sleeping in that chair."

She meant it. He knew she did. He would have to wait, and see if she calmed down any, before he could try to persuade her to stay. Sighing, and not looking at her, he got up from the side of the bed and sat down in a beat-up recliner that looked like it might have literally fallen off a truck.

It was then that the voice he had been hearing in the night, the one that awoke when he slept, broke into his waking world for the first time, and the message it delivered inside his head was terse: "I hope you haven't made this unrecoverable for both of us."

He knew the voice too well. It was his own.

IT WAS MIDNIGHT IN ONE OF the better neighborhoods in Hapeville, some five miles south of downtown Atlanta.

Two nondescript men waited inside a service van parked at an equally nondescript one-story house. That van occasionally made trips around the town, making lunch runs and similar errands, but its real purpose – as well as that of the house – was for surveillance.

The two were from the Intelligence and Analysis agency within the Department of Homeland Security. They, and the rest of their team, had been tasked two months before with monitoring one man – a questionable actor named Alfonzo Reyes. He was suspected of numerous connections to dubious individuals, mostly militia types along with the entire assortment of end-of-the-world mixed nuts, but most of those associations were little more than background noise. His record was essentially clean, and he was a native U.S. citizen. Ordinarily, he would have been considered a fairly low-level threat.

That had changed the moment that his younger sister had blown up a laboratory at the university downtown, killing a researcher that had happened to be her boyfriend. Apparently, she had used him to get close enough to destroy the project, and had gotten away nearly clean; no one had seen her in two months. Her actions had not been publicized, in large part because of concerns over who she might have been working with. She had been, until the moment that that lab exploded, a complete nonentity.

Alfonzo had been questioned twice about her in the days after the incident – once by FBI, and once by GBI, the Georgia Bureau of Investigation – and had had nothing to say. He claimed that he had not seen her, and that he had been eating at a popular local hamburger joint at the time of the blast. His story checked out, but his connections had been suspect, and over the ensuing six weeks, a number of different bugs had been planted in his house and truck. Through all that time, they had seen and heard nothing, and there had been talk of ending surveillance – until that morning.

The man had been in his truck when he received a call on a cellphone he had not used even once in the months since he had bought it. The girl had called him, and he had said he would go to see her; and he was loading the cab of his truck as they watched.

"Subject looks like he's about to leave," one of them said quietly into a headset. The van's interior contained multiple monitors; all of them were linked to cameras equipped with night scopes, and most of them were trained on the van.

"Roger that. Beacon is transmitting from the vehicle. We'll trail him by a half mile until he gets out of the city, then hand him off. Wherever he goes, we'll be a minute or two behind him," came the reply from the headset.

The other man was silent, and only pretending to be monitoring the driver; his job at I&A was a cover for a much more secret organization, one that only a handful of people outside of it had ever heard about. He already knew the truck's destination; Ius Divinum had already developed its intelligence on Phoebe Reyes and her brother.

They also knew that the explosion in the lab had not been caused by a bomb – and that its actual cause was a matter of the uttermost severity. They rarely engaged in field operations, except in cases such as this one – incidents with the potential to alter human history in an immediately negative fashion.

The manner in which the Einstein-Rosen bridge had been destroyed was just such an incident. Ius Divinum had assigned him to monitor Alfonzo Reyes in order to find his sister, and to inform them as soon as she was located.

The man finished loading his truck and climbed in on the driver's side, A few seconds later, its lights came on as the vehicle roared into life, and began to make its way slowly out of the sleeping neighborhood.

The agent said, quietly, "Subject has left the residence. Will continue monitoring until the handoff." He would not need to do or say more; once he confirmed the handoff, Ius Divinum would know that Reyes was going where they expected him to go.

They would need to be certain, so that they could get there first.

Chapter Five

GENERAL HAVERHILL HAD TEMPORARILY commandeered an office two suites down from Colonel Mangum's on his arrival, issuing orders for a meeting at seven the following morning. When that time arrived, the Colonel was seated across his desk from him. Major Eier sat beside Mangum, and in a third chair was an unimpressive, fiftyish man whom they had introduced as Dr. Robert Tinsworth. All of them were waiting for him to speak.

The morning had brought new intelligence: Phoebe Reyes' brother had received a cellphone call from her the previous day, and had left overnight. His source had last reported that he was bypassing Cincinnati on I-275.

Haverhill looked each man over for a few moments before he spoke. "Dr. Tinsworth, I've been briefed concerning the call you received yesterday. What would you say are the odds that Anderson is still alive, and made that call?"

"Very low, General." Tinsworth was all too obviously nervous, but doing a decent job of maintaining control. "It's possible, but it's also possible an asteroid will hit the earth this year."

"Did he say whether the girl was with him?"

"He didn't say. He didn't expect that she would be blamed for it, and he didn't sound like he was acting. He was genuinely surprised." Tinsworth leaned toward Haverhill's desk. "But one thing bothers me. How in the world did he know about Bryant's lab? *I* definitely didn't tell him about it. If he really knows what's going on in there, then he probably isn't bluffing about the DNA match."

Haverhill glanced toward Mangum. "Your thoughts, Colonel?"

Mangum looked troubled. "Tinsworth's point about the lab is the key, General. If this man knows about the lab, he *could* be using that knowledge as a bluff – although I can't imagine how he would make that work to his advantage."

"That's also what I don't understand, General," Eier added. Haverhill's gaze shifted between the two officers for several seconds before he looked back toward Tinsworth.

"That call you received yesterday – we traced it to a town north of Cincinnati, called Hamilton. So, we know your caller is somewhere around there. We've also been monitoring Phoebe Reyes' brother, Alfonzo, and – " sarcasm crept into Haverhill's voice – "by some odd coincidence, Alfonzo Reyes left his house last night around midnight. My people have been tailing him, and they tell me that he's on I-275 bypassing Cincinnati right now. So whether or not that was Jason Anderson, there's good reason to believe Reyes is going up after his sister."

"Her brother would have known she was a suspect," Tinsworth interjected. "If he's just now going up there, after the call yesterday, then it sounds like she and Jason really are together."

"More to the point – if she's with whoever made that call, then one of two possibilities remains. Either she's a terrorist, and her organization knows a *lot* more than it should – or that really was Anderson, and we have a different situation completely, but one that might be even more dangerous." Haverhill sat back in his chair slightly, looking at Tinsworth, then Mangum. "Let's say that this really *is* Jason Anderson we're dealing with, and that everything he said was true. What are the implications for the bridge project, in that case?"

Mangum looked slightly surprised, but Tinsworth's eyes widened in horror. "If future technology can detect and modify an intact bridge, then any bridge we build in our own time might be used to create a rift – or be turned into a bomb."

Haverhill nodded as appalled comprehension dawned in the eyes of his officers. "Exactly. We have to find out, one way or another, whether this man really *was* Jason Anderson. We have a team set to move in on Alfonzo Reyes as soon as we have his destination pinned down." He glanced at Tinsworth. "If this really is Anderson, I'll need you to help us out on the debriefing. I'm pretty tech-savvy, but this project is for the *serious* eggheads."

"And if it's not Anderson?" Mangum asked.

"If it's not, then it will be much harder to take them alive, and they'll wish we hadn't, if we do." Haverhill's voice carried a very slightly colder tone than it had. Tinsworth paled visibly, but Eier and Mangum only nodded in response. Haverhill stood, and the others stood with him. Motioning toward the door, he said quietly, "Dismissed. I'll call you in as soon as the team closes on – Anderson, or whoever it is."

JASON HAD SPENT ANOTHER mostly sleepless night in even greater discomfort and worry than normal, and had wakened from a brief doze just before dawn to see Phoebe stuffing clothing and personal articles into her gym bag. She hadn't even looked at him since he had told her what had happened, and her anger had not abated one bit. He sighed to himself; they were about to have another argument. There was no way around it: he could not allow her to leave when she was a prime suspect in his murder.

He got painfully to his feet and watched her; she pointedly paid him no attention. After a minute had passed with no acknowledgement, he clambered across their bed to stand beside her, and finally said, quietly, "Phoebe, it's not safe for you to leave. I know you're angry with me, and I understand why, but if you go out there without me and someone recognizes you, you'll be arrested – maybe even shot. They think you blew up my lab – that you're a terrorist. You've got nowhere to go."

"That's what *you* think." She stuffed a few more articles of clothing into her already-bulging bag and rounded to face him. "Al gave me a phone and told me to call him if I needed him. He's on his way up here. As soon as he gets here, I'm leaving, and I never want to see you again after that."

Jason's face paled so noticeably, and so much fear overcame his expression as she spoke, that instead of continuing to pack, she simply glared at him. It took him several seconds to get any words out.

"Shit. Phoebe, do you think whoever's looking for you isn't watching him, too? They'll follow him, and once they know he's heading into Ohio,

the whole shitstorm is going to break. We have to get out of here. *Now.*
And you *can't* leave without me. I know you want to get rid of me. I'm not
staying because I want to, even though I gave up *everything* to get you back.
I'm staying because unless you're with me, you can't defend yourself.

"I don't want you to go to jail for the rest of your life. They might even
give you the death penalty, because bombing a research facility like that
would be considered a terrorist act." He was breathing heavily, nearly in a
state of panic; she was still glowering, but he could see the doubt coloring
her eyes. He had spent so much time studying her expressions since his
return, remembering how dead those eyes once had been, that he could see
that he was finally getting through to her.

"I'll leave with you. Give me five minutes to fill my bag, and we'll leave.
We can leave a note for Al – he's going to get picked up no matter what,
and he'll have to acknowledge that he was coming to see you. I'm sure
there's someone tailing him. It might even help you if he's caught, because
he knows I'm alive."

Phoebe still glared at him, her eyes more slitted than before. "You'd like
it if he was caught, wouldn't you? He's the only one who can help me."

"If he's caught, I'll turn myself in to make sure that you and Al, and
Wiley, are all let go. *I'm* the one who actually blew up Williams Hall. *I'm*
the one who killed the version of myself that was in the lab. I risked
everything else for you – I'll do whatever it takes. I just wish you would
realize one thing, Phoebe." As he stared at her, she once again had that sense
of more than one person behind his eyes – one who she had always known,
but the other, while not a stranger, had been in places and seen things that
had made him somehow dark, and terrible.

Even as her fear of that other made her flinch slightly, she thought saw
something else there, as well. She could see terrible pain and regret, but
both of those only cloaked something deeper and more indomitable. It had
been two months since they had left Atlanta, and in that time, the sense of
immediacy in what had happened to him had faded. That sense had
returned, powerfully, and she realized that she would have to choose – then
and there – whether she would trust him, or run from him.

He was still watching her, waiting for her to decide, and he continued quietly, "I want whatever is best for you. If the best thing for you is for me to disappear, then I'll disappear. I love you. The one thing you have to understand is that I will never hurt you, and I will never let you be hurt if I can stop it. That was why I did what I did. I saw what had happened to you, both outside the lab and in the future, and I promised the – the thing Bryant turned you into – that I would make sure that that never happened to you.

"It tore my heart up to see what had been done to her – to *you* – and I *will* keep that promise. I already kept part of it by wiping out that timeline. The people I met there will never exist, except as I remember them. I know you'll never really understand that, and that's okay. I don't *ever* want you to go through what I went through, even if it means we can't be together. Can you understand that? Can you at least realize, even if you think I'm not the same person, how much you mean to me?"

Her lips trembled, and tears sprang into her eyes; even with the anger that surged, fighting her instincts, she had heard what both the voice in his head and the voice in his heart had said to her. For a moment, Jason thought she might have heard both voices as he spoke – even as he had once heard two voices speak through her mouth, telling him the same thing he, less simply, was telling her.

In truth, she had; that other one behind his eyes seemed to have whispered molten, golden love directly to her soul. She was still frightened, and unsure of the man her Jason had become – or had he simply revealed himself, and been that man all along? – she could not be certain. But she knew she could not turn from him, try as she might. In her heart, she knew he was telling her the truth as best he knew, and that her world – the whole world – had changed forever.

So she stared back at him, trying to fathom him even as she knew she would commit her course to his, and tried to find words, but all she could muster was: "I don't understand at all. I don't want to.

"But I believe you love me. I believe you are who you say you are. I'll come with you. But I'm scared to death of you."

This time, the tears sprang into Jason's eyes, and his voice broke as he answered. "You don't need to be, but I understand. Can you give me five minutes to pack a bag?"

She nodded, as tearfully as he. It actually took him less than three minutes to stuff the things he knew they would need – the hidden money, two burner phones, some clothes, toiletries, and a few other articles – into another bag. He grabbed a pad and pen and dashed off a quick, terse note to Al before he led her back through the decoy box, and out the storage room door.

Once outside into the access hall, he locked the door behind them, shoved the key back under the door, and together they made their way to the exit.

Chapter Six

AL REYES WHEELED HIS TRUCK into the parking lot behind a cut-rate grocery store in northwest Dayton, some ten hours after he had left Atlanta. He had monitored his rearview mirrors the entire trip, and while not entirely certain, he thought he had made the trip clean.

Behind the discount store lay the commercial storage facility where he had sent his sister, along with her boyfriend, the scientist. When the government goons had questioned him, he had learned that they thought Jason Anderson was dead, and that his sister was suspected of killing him – and that put him in a terrible position. He could not clear his sister without giving up her boyfriend, and he was likely to end up in hot water himself. As a result, he had not been very forthcoming when questioned.

He pulled the truck into a space near the entrance and parked. After shutting the engine off, he sat for a moment in the relative quiet, listening to the sound of nothing. In spite of everything, he was nervous, and though he had watched his rearview like a hawk for anyone tailing him, there had been no one that he could pick out. To his best knowledge, he was unmarked.

He got out of his car, drawing his wallet from his pocket as he walked toward the entrance. At the door, he held up the key-card that allowed him entry to the facility, and opened the door when he heard the confirming chime indicating that the card had been accepted.

He walked past a closed kiosk that, when open, served as the rental office. A nondescript man in a T-shirt and jeans passed him as he turned left and began making his way toward the unit where Phoebe and Jason were hiding.

He came to a halt about two thirds of the way down the hall. He glanced behind him, then forward, but saw no one; using the knock he had given

Phoebe before they had left Atlanta, he rapped several times on the door, and then drew out the key to unlock it.

The key was in the lock when several men burst out of the two adjacent units. Several more emerged from the door directly behind him. All of them had guns drawn. He knew at once it would be useless to fight; he would accomplish nothing but getting his ass kicked, or shot.

He put his hands up even as one of the men barked, "Get your hands up where I can see them!" He turned and faced them; there were at least eight men there. None of them wore police uniforms. He nodded to himself, then asked, "FBI?"

"That's right. You mind telling us what you have in there that's so important that you drove overnight from Atlanta for it?" An older agent on his left replied.

Al shrugged. "I don't suppose you'll believe me if I say it's my baseball card collection."

His response was received with few humorless smiles. "You wouldn't be hiding your sister Phoebe in there, would you? We've been looking for her for a while now," the older guy said.

"Yeah, she's there," he answered, nodding resignedly. "Her boyfriend's with her."

"I thought she blew up her boyfriend with that bomb she planted in his lab," another agent answered coldly.

Al smiled in spite of himself. "Nope. He's with her. I saw them before they left Atlanta. He's definitely with her, and he's *definitely* not dead."

"You sure about that?" another agent asked. The news that Phoebe was not alone inside the unit had visibly changed their demeanor; Al realized that they were thinking that they could be facing two armed fugitives, rather than one.

"You want me to go in first?" he offered. "They're not going to shoot you, but they're *really* not going to shoot *me*."

Several of the agents looked at each other, thinking, before the old one – he was probably in charge, Al thought – answered, "all right, you can go in first. Bell, unlock that door and open it."

A younger agent came forward. He wore a suit and fedora that made him look like a caricature of an actual agent, but amusing as Al might have found his appearance, he was in no mood to laugh. The agent turned the key in the lock, then withdrew it, and opened the door carefully.

Al happened to be looking down as the door slowly opened, and at once he said, "they've left. They're not here."

"What makes you so sure about that?" the young agent snarled at him. Al grinned back, and keeping his hands up, pointed toward where their key lay on the floor.

"You go first and walk in, *slowly*. Keep your hands up, and no sudden moves." The voice came from behind him, but he couldn't identify which agent had spoken. He complied. Two agents followed him with guns drawn.

Inside, the setup was the same as in the storage unit in Atlanta – a blind wall of loaded boxes was stacked nearly to the ceiling. The light was out; one of the agents flicked it on. The room was silent.

Al pointed to one box on the bottom row. "That one. Pull it out and there's a way through to what's behind this wall."

One of the agents called out, "Phoebe Reyes! FBI. We have your brother here."

He received no response, and Al shrugged again, smiling slightly as he said over his shoulder, "I told you. They're not here."

ABOUT TWO MILES AWAY, Jason and Phoebe were walking in the general direction of downtown Dayton, following a sidewalk beside a four-lane road that was seeing heavy morning traffic.

They had left the facility together, and had not spoken since then; they were each lost in their own thoughts. Phoebe was desperately worried about her brother, knowing that he might be walking into a trap. Her thoughts about Jason were so confused and tangled that she didn't know where to begin to address them.

Jason's worry was much more immediate – they had no place to go, and no way to get there. They had money, enough to survive at least a little while, but there was no way that they could get a hotel room or ride any form of transportation without presenting ID – and that would almost certainly give them away. They could take a taxi as far as Cincinnati, but that would take more of their money than he felt they could spare. Already, he was beginning to suspect that they might have to give themselves up, if only to keep from living on the streets.

A fast-food chain restaurant lay on their side of the road a short way ahead, and he motioned toward it, saying, "we'll need to eat something, and we need to sit for a little while and figure out our next move."

She nodded, not looking at him, and together they walked toward it and entered.   Phoebe went to take a seat, while he got in line at the counter. Several minutes later, he was returning to her table with biscuits and drinks when he saw that she was not alone.

He stopped short, just as Phoebe cast a stricken look at him, and as she did, an iron grip closed on his arm, guiding him toward the table as a quiet, unsettling voice behind his ear suggested, "why don't we sit down?"

His legs felt like they were about to turn to water, but he managed to keep his feet as he was led, not painfully but very firmly, to sit at the table. An expressionless woman in a dark business suit and sunglasses sat next to Phoebe. Jason sat across from her, and the man who had taken his arm sat beside him.

For a moment no one spoke; then the woman leaned forward and said, quietly, "aren't you going to eat?"

"I've suddenly lost my appetite." Jason glanced at Phoebe, who nodded.

"And why would that be… *Mr. Anderson?*" The man asked, saying the last two words with odd emphasis.

In spite of himself, in spite of his fear, Jason could not help giving the man a strange look. He grinned back with apparently genuine humor.

"Sorry, but I always liked *The Matrix*, and I've always wanted to – interview – someone with that name. Couldn't resist the opportunity when it came up." He motioned toward the bag. "Go on and eat, even if you don't feel like it. You might not get another chance for a while."

"Aren't you going to arrest us?" Phoebe asked, her voice trembling.

"That depends on how much you can help us," the woman replied. "We've known where you were for some time, but we left you alone. We know most of the circumstances surrounding your, ah, sudden departure from Atlanta. We know why Mr. Anderson felt it necessary to drop out of sight – wise choice, incidentally," she added, looking from behind her sunglasses toward Jason. "And another wise choice in leaving when you did. That storage facility was crawling with FBI not ten minutes after you left."

"You mean you're *not* FBI?" Jason asked in surprise.

"Heavens, no. You think the FBI could be trusted to assess this situation correctly? Don't get me wrong, on their own ground they're as competent and dedicated as you could ask, but time travel really isn't their thing."

Jason's blood ran cold, and his skin crawled; across from him, Phoebe's eyes suddenly went round. The woman gave him a small, self-assured smile; he couldn't see her eyes, but he would have bet a lot that that smile had failed to reach them.

"So you know Phoebe didn't blow up the lab?" Jason asked, stalling for time while he tried to think.

"We know it, and *you* already know we know it. What we *don't* know who actually *did* blow up that lab. We're trying to learn why, and how. Now. *Eat.*" She reached into the bag and pulled out a biscuit, handing it to Jason.

"That's hers," he said, handing it to Phoebe; she looked completely confused and very frightened. He nodded to her, and she took it from him and began unwrapping it as he reached into the bag and drew a different one out for himself.

"So if you're not going to arrest us, and you know Phoebe's innocent, are you going to let her go?" Jason asked.

"That we cannot do, not yet. Miss Reyes' brother has been taken into custody; according to our sources, he will be transported back to Atlanta for questioning. It seems he had quite a few interesting artifacts stored in that unit you were hiding in." She looked over at Jason. "And he also had a quantity of depressants, with no prescription for them."

Phoebe looked stricken, but the woman waved her hand her placatingly. "All of that will go away once we get a few matters settled, but for now, we will need your boyfriend's help. Our organization has embarked on a project similar to the one that was so thoroughly wrecked two months ago, and it has developed an issue that we can neither control nor explain."

"Is this the only reason you were looking for me?" Jason quickly asked.

"Of course not. We're going to have to interview you both, quite thoroughly – you in particular, Mr. Anderson. For that, we will have to return to our local facility, and before we do that, *you – need – to – eat*. Don't make me tell you again." The sunglasses hid what was clearly an impatient glare.

Phoebe and Jason exchanged another look; Jason shrugged. "If you were going to arrest us, you already would have," he said aloud. He glanced toward each of their two unexpected companions before meeting Phoebe's gaze again. "I think we should go with them."

"I don't think we really have a choice," Phoebe answered. She still looked afraid.

"That's essentially true," the man answered her. "We don't *want* to be unpleasant about this, and you'll certainly benefit from your cooperation with us. But if coercion is necessary -" he shrugged, his eyebrows raising slightly – "then we will do what is required."

"So if we come with you peacefully, there won't be any handcuffs or jail cells or anything?" Jason asked, looking steadily at him.

He removed his sunglasses and returned the look directly. "You'll be in a secure facility. But otherwise, no, none of that."

Jason looked at Phoebe again. "You're right, we don't have a choice, but I like this option a hell of a lot more than the FBI." He then glanced at the male agent again before addressing the woman. "We'll come with you. I assume you want us to finish eating?"

One of the woman's eyebrows raised above the top of her sunglasses. With a smile that he knew looked slightly insolent, he said, "it'll take a minute. We each have two. Unless you'd like one?" When no further response came, he began to devour the still-warm biscuit in his hand, and Phoebe, though still nonplussed, did likewise.

Chapter Seven

AL REYES RODE, NOT very comfortably, in the rear of what he believed was an unmarked FBI vehicle. He was handcuffed, his ankles shackled, and a chain had been drawn between the two sets of restraints that made it impossible for him to move any limb more than a few inches in any direction.

One of the goons who had arrested him in Dayton rode in the back with him, and two more were in front; all were armed, and none of them looked even remotely friendly or sympathetic. Al sighed. The only real hope he had of evading prison – which looked damned unlikely at that point – was by convincing those men's superiors that Jason Anderson was still alive.

They had taken Interstate 75 south of Cincinnati through its Kentucky suburbs; they had circled the city on its west side. For a few minutes he had dared to hope that they might fly him back to Atlanta, but they had passed the airport without stopping.

It was past noon; he guessed that, given the rate at which they were driving, they would be back sometime around ten, or a little before. He had little reason to hope that anything pleasant would be awaiting him there – or wherever it was they were taking him. His only faint source of hope was in the fact that, while his captors had generally gone out of their way to be unfriendly, he had not actually been abused at all. He hoped that full cooperation with them would keep things that way.

The ride up had been boring in the night, and daylight had failed to improve it; he found rural Kentucky shockingly dull. He could see that they were already nearing the mountains; that would at least make it a slightly more interesting ride, if not a more bearable one. He couldn't decide whether he wanted it to be over, where the cuffs could finally be taken off him, or whether he wanted to avoid wherever they were taking him for as long as he could.

He leaned toward the side of the car and closed his eyes, trying to catch up a little of the sleep he had missed, and hoping that somehow he would be able to extricate himself from his situation. For a few minutes he was close to dozing off, but then his brain reminded him that without a safe house, Phoebe and her boyfriend would probably have to spend the night without shelter, and that worried him even more than his own plight – especially knowing that Anderson might be mentally unstable. He could only hope that Phoebe would call the police if she became desperate; once Anderson was found, they all might be released without charges, given that he had cooperated fully.

He twisted his head around, trying to clear his thoughts as well as relieve an incipient crick in his neck, and settled back into the best sleeping position he could achieve. This time, his mind allowed him to drift off without further interruption.

GENERAL HAVERHILL SAT IN his borrowed office, mulling over the latest reports he had received on the situation in Ohio. In one regard, his job had just gotten a lot easier; in another, he had just been given something truly terrifying to worry about.

He had summoned Mangum and Eier; Tinsworth was not to be part of this discussion. The DARPA agents would need to know some of the basics of the situation at least; Tinsworth's security clearance, while higher than most, prevented his inclusion.

He was still trying to figure out how Anderson could possibly be alive, when the body in Bryant's morgue was clearly his. There had been a medical history search done, and sure enough, he had visited the campus clinic for an ear infection a year before being named to the bridge project. The DNA from the blood test taken at that time had matched the battered, burnt corpse Bryant had inherited. Jason Anderson, for all intents and purposes, was very obviously dead.

Except that he just as clearly wasn't. Another organization – the one he couldn't even name, not to his DARPA subordinates – had reportedly picked up Anderson and his girl in Dayton, not far from where the girl's brother had been caught, and they were taking both of them to their laboratory in the same city. It was sheer luck, for all concerned, that their chosen hiding place had been less than two miles away from a facility that was – secretly – doing almost exactly the same experiments that Tinsworth's team had pioneered.

He glanced up as Eier and Mangum entered; they saluted, and stood at attention as Haverhill studied them each for a moment, before he muttered, "at ease," and they relaxed. "Sit," he said, gesturing toward the chairs as he himself dropped back into his own, more comfortable one.

They looked at each other for several seconds, as Haverhill sought to frame his words correctly, but at last he almost blurted, "men, there's no getting around it. I have confirmation from sources in Ohio that Jason Anderson is definitely alive."

Eier's eyes widened slightly; Mangum's brow furrowed. "So Tinsworth was right. Any reason why he hasn't been brought here already?" Mangum asked.

"Security reasons." Haverhill's response was curt. "Anderson has been – commandeered – by an ongoing operation in Dayton. It relates directly to his own line of research, and is classified even beyond your clearances. I can only confirm to you that he is in fact alive, that he is reportedly cooperating with this operation, and that Phoebe Reyes is with him." He snorted. "They also confirmed that Phoebe Reyes should no longer be considered a suspect in the lab explosion."

"Obviously not, if Anderson is alive," Mangum answered. "Phoebe Reyes' brother was apprehended this morning and is being renditioned back here. With your permission, I'd like him transferred to the facility where Grant's being held."

"Why d'you want him transferred there, Colonel?" Haverhill asked guardedly. He knew Alfonzo Reyes was considered a bad actor, though not much of a credible threat. "If the girl didn't destroy the lab, then Reyes' communications with her weren't criminal. He hasn't actually done anything to justify being held."

"Grant's been saying all along that he didn't have anything to do with what happened. Maybe putting those two together will tell us something we don't already know, before we let them go. We're going to have to release Grant as well." Mangum sighed. "I don't want him on any more DARPA projects, but that may be unavoidable. He knows the project about as well as Anderson did. He's probably the second-best graduate assistant available here. But he's got a lazy streak, and frankly, he could use a personality transplant."

"He might be slightly different once released, Colonel," Haverhill pointed out. "He's not likely to forget that experience anytime soon. Renditioning is designed to fuck with the subject's head."

"That's true." Mangum chuckled. "He griped about the food he was getting – and he was better fed than just about anyone I've ever seen in his situation – so we decided to have some fun with him, and gave him TV dinners until he broke."

Haverhill looked puzzled. "I'll grant those aren't military standard, but what was his problem with them?"

"He seemed disappointed that they weren't heated before they were served," Mangum said, with a slightly nasty smile.

Haverhill stared back at him for several seconds before erupting in laughter. "That might have been a problem," he replied a few seconds later, still chuckling. "So what do you think you might learn from having them interact?"

"Alfonzo Reyes is not his sister," Eier spoke up. "Phoebe Reyes was absolutely clean up until the lab explosion, and she's been cleared of that. Alfonzo was apprehended with a controlled substance with intent to distribute, and there were several firearms in the storage unit where he was arrested."

"There may still be more to this story than we know, General," Mangum continued. "We've got one logical impossibility – Anderson being both dead and alive – and there may be things behind the scenes that we don't know about. The fact remains – Grant left his station, and not two minutes later, it blew up in a way that shouldn't have been possible. There may still be some link we don't know about. While we have them both in custody, it makes sense to try to find out more of what was happening."

Haverhill considered. "All right, I'll give the order, but you have twenty-four hours. If they're not released after that, it'll be on your head, Colonel." He rose, and the two officers rose with him as he added, "dismissed."

PHOEBE AND JASON RODE in the back seat of a black SUV that fit every secret-government cliché imaginable; their two captors, again in sunglasses, rode in front.

Phoebe was watching Jason, who in turn was watching where they were going; they had left the restaurant and were driving north. She was struck by how relaxed he looked; he had always been tense and worried when they were in hiding. Maybe, she thought to herself, he only needed to be actively controlling his destiny, even if only slightly – as was the case in this situation.

She had expected a long ride, but it turned out to be quite short: within ten minutes, the SUV had pulled into the parking lot surrounding an abandoned arena complex and was driving around to the back. The lot was empty, with a widespread, grass-sprouting delta of cracks running through it, and as they drove behind it, the asphalt expanse was bordered by overgrown, neglected lots of scraggly, wild trees. Not even one vehicle was parked there. Phoebe looked fearfully toward Jason, but he seemed unperturbed.

"Welcome to Hara Arena," the man in the front said, not ungenially. "The old minor-league hockey team, the Gems, used to play here, but the place wasn't generating anything like enough revenue to cover the cost of keeping it up."

"Doesn't look like anyone's spent anything on it since then, either," Jason replied, looking at the structure with some uncertainty.

"It's more convenient for us if it looks like this on the outside." The woman, who was driving, glanced back at them as she drew close to the arena's rear entrance; as she did, she pressed a button mounted on their vehicle's dashboard, and the freight door began to lift. Inside, up a short incline, there was just enough room for the SUV to park beside a forlorn-looking, orange Zamboni whose front was emblazoned with "I saw it at Hara!" in black lettering. Jason and Phoebe glanced at each other again.

"I hope you don't have any jail cells in here?" Phoebe's words began as a statement, but ended as a nervous question. The man in front took off his sunglasses as he glanced back, smiling again with surprisingly genuine green eyes.

"Of course not. We normally keep a few motel rooms reserved a few miles from here, in case we have need to put up individuals like yourselves. I assume you'll be in one together?" The woman had opened her door and was getting out, but the male agent continued to watch them closely in the mirror.

Phoebe hesitated for a moment, glancing at Jason, and then looked straight at him. "You said he traveled in time. How do you know that?"

"Because there's no doubt that this man you're with is Jason Anderson, and there's even less doubt that the body in storage back in Atlanta is also Jason Anderson," he answered. "No one on earth has that kind of cloning technology – not even remotely close. Time travel is the only way to explain that one." His shaded eyes appeared to be watching for her response.

Phoebe gave Jason, who had listened with one eyebrow lifted as the man spoke, a surprised look before returning the agent's gaze and nodding affirmatively. She finally answered, "But he's not the *same* Jason – is he?"

"I told you, Phoebe," he said quietly. "Until the moment when I made my lab go up, I was exactly the same. At least I think I was. I know the differences were so small that you would never have known. I know you're *exactly* the same."

Tears sprang into her eyes again. "But that means… that means you died in the lab."

Jason closed his eyes. Of all of the things he had done to get back to her, that had been his one regret: he had killed another version of himself.

"Phoebe, I would not have done that if I had not been completely willing to make the same sacrifice myself. If the Jason in the lab had known why it happened, he would have accepted it. I know because he's me, and I would have," he said, his voice cracking.

The man in front glanced at each of them, then turned and began exiting the SUV, saying as he did, "We can discuss this more later. Right now, we have a more pressing problem that could cause a similar explosion at any moment, in this building. We'd appreciate it if you'd come with us now." He closed the door behind him and went to stand beside his counterpart. They were alone inside the vehicle.

"I don't know what to think anymore," Phoebe said sadly.

"No one would, Phoebe. No one has ever had this happen. Believe me, I get it," he replied. Tentatively, he reached across and took her hand with both of his. She stared despairingly at him, her lips pursed and trembling.

"We need to help these people now, if we can. If what I did is something that can be repeated, it means that a bridge like we made in my old lab could be turned into a remote-control bomb." Jason squeezed her hand gently, once, and then let go, opening his car door and getting out. A moment later, she did the same.

Chapter Eight

DR. ALLEN BRYANT'S OFFICE in the basement of Nesmith Hall had been converted from a Cold War-era bomb shelter, and it looked the part; unlike many of the professors on campus, Bryant preferred function to form. The walls were whitewashed cinderblock, most of which were lined with bookshelves that were crammed with medical texts and journals. As it was below ground, it had no windows, and could only be accessed down a short staircase. Bryant had eschewed fluorescent lights, preferring two incandescent fixtures attached to the concrete ceiling and several lamps. His desk was stacked with papers and textbooks, but was orderly, and there was not a speck of dust anywhere in the room.

In front of the desks were several chairs, and those were occupied by the two DARPA agents assigned to this campus, along with Dr. Tinsworth, who looked singularly unhappy to be there. Bryant looked across his desk toward the three men, nonplussed and slightly puzzled.

"I don't know why you wanted to call a face-to-face in here, Colonel," he said, watching Tinsworth. The man's research was unrelated to his, and while he was quite competent in his field, his recent successes had largely rested on his good fortune in recruiting two of the best graduate assistants the university had ever produced. Until the disastrous failure in Williams Hall, he had appeared to be riding them to a Nobel Prize in physics. "I haven't had any explosions in here recently."

Tinsworth's face darkened noticeably. "Not yet, you haven't. But that may be about to change," he answered in what was almost a snarl.

"Gentlemen," Mangum said firmly, "the reason we're meeting here, in person, instead of on a conference call, is related to the explosion in

Tinsworth's lab. What we're going to discuss here is classified." He glanced over to Eier, who continued, "we have reason to believe that the security of this facility may have been compromised."

Bryant's annoyed bemusement hardened into disbelief. "That seems unlikely. I've got four GA's working with me on the cyborg project, and they're all trustworthy. No one who's left the project had any information on it beyond the morgue, and that's nothing unusual for a medical research facility. If there's been espionage, I think I would have been aware of it by now."

"This isn't an inside job, Allen," Tinsworth interjected. "This is something you might not be able to believe."

"We aren't certain of that yet," Eier shot back.

Mangum cut across them both. "At the moment we have two working hypotheses of how this happened, but for practical reasons, it doesn't matter so much how this information got out as what measures need to be taken."

Bryant was watching them all with growing anger and suspicion. "What are your two theories, Colonel? I want to know who I'll be firing as soon as we're done here."

"We're not sure. The first possibility is that someone – we don't know who – was passing that information to a subversive operation, and that that operation was responsible for the explosion in Williams Hall." Mangum looked directly at Bryant, whose eyes narrowed as he glared back. "The second possibility is that there was no insider, and that the information was conveyed by another means."

Bryant snorted. "You're telling me nothing. 'Either there's a mole in your department, or there's not.' No shit, Sherlocks. And you still haven't explained why this hack –" he pointed at Tinsworth – "is even in here. So are you going to keep wasting my time, or are you going to tell me what's really going on?"

Tinsworth's reply was low and quiet, but venomous. "They want me here so that I can explain to you why Williams Hall shouldn't have blown up. There's still the possibility that a terrorist left a bomb in the building, but there was no residue in anything that was examined in the lab. Nothing.

But the other possibility is that the explosion was caused by a velocity differential between two bridge endpoints."

Bryant looked at him for a moment, surprised despite himself. "You know, I'm just a medical doctor, so I don't have the physics background you have, but it seems to me that there shouldn't *be* a velocity differential between the endpoints of a bridge in your lab. Not unless you were moving them."

"That's the point." Tinsworth's voice still dripped acid. "*We* didn't move them. Someone else did, and we don't know how it was done. The bridge by itself would have just winked out. But if the endpoint had a temporal dislocation, that could create a big problem – especially if the dislocation were accompanied by an expansion of the bridge diameter."

"Wait. You're saying something made it bigger, and moved it – in *time*? How is that even possible?" Bryant glanced at the two DARPA agents; their expressions were impassive. "And what reason do you have to believe that happened?"

It was Tinsworth's turn to look over at Eier and Mangum; Eier nodded, and Tinsworth glared back at Bryant. "Yesterday, I got a call that was traced to a cell tower in a town north of Cincinnati. The caller identified himself as Jason Anderson, and said that his DNA was an exact match for the body you've got stored in your lab."

"And you believed him?" Bryant's momentary incredulity dissolved into a contemptuous sneer.

"The point is, he knew about your lab. *I* certainly didn't tell him about it," Tinsworth shot back. "So either there's some sort of terrorist cell out there that knows a *lot* more than they should, or Anderson *is* alive, even though his body is in your morgue – and that would mean that the bridge was changed into something that could be traversed relatively safely. But also, that might mean that any Einstein-Rosen bridge built anywhere in the world can be turned into a bomb."

Bryant scowled, first at Tinsworth, and then at the DARPA officers. "I'll assume it's the terrorist cell. Again, I'm not a physicist, but from what I do know, the idea of a passable bridge would indicate time travel, and that's insane. Besides, I know for a fact Anderson showed up in my lab as dead as George Fucking Washington."

Mangum looked hard at Bryant. "If you assume that this was a terrorist act, then you won't mind if we question your assistants?"

"You know I answer directly to Haverhill. When *he* gives the order, you can talk with them. Not before." Bryant rose to his feet. "So until then, officers, I believe you've taken up enough of my time. You can show yourselves out."

Mangum didn't move. "And who exactly did you think sent us to speak with you?" he growled, his normally polite voice slightly roughened by suppressed anger. "Haverhill's here now, and he agrees with Tinsworth – but you might want to think about talking to your people, just to make sure your ass is covered. After this conversation, I'm not going to be tripping over myself to cover it for you."

Bryant glared again at Mangum, who glowered right back. Eier looked slightly uncomfortable, and Tinsworth looked uncertainly at each of them in turn. Seconds ticked by before Mangum rose, slowly, his stare never wavering, and said quietly, "we'll show ourselves out."

He turned, and made his way back toward the low flight of cement stairs leading to the door. As he passed them, Eier and Tinsworth rose and followed. Bryant stared after them long after the door to his office had clicked shut.

Once outside, the three men made their way back through the Nesmith Hall basement to its entrance, and exited the building. Tinsworth nodded to the two officers, but said nothing more before leaving them and making his way toward his aging pickup truck. Eier and Mangum watched him depart.

"Not a lot of help from Bryant. You think he'll talk to Haverhill?" Eier asked.

"Most likely," Mangum responded. "And I'd just as soon let the General tell him that we don't trust him."

"I'M AGENT GREENE, AND my associate here is Agent Jensen. Sorry not to introduce ourselves before, but we have to be pretty tight with information about ourselves when we're in public." The male agent's friendliness seemed genuine enough; Jensen seemed somewhat more aloof. Jason guessed that she was the senior partner of the two.

They had made their way around the old hockey arena; from the few glances he got of its interior, it was apparent that nothing was being done with it. The ceiling tiles were often black with mold, when they weren't missing; the seats were a faded, mustard-yellow color that probably had not ever been particularly attractive even when new, and the boards surrounding the concrete that had underlaid the rink had not been painted in at least a decade, so that they went from a flaking, dingy off-white to a dishwater-gray at their base.

"Did you try to use the arena as a staging area?" Jason wondered aloud.

"I asked the same question when I was assigned here," Jensen answered. "I was told that the magnetic fields were too close to allow experimentation within a single building unless it was very large – too large to escape notice easily if it were abandoned. There were a few buildings – closed auto plants in Detroit, for example – that might have served, but there were other problems with those locations.

"There were a lot of factors involved in the decision of where to conduct this research. Above all else, nothing about it could be notable – we didn't want to attract any attention. Dayton's perfect for that – it's a place everyone's from, but where no one stays. It's a dead-average small city in every way you can imagine. It's completely generic. This arena is a perfect example of how the outside world sees the whole town – out of date, past its prime, nothing new. It's just Dayton. No one gives it a second thought, just like no one gives this arena a second thought. It used to be a place. Now people just drive by it and if they think about it at all, they forget about it a minute later. It's been here forever, and it's as dated as the rest of this part of town."

Jason thought about that. "I guess that was initially because you wanted to discourage espionage."

"Exactly," Greene replied. "If anyone decided to come snooping on us here, we'd know it immediately. There was no sign of any outside interference for two years – but then your lab blew up, and since then, it's become clear that we're being watched, at the very least. We think they may know what we're up to, though we're not sure. That's why we came for you, once we knew the FBI was about to raid your little hideout. Absent that, we were prepared to wait until you were ready to come out of hiding, but once this – phenomenon – started, we knew that eventually we would have to enlist you."

" 'Enlist.' You'll forgive me if I don't quite like the sound of that." Jason shot a glance at him as they drew to a halt, a little less than halfway around the disused, grimy concourse that ringed the arena. A sign indicating that section twenty-eight was to their right hung askew from one of its original two chains. To their left, a dim hallway crowded with discarded, superannuated chairs and folded convention tables led deeper into the complex, away from the arena itself.

"You wouldn't believe what's in that conference room to the right," Jensen said as they passed a pair of heavily-locked doors. There was just enough light for them to see where they were going, and just enough space left in the hallway for them to walk two abreast – Phoebe in front with Jensen, with Jason and Greene behind them. The hallway darkened again, until they reached another door to their left. It also was locked, but that lock looked newer than anything else in the place. It and the doorknob were set in a postcard-sized metal plate.

Jensen held a small key ring in her hand; she fitted a key into the lock, turning it, so that a small panel with a number pad was revealed behind the metal plating, just above the doorknob. She glanced back at Jason and grinned; her white teeth gleamed slightly unnaturally in the near-dark. She had removed her sunglasses during their walk, but it was still too dark for him to see her face clearly.

"Anyone busts this lock without the code, and all they'll find is an empty room." She looked back at the keypad. "Normally we'd use an electronic key or a fingerprint scan, but this method actually works better in this case. Someone trying to get in who doesn't know the code will trigger a master alarm after two bad entries. That automatically resets the system so that no one can get in. If any of us were kidnapped and interrogated, we would all know to give our captors a phony access code, and that would lock them out – and we wouldn't be able to tell them how to get in after that,'

"But wouldn't that be dangerous for you?" Phoebe asked. Greene chuckled slightly, but Jason shuddered. Jensen looked meaningfully at him.

"Mr. Anderson seems to understand the danger implied in this – project," she replied. She quickly tapped a five-digit code into the system, then turned the doorknob. After she removed the key from the lock, she closed the panel, and the four of them all entered the room, Greene closing the door behind them as he entered last.

They were in a small, dark, windowless conference room with faded seventies-era décor, walled with heavily dated wood paneling. A section of that paneling had sprung open, leading to a much more brightly lit – and much more recently and solidly constructed – stairwell leading straight downward.

Jason glanced knowingly toward Jensen. "I knew this complex was too small for a bridge to be built here. If you've managed to construct one, where'd you put the other endpoint?"

Greene's smile faded completely for the first time since the two agents had joined them. "The second endpoint was built underground. The access point is in the maintenance shed of a high school about a half mile southeast of here."

Even in the dimness, Jason paled. "How close is the other end to the school?"

"Too close," Jensen answered seriously. "We thought that if our bridge failed, the energy release would be negligible, but the event in your lab changed that."

Jason thought about that as Jensen started down the stairwell. Phoebe looked questioningly toward him; he nodded to her, indicating that she should follow. As she turned, he saw Greene watching him carefully.

"I don't like the idea of being underground with an intact bridge," Jason said. "Especially when I know how wrong something can go with it."

"Understood. We considered shutting the bridge down after the first few instances, but it took months for us to create it, and we weren't certain whether the problem was a by-product of the bridge formation, or something else. It's still happening, and we've been concerned that it might be the lead-up to another explosion like the one in your lab."

Jason thought for a moment. "That's unlikely. I know why my lab blew up. This probably isn't the same thing at all. I don't know what it is. At least, I *hope* I don't."

Greene shrugged. "We can talk about what happened in your lab after you see what's going on here. After you," he added, motioning toward the stairs.

Jason moved past him and began to descend. The walls of the stairwell were whitewashed concrete, with a tunnel at the bottom about fifteen feet below and about twice that far ahead. About halfway down, he heard the voice inside his head speak again, so abruptly that he stopped in his tracks. Greene halted behind him.

"What is it?" Greene asked.

"I'll tell you when we talk about the lab explosion," Jason replied, his voice barely above a whisper. He could only force himself to move forward again with difficulty, his thoughts suddenly roiling in fear.

Chapter Nine

ALFONZO REYES WAS extremely worried.

He had expected to be taken to the Atlanta Penitentiary, or to the Atlanta City Detention Center, and booked there. Instead, he had been hooded as soon as the sun went down, as they neared Chattanooga. He had no idea of where he was, except that they had driven for about as long as it would have taken to get to Atlanta – but that proved nothing. They might well have taken another route into Nashville or Birmingham. The only thing he knew was that they had remained on the interstate for quite some time – more than ninety minutes, by his best guess.

When the hood was finally taken off, they were in an underground parking garage, but his relief at breathing fresher air was short-lived. The size of the place told him that he was probably underneath a fairly large building, meaning that in all likelihood, he was in a city large enough for such a building to exist.

He had been taken into a stark, windowless concrete processing cell and left there in handcuffs for perhaps thirty minutes; the person who finally retrieved him had not asked him a single question. Instead, he had been taken down a flight of stairs (*but they were already underground*, he thought to himself – *this was a dungeon!*) into a small prison where all the cells were defined by floor-to-ceiling bars, except those that bordered the walls. The prison was empty, except for one sleeping, unkempt-looking man who looked pale and unhealthy, as though he had lost a lot of weight in a short time. He was in one of the cells against the far wall.

Al's captors led him to the cell next to that one. As they neared it, a loud buzzer sounded, and the metal-grilled door swung open; the unkempt man was startled awake, and watched them all with the appearance of someone too scared to say anything.

After frisking him again, one of the men waited outside with his weapon drawn while the other led him into the cell; that one undid the handcuffs Al had been wearing for the last twelve hours before shoving him, though not very hard, into the cell as he backed away. The door clanged shut as Al turned around, rubbing his wrists; his captors were already walking back to the stairs. They did not look back, and Al did not call after them.

He went and sat down on the bunk set into the cell's rear wall; he was in a space measuring less than eight feet by six feet, with a metal toilet/sink on one side and a small, bare table on the other; the table was low, and close enough to the bed that it could be used as a desk. In addition to the bars, a metal mesh separated the cells from each other. It would be impossible for anyone to get a finger more than two inches into the next cell.

He sensed the other inmate watching him, but refused to acknowledge that. Still trying to work out the stiffness left behind after twelve hours in handcuffs, he twisted his neck and stretched his arms as best he could. He was very sore.

"Was it your sister that blew up our lab?" The words came unexpectedly from the next cell. Al glared over at the inmate. He was younger than he had initially thought – probably Jason's age, he guessed, and as that thought came to him, he realized who he was.

"If you say another word about my sister, you'd better hope that one of us stays in here for life. I'll rip your fucking head off." Al glared straight at him. The other man flinched, but did not give up.

"All I know is, *I* didn't blow it up. If the bridge had gone down normally, it wouldn't have caused anything like that explosion. The girl was in Williams Hall talking to Anderson when I went to the can. The place blew up less than two minutes later. And you look enough like her that you're either siblings or cousins." He paused. "I'd already worked out that she did it. Did you help her?"

"Go fuck yourself," Al growled back.

"I'm already fucked, but thanks for the invite," the man replied. "You're fucked too. You just haven't figured it out yet. They're going to nail you for a terrorist act and first-degree murder. You'll get the death penalty."

Al slowly turned and looked at the other inmate for several seconds. Silence fell, and stretched out, before he answered: "They can't get me for either one."

"Looks like they already did. Where do you think you are, anyway? This isn't the Atlanta jail. I'd bet no one knows where we are except the guys who took us here." The other inmate smiled nastily, though fearfully, at him. "They might just dispense with the trial and carry out the sentence."

"That won't happen." Al tried to maintain a confidence that he suddenly no longer felt.

"You don't think so? All *I* did was leave my station. That was enough to make them think I was a part of what happened, and that got me locked in here about two months ago. I haven't seen *anyone* since then. You can forget the phone-call-and-lawyer shit. Guys who end up in *these* cells aren't supposed to come back out." The other inmate suddenly sat back on his bunk, looking as defeated as Al felt.

Al thought about that for a minute, considering, and decided he had no choice. He leaned forward, looking at where the other inmate was slumped, and asked, "What if I told you that Jason Anderson is alive, and that his girlfriend – my sister – is with him?"

The man sat up quickly, but a wary cast quickly replaced the surprised hope that had momentarily wrested control of his features. "Are you fucking with me?"

Al considered again. It would probably serve the ugly bastard right to leave him hanging, but if he could be turned into an ally – even if only partially – then that would be to his advantage.

It was an easy decision.

"I'm serious as a heart attack." He moved down the bunk, closer to the bars that separated them, considered his next words briefly, and spoke more quietly once he chose them. "Who are you?"

"Name's Wiley Grant. Like I said, I was with Anderson on the bridge project. You said his girlfriend is with him? That he's alive?"

"I'm Al Reyes. Yeah, he's with her, or he was until this morning. They left Atlanta a few days after the lab went up." Al sighed. "Look, I'm tired, they haven't given me any food, and it's been a *long* day. I'll tell you the whole story in the morning. But I'm sure she didn't blow up your lab, and I'm even more sure that Anderson's alive. I'd met him before, and it was definitely him." He nodded to Wiley as he turned and stretched out on the thin, sheeted padding that failed to soften the hardness of his metal bunk. He closed his eyes, hoping that food would be brought before morning, and aware that the other inmate was still watching him.

He didn't need to act. Within a few minutes, the sleep of exhaustion overtook him.

AT THE BASE OF THE stairs leading under the arena complex, a narrow hallway stretched forward until it shrank to a point in the distance; a low door was set in the wall to their left, with an identity scanner beside it. It somehow looked both bright and forbidding.

Phoebe was watching Jason closely. He looked visibly shaken. "Are you all right?" she asked.

Jason nodded affirmatively. He was still pale, and breathing heavily, but he refused Greene's proffered arm of support. Instead, he bent forward, his hands on his knees, and lowered his head for a few seconds as though he had just completed a race. Phoebe shot a worried look at Jensen, who alone among them remained unmoved by the scene.

"This looks like a stress reaction," she said quietly. Greene looked askance at her, and Jason looked up as well. "We're going to show you where we are on this project. Are you up to that?" she asked him.

"I think so," he replied, more than a little unsteadily, but he stood up again with a sigh, and seemed to be recovering himself. Greene and Jensen exchanged another look before Jensen shrugged, and turning back toward the door, held her thumb over the scanner pad. A second later, a muted buzz sounded from the room beyond, and the door swung inward.

In spite of his recent distress, Jason was surprised by what he saw: the facility was a near-duplicate of his own lab, including the intercom; beyond the airlock, a technician some ten years older than himself sat at a decidedly more advanced-looking console than his own had been. He looked at Jensen again.

"Whoever you're with, it's obvious you're well-funded," he said. Jensen responded with the first completely genuine smile he had seen from her.

"That we are," she replied. "How much of this looks familiar to you?"

"I recognize the overall setup. It looks like you had access to our design, and duplicated a lot of it, except you upgraded the console." Jason looked at the lab again. A long tube ran away from them, parallel to the hallway they had just left. He smiled. "Neodymium wiring to manipulate the fields?

"Samarium cobalt. We thought it might remain more stable in the event of a fire." Jason nodded, looking thoughtfully at the lab setup. The man at the console remained focused on what he was doing, apparently unaware – or, at least, dismissive – of the people watching him work.

Nothing happened for nearly a full minute, until Jason asked, "so, what's this thing you say is happening, and why do you think I can help with it?"

Jensen's eyes never left the lab as she answered. "Every so often, there's an anomalous energy discharge. It seems harmless, but it's large enough to be noticeable, and after what happened in your lab, we're all concerned that there may be more going on here than random energy discharges."

Jason was deep in thought as he watched the lab, and did not reply. More time passed. Phoebe watched Jason as he stared intently toward the console.

It happened so fast that none of them saw it directly: there was a distinct popping sound not unlike that of a cork leaving a champagne bottle, and a very brief, very faint flash of light. All of the observers were startled, including the man actually in the lab; he recovered more quickly than any of them, and turned, acknowledging his visitors for the first time.

A red light on the intercom next to the airlock door flashed; before Jensen moved, Greene shot forward and pressed it, saying without preamble, "we saw that."

"I did, too." The voice speaking through the intercom was altered by the medium transmitting it; for a moment Jason felt a pang of regret. He had never realized how unlike himself he must have sounded when he had talked with her over a very similar intercom, in a universe he would never again reach.

He glanced toward Phoebe, and saw her watching him. He moved closer to her, and said very softly, "I never thought about how I sounded when we talked over that thing. I'm sorry."

Her evident sadness matched his own as she answered: "I know you didn't know."

He looked deeply into her eyes. He was still trying to recover from what the voice had said to him, and from the implications of the sound of the intercom for his memory of a place that he had himself sent to oblivion. Like then, he knew his strength was waning, even though it was not quite midday, and that he would have to rest soon.

"I'll explain why this hit me so hard after we get away from here." He looked around toward Jensen and Greene, quietly adding, "Get that man out of there and leave the bridge intact. If someone's on the other end, get them out, too."

Greene and Jensen both looked puzzled. "Why? We've seen those happen before. We were hoping you could explain them."

"That's what I'm going to do – when we get out of here. *Now.* We don't have any time to waste. If you can access the bridge console remotely, we need to do it that way, instead of staying here." Jason was growing agitated. "Get them out. We *all* need to get out of here."

Jensen walked toward him until they were nearly nose to nose, and spoke firmly, but not angrily. "I'll do as you ask, if – and *only* if – you can tell me what you think that was."

He looked into the lab. The man inside was watching their conversation as well. Jason realized that he intercom was still transmitting.

He then looked back at Jensen, and replied, "I think that sound was a missed attempt to latch onto the bridge. Someone was trying to alter that endpoint's position. If they succeed, and they're from where I went, this lab could go up just like Ham – like Williams Hall did." Without waiting for an answer, he looked toward the tech still in the lab. "You can do what you like, but *I* wouldn't stay in there unless *her* life depended on it." He motioned toward Phoebe. The man's face drained of color.

Jensen stared at him for two more seconds, then looked back at the intercom, barking, "confirmed. Get out of there. Send the order to Swartz to evacuate, and *get out.*"

"Leave the bridge intact!" Jason shouted as the tech began to open windows on his console. He rounded in his chair again, staring back at Jason in disbelieving incomprehension. Jason gave him a seemingly inexplicable thumbs-up.

"Just leave it up. We have to go. *Now.*"

Jensen glared at Jason; the look echoed a look he had received from Tinsworth in another place and time.

"Do it!" she half-ordered, half-snarled.

A minute later, they were all walking rapidly out of the arena complex, back to where their vehicle awaited them. They all climbed in except the tech, who had already gotten into his car and left. Jensen gunned the engine into life, and another minute later, they were on a road leading away from the complex.

"I think we should monitor the bridge remotely for the next twenty-four hours, and then return," Jason said. He looked exhausted, but determined, and focused on the situation.

It was Greene's turn to look back at him, a questioning – but not angry – expression on his face. "Why would we go back in twenty-four hours?"

Jason looked at Phoebe, and took her hand; she was clearly as bewildered as Greene. Then he looked forward again, and answered, "If the attempt to latch onto the bridge is a rogue attempt, then they're going to succeed. Soon. I didn't see exactly where the probe was, but it was only a few feet away from the endpoint.

"What you heard – I'm thinking - was a package of nanoelectronic sensors being destroyed by the velocity differentials between two widely separated points in space-time. The problem is, since they're nanoelectronic, it's possible that they survived long enough to transmit data back to their source, and that will allow whoever sent the probe to get a better fix. If they're that close, they'll succeed in creating another rift – or blowing up the lab, or both – within twenty-four hours."

Jensen and Greene both responded at once: Greene asked, "*another* rift?" while Jensen said, "and the new rift will cause another explosion."

Jason answered Greene first – "I'll explain when we get where we're staying tonight –" before looking askance at Jensen. "Probably," he said to her after a moment's pause. "But I'm pretty sure that's what's happening, and that's a powerful argument against building any more of these bridges. Once they're activated, they become permanent space-time beacons, and anyone in a future date with the right tech can try to latch onto them – and that's beyond dangerous."

Jensen only nodded into the mirror and continued driving, albeit with less intensity. Jason sighed, and looked at Phoebe again.

"I had hoped to avoid this, but I think everything that happened before – that brought me here – is about to go down all over again."

Interlude

April 2032

DR. ALLEN BRYANT WOKE to another day in his shitty, postapocalyptic life in his usual foul mood.

He sat up in bed, grumbling as the auto-alarm sensed his movements and shut off; as considerate as it had been, it was still too late – again – to prevent his sense of irritation as he shuffled toward the shower.

He was the last real hygienic holdout, he reflected, as he cranked the hot water – this might be the only place left in Atlanta where that still worked – and disrobed. Their facility had been completed not a day too soon; as much as he had disliked Anderson, he had to admit that his initial projections had been enough for him to task his own major research at least partially toward those conclusions – and the confirmation of their accuracy had been so immediate, and so dire, that he had had to form an alliance with two men he detested in order to ensure his survival through at least the first stage of the fall of civilization.

The warm water felt like balm on his sore body. He had been obliged to help with the manual labor in the final stages of the Drome's construction, in order to get everything online before the projected date for the start of the disaster. In any other situation, he would have refused to do the work, but the data was so compelling, the projections so closely packed together, and their options so limited that he had had no choice. The work had gotten done, and he had worn himself out doing it.

He washed himself quickly; the shower was a combination of habit and superiority as much as anything else. He knew that it would not be long before he would take his last one, but it couldn't be helped. They had been lucky beyond belief to have salvaged as much as they had.

He tasted bitterness as he stood under the shower head. That bastard – Anderson – had turned into something so weird, but so intelligent, that even he had found himself forced to back down in the face of climate forecasts that were both insanely accurate and insanely horrifying. That asshole Tinsworth had been even worse. Once he found out that his star pupil had been brought back to life, and was doing what was possible to save as much as could be saved, he had gone all-in on the Station project, and there was no getting rid of him – not without alienating the being that he himself had created, but had realized he could no longer control.

The lone saving grace in what would otherwise have been an unacceptable situation was, strangely enough, Anderson himself. He had been the first survivor of the process Bryant had engineered, and had wakened with enough intelligence to be able to assist with further conversions within weeks. More importantly, he had ceased virtually all of his glandular functions at death, with the result that he expressed almost no emotions. Bryant usually sneered at science fiction, but he had to admit that he had managed to create a reasonable (and incalculably useful) facsimile of Mr. Spock.

He washed quickly, drying himself with the towel hung from the bar beside the shower, and dressed as quickly as he could. It was still early spring, but the temperatures were already summerlike – and it had gotten worse every year. July would bring hell, when it came. It was barely past sunrise, and the digital thermometer read seventy-nine degrees.

Within fifteen minutes, he had left his comfortable, if not very sumptuous, quarters and entered the low, concrete building next to the station where the server banks were housed. As usual, Anderson was already awake; he glanced up with his usual, disinterested, yet succinct "good morning" before returning his attention to the bank of monitors before him.

"Morning. Anything new?" Bryant's curt response was typical; Anderson, he knew, would not take offense.

"Several possibilities, none of which seem likely to be productive without massive resources." He glanced toward Bryant for an instant.

"Human survival this far inland will be less problematic long-term than along the coasts, but there will be severe climactic anomalies nevertheless."

"No shit. This heat's a killer." Bryant had unlocked his own computer bank; two screens that he had dedicated to one of the few remaining operative news sources online were returning 404 errors. "Shit. NPR's gone."

"NPR was certain to shut down, once the government ceased non-emergency operations. Weather.gov is still functioning in emergency capacity for the time being, but most of the NOAA ancillary functions are out." Anderson glanced again toward Bryant. "The NHC page is unresponsive. I have not been able to learn whether that shutdown is permanent, but with the changes in the coastlines worldwide, I would expect that it will be restored to at least partial functionality within the next few weeks."

Bryant groaned. "I don't need to be worrying about hurricanes. Just keeping this installation going is going to be enough of a challenge. Have you decided on a solution for the maintenance team?"

Anderson's reply was as immediate, as were all of his responses; Tinsworth had insisted that his behavioral software not be modified with the humanizing algorithms that had been implemented with the others of his kind. As a result, Anderson was less human-seeming on the surface than any of them.

"The best solution will be for this installation to maintain multiple teams, each dedicated to one axis of the rail system. Annette and Darleen are most effective when working together; I recommend that they be assigned to maintenance on the north-south line." Anderson's voice was inflectionless.

"What about this line, the east-west?" Bryant asked.

"This line should have at least three teams trained in maintenance and operation, taking on the task in turn. I do not expect that the north-south line will ever be put into use again - certainly not in the short term – but it must be kept intact if it is to serve the purpose I have in mind for it." Anderson did not look at Bryant; he was studying a complex equation carefully. It took Bryant a moment to make the connection.

"You've stared at that for almost a full minute. That's like me staring at it for a week. What are you working on?"

Anderson looked briefly toward him. "There's no way to reverse the climactic trends that are driving the current crisis, and no viable methods to alleviate them. I've decided to look into a different possibility that might have a better outcome, but will take some time to develop, and longer to implement."

"I had thought that our best chance would be with immediate or short-term measures. The longer we wait, the worse the situation will become." Bryant favored Anderson with an unusual expression, a puzzled glare, that was returned with the usual blank look from the latter.

"That is correct, and I am continuing research along those lines, but in the probable event that they are unsuccessful, it would be sensible to develop a longer-term strategy." Anderson looked back to the equations on his monitor before he continued, "These equations were derived from the work Dr. Tinsworth was pursuing at the time his laboratory was destroyed. It appears that an Einstein-Rosen bridge in a given position in space-time might be detectable with the right instrumentation, and that it might be alterable."

"I'm not a physicist. You'd need Tinsworth in here to understand what you're saying." It galled Bryant to have to say it, but it was true. Even more galling was the knowledge that Anderson was equally knowledgeable about his own field, and would surpass him before much longer. The only saving grace, again, was that he wasn't an asshole about it. Bryant frowned again, realizing that Anderson was getting close to unlocking the chain of events that had led to his re-creation in this form.

"I'm not sure Dr. Tinsworth could follow this idea any more than you. But I will have to talk with him. We're not going to stop the fall of civilization from where we are, but there may be a way to buy ourselves more time." Anderson leaned closer to the monitor; even with eye replacements – his own had been damaged in the explosion that had killed him – his vision remained subpar. Bryant grimaced slightly; that remained the only minor failure in what otherwise had been, by far, Bryant's most successful conversion to date.

"What did you have in mind?" he asked Anderson, reluctantly.

"The first thing I will require is more knowledge about the terrorist who called Dr. Tinsworth from Ohio after the lab exploded. If my theory is valid, then I think I know who he was, and if he actually was in Ohio, I'll need to know roughly where he was at the time."   Anderson's expression did not change even as his answer failed to satisfy Bryant – not that it ever changed much, at any time, for any reason.

"That didn't answer my question."

"From my perspective, it did."

"So you're not going to tell me."   Bryant rolled his eyes as he turned back to his monitor bank with a disgruntled snort, trying to hide his sudden worry.

Anderson replied without looking up.   "The fewer people who know what I'm going to attempt, the better."

"Is it dangerous?"

"Potentially catastrophic."

Bryant mulled that over as he opened his email application. Each month, there had been fewer communications than the month before, and for the last few weeks, his email had been empty more often than not – as it was today.   A major winter storm had hit the eastern United States in early March, and since then, communications with points north of Washington had been virtually nonexistent.   The few satellite radars he could still access painted a grim picture; shorelines had advanced inland along all American coasts.   Nearly one-third of Florida was underwater.

The longer they waited, the less of everything they had known would be left.   Bryant realized he didn't particularly care about that, but whatever Anderson was contemplating might become a huge problem.   Trying to sound neutral, he asked, "About how long do you think this will take?"

"Years," Anderson responded, his eyes never leaving the monitors.   "If I have a starting area to work with, it'll take less time, but it will still be five years at the least."

"What's the high end?"

Anderson looked at him. "It may prove undoable."

Bryant was about to shout an angry response at him, but the door behind him opened. Tinsworth was usually the last of the three to arrive, and this day was no exception. "Good morning, gentlemen," he said quietly as he passed them both and sat down at a desk some few feet away from them both. He wore the perpetually tired expression he had had for months as he logged into the network and studied the monitors on his desk.

Bryant grunted in annoyance. "Anything new we didn't already see?"

Tinsworth looked up at him with a long-suffering expression. "Must you always ask me that? I sleep later than you do because I think better at night." He glanced briefly back toward his monitors before continuing, "and no, I've had no communication of any kind."

Anderson asked, quietly and without preamble, "Dr. Tinsworth, when that terrorist called you from Ohio after the accident, do you remember the city where he was traced?

Tinsworth's eyes snapped toward him and held their gaze; Anderson stared back in solemn emotionlessness. Bryant's eyes darted between them. Tinsworth seemed to consider for a few moments, then said quietly, "The call came from Hamilton, Ohio. From what I was told, the caller was tracked down in Dayton a few days later and arrested. Why do you ask?"

"Did you ever learn the identity of the caller?" Anderson asked in reply, ignoring Tinsworth's question.

The professor glanced briefly toward Bryant, and then sighed. "I tried to find out, but the government types closed in on whoever it was, and I never could find out more." He looked hard at Anderson. "Again, why are you asking me this?"

A human being might have hesitated before speaking, weighing his words. Anderson might actually have done just that, in the microsecond it would have taken him, but to the true humans in the room, the pause would have been imperceptible if it happened. "I believe that man could hold the key to changing what is happening. He may be our best chance."

Tinsworth and Bryant exchanged a glance, and then Bryant said, "and you're still not going to tell us who you think he is."

"I cannot tell you that.   There are causality issues at work here." Anderson looked at each of them for an instant before looking again to his bank of monitors; both men realized belatedly that they had been very carefully studied, so quickly that anyone else would have missed it. "It's best that you know as little as possible for now. I will look more closely into this matter."

As Anderson fell silent, Bryant shot an annoyed look at Tinsworth, who replied with a "what can I do" shrug and resumed studying his own pair of screens. Pursing his lips with dim, frustrated rage, Bryant likewise returned to his own work as the familiar, faintly desperate, hopeless silence of their plight fell once more in the room.

Chapter Ten

JENSEN AND GREENE HAD checked into a rebranded, once-popular motel some ten miles from Hara Arena in Fairborn, a suburb northeast of Dayton. Jason and Phoebe shared a room accessible from theirs via a connecting door, and Jensen had joined them there almost as soon as they arrived.

Jason noted that the town looked as though it hadn't changed in at least thirty years, and remarked on that fact to Jensen after the connecting doors had been opened: "Are you sure we didn't go through a time warp in that arena to get here? This looks like the pictures my dad took of where he grew up."

Jensen looked appraisingly at him. "It's odd you should say that. As I told you, Dayton was selected for this project because it's – what it is, I suppose. The whole city seems like it's in a bit of a time warp. It's so far off the cutting edge that it might be overlooked."

"In any other case, you'd be right, I think," Jason answered. Phoebe had lain down on the bed, resting while she could, but she watched the conversation intently. Jensen's face betrayed a slight annoyance with Jason as Greene entered the room, carrying a laptop computer and a can of soda.

"So. I know it's not that late in the day, so we've got some time to kill. I was hoping you could tell us what you think's going on in that lab." Greene glanced toward the bed where Phoebe was resting, decided there was enough space, and sat on the edge.

Jason looked from one agent to the other, sighed, and moved to sit down next to Greene. His eyes narrowed as he looked at Jensen. "First thing. I have to know what our outcomes are, especially hers."

Jensen and Greene both stared back at him. "We're field agents," Jensen finally said. "We'll advocate for you if you help us, and our organization can certainly offer you protection you wouldn't otherwise have, but that decision's above our pay grade."

"If what you're telling us about the thing we saw in the lab is true, then you might have saved lives by getting us out," Greene added. "Our organization is not unmindful of people who do that sort of thing."

Jason motioned toward Phoebe, letting his eyes linger on her for a moment before he continued. "I've already had to go through hell to get her back, and to save her from something I don't even want to talk about here. I don't think even you guys know about that. I didn't go through all of that just to have you disappear us."

"Maybe it's time that you tell us, then," Jensen answered. She seated herself in a chair near the window of their room and looked expectantly at Jason, who cleared his throat uncomfortably, shot a resigned glance toward Phoebe, and began to speak.

He told them briefly about the bridge project as he had known it, up until the day that Phoebe had come in and left him over the intercom. He described the explosion that had taken place and his escape from Williams Hall before the second blast at the other end of the tube, but when he reached the point where he had found Phoebe's body, his voice failed him.

Phoebe had sat up, her back against the headboard, and was watching him as he retold the story he had told her. When his voice trailed away, she said quietly, "you have to tell them."

He looked back over his shoulder at her, his eyes again seeming to radiate the dual personality that was so unsettling for her, but then he sighed. "The only way back is forward," he said quietly, and turning back to Jensen, he resumed his story.

Jensen and Greene listened attentively as Jason described his visit to Nesmith Hall, his passage through the rift, the post-Seaflood world, and the Cybwomen he had encountered. Several times Jensen interrupted with questions about Seaflood details; of those he had known little, other than that the event had disrupted civilization to the point where it had fallen, and that it had started at least ten years after their current time. Both agents looked deeply troubled, both by the extent of the destruction and the collapse of the food supply chain that had followed.

When he reached the point where he had reversed the directional collapse of the bridge, Jensen stopped him. "How were you able to latch onto it at all, let alone change it?"

"Wiley was the one who did that." Jason hesitated. "Dr. Bryant made him into something completely different, almost like a supercomputer, but paranoid and power-hungry. Supposedly it took even him decades to figure out how to do it. I didn't have time to decipher all of the math, but I didn't have to. Professor Tinsworth and – the other me, the one in that timeline – figured out how to change the direction our bridge collapsed, and reversed it."

"But you think someone's trying to do the same thing with our bridge?" Greene interjected.

"*Yes*," Jason answered emphatically. "That's why I said we should clear the building, but leave the bridge in place. If it's an enemy trying to turn the bridge into a bomb, they'll probably hit it within another day of trying."

Jensen studied him. "What if it's not an enemy?"

Jason thought. "If it's not an enemy, then they may still be trying to create another rift, but the packet we saw wouldn't just be a sensor – it'd be a signal. Whoever it is, they're telling us to get out of there."

"How would they know if we understand a signal like that?" Greene asked.

Jason turned to look back at him. "Because they're in our future, and they already know what's going to happen. They know that I'm here, that I understand what's happening, and they're telling us – clear out of the way."

"Are you sure that would work?" Jensen asked, somewhat skeptically.

Jason nodded. "In my timeline, the rift formed at the same time that Wiley slipped out of the lab to go to the john. If it had formed any other time, none of what happened next could have happened, because the blast would have killed one or the other of us, and he needed for both of us to come through."

Greene looked awed, and more than slightly horrified. "But wasn't he killed as soon as he went through? Isn't that what you said?"

"That's the most cold-blooded part of it," Jason answered. "When I came back, I changed the collapse direction so that I could try to save Phoebe from ever being turned into what she became. I had to kill the version of myself on this timeline in the process. I don't think I could have done it if..." As Jason spoke, his eyes suddenly widened, and he whispered, "Oh. *Shit.*"

Phoebe was staring fearfully at him, and Jensen and Greene both realized something was very wrong. "What is it?" Jensen asked.

Jason buried his head in his hands. "I think I know who's doing this. What I don't know yet is why. But now I'm *sure* that another rift is going to form. This might get really bad, really fast."

Late Winter, 2048

ARGO WATCHED THE MODIFIED readouts carefully as the data transmitted back through the temporary bridge to the instruments he had spent so much time constructing.

It had been fifteen years, ten months, and two days since he had concluded that there was no mitigating solution for the catastrophe that had come to be known as the Seafloods. Bryant and Tinsworth had insisted that he continue pursuing shorter term options, and he generally had acceded to their requests. Occasionally, he had been able to find answers to some of the issues they encountered, and had lessened the suffering in the area outside their installation.

Their health was failing now, both of them; Bryant's obesity, and Tinsworth's blood pressure – either of which could have been treatable with diet and exercise, had they been willing – was slowly killing them, Bryant the more rapidly of the two. He estimated that both would be dead within eighteen months, and after that, he would have to carry on alone –

– unless he could execute the plan he had formulated.

With little else to do, Tinsworth had taught him chess years earlier, attempting to determine how quickly Argo could learn from calculable algorithms. Within hours, he had been able to defeat every program

Tinsworth had had in his library, and had been able to expand upon those strategies. He had learned the principle of maximizing control, and not only over the installation where he lived. Through communication and manipulation of the others of his kind Bryant had created, he could extend his influence throughout most of the now-fallen city that lay beyond his immediate environs.

The area around what once had been Grant Park had been a significant concern; a particularly aggressive group of survivors had congregated there in the years after the local governments had ceased functioning, and had terrorized the surrounding neighborhoods until he had dispatched a team of the Cybwomen to subdue them. That team – Lisa, Julia and Rosamind – had become the liaison between the new faction, who had adopted the local football team's logo and styled themselves as "Black Birds," and his own installation, which had come to be known in the surrounding territory simply as the Station. When the sickness that came in 2034 had wiped out the tribe, the three – who had been given the moniker "Threebirds" – had been reassigned to another, even more problematic enclave.

All of these reflections – along with countless streams of input data from sensors, Cybwomen, and other sources – coursed through his mind in a fraction of a second as he considered, until a hail from one of the Cybwomen reached him. It was Ellen, one of the guards on the Station's perimeter.

"Signaling Argo. There are two people at the perimeter requesting a meeting with you."

"Acknowledged." He knew that these were likely strangers; Ellen would have named them if she had known them.

"I have not seen them before. They are unarmed, and do not appear to pose a threat."

Argo thought for a millisecond before responding. "Did they identify themselves?"

"They say that they belong to an organization that works within the old government, seeking to advance the betterment of humanity. They have requested to meet you based on intelligence they have which suggests that you are attempting time travel."

If anyone other than a Cybwoman had given him that information, Argo would have had to evaluate it through a diagnostic verification that might have taken him as much as a full second. However, he knew Ellen would already have done a preliminary analysis of the visitors' voices and demeanor to determine the veracity of the claim. It therefore took him less than a millisecond to respond.

"I have no direct information concerning any such organization. Assuming that it is clandestine, I have seen indications that at least two such entities were in operation at the time the danger of coastal inundation became publicly known. However, no further activity of that kind has come to my attention since communications from most of the government ceased. Did they name their organization?"

A few seconds' hiatus followed; Argo knew that Ellen was questioning the visitors. He could have tapped directly into her CPU and followed the conversation himself, but he had discovered that each of the Cybwomen perceived their environment uniquely, and knowing this, he often received more information when it was relayed to him than he might have garnered by gathering it directly from their brains.

The response, when it came, would have surprised a human being, but Argo had already considered all known possibilities. "Affirmative, Argo. The organization may be defunct at this time, as its internal communications have been disrupted by both the crisis and through conflict with another organization, but it was known as the Keepers of the Prime Order – KOPO."

Argo considered. The possibility of strife between two or more warring, covert factions within the government explained a number of anomalous occurrences – most particularly, the apparent paralysis that had characterized that government's response, and also the relative swiftness with which it had fallen, once the situation had gotten beyond any hope of control. The name of the visitors' organization was unknown to him; a few milliseconds' mental search for relevant data turned up nothing that he could correlate.

He was not curious by nature, not any more than any other of his kind, but it was Argo's practice to pursue any new knowledge he encountered.

The two visitors were unlikely to pose any sort of security threat, even if they had knowledge of the installation – which they likely had, since they knew about the line of research he had been pursuing.

"Bring them to the command center," Argo responded, and received a nearly-instantaneous "acknowledged" in reply. They would arrive within a few minutes; Ellen had been stationed at the northeastern gate.

He returned his attention to the instrumentation before him; in the past few years, he had created a new bank of displays that represented data in a shorthand he could read easily, but which was incomprehensible to any human being that might view it. The readouts came in an endless loop of streaming, pipe-like vertical holographs, enabling him to fine-tune his target destination. The display lent an added dimension to the information that direct, digital transmission to his brain would have failed to capture, revealing patterns within the data more readily.

Nothing new was streaming through the pipelines at that time, though. The weather data was consistent with his projections. A new hurricane had formed in the Atlantic, on a latitude roughly even with New York City; it would likely grow to significant size before brushing Nova Scotia as it turned northeast. A line of storms crossing Texas would roll over the Station in roughly forty-five hours; they would be severe enough to merit warning the surrounding tribes. He determined that he would send Ellen to notify the Covingtons.

Another communication cut across his thought, one that might have been unwelcome had Argo not been the creature he had become. "Acknowledged, Allison," he responded wirelessly.

Allison was unique among the Cybwomen, both in her mode of communication and in her behavior. She had undergone several system failures when she had first been brought online, one of which had been so severe that Bryant had come close to aborting the attempt. When she had finally reached full activation, the extent of the damage had become apparent: she had suffered the equivalent of several mini-strokes. She was still fully functional, but unlike any of her counterparts, she retained echoes of personality and temperament. These made her the most humanlike of any of the Cybwomen, but the vagaries of that temperament made her unsuitable for most of the tasks the others of her kind routinely performed.

Argo had observed her carefully throughout her life as a Cybwoman, and concluded that she had developed what would have been called a dissociative identity disorder, though with a few differences. She had two starkly different behavior patterns, but with none of the memory-lapse issues that a human would have exhibited. One of the personalities was almost normal for a Cybwoman, except that she seemed almost anxious to please the human denizens of the Station. At those times she was assigned duties that did not require her to leave the grounds, and which would not overtax her.

The second personality was much more problematic, and it was this one that had contacted him; Allison was prone to fits of deep depression. When in that state, she ordinarily cut off all communications and went to the southwestern edge of the grounds to brood. At first she had simply stood amongst the trees, oblivious to the weather, until Tinsworth had learned of her condition from Argo, taken pity on her, and built a small, crude shelter for her use.

This would not have been an issue in itself, except for one thing: somehow, she had fathomed what Argo was attempting to do, and during each bout of her depression, she would rouse herself long enough to ask after the progress of his research. He told her as little as was possible, not wishing to jeopardize the secrecy of his project, but she had somehow developed an understanding of what was required.

"Request update on the status of Project Red." Argo had adopted that name strictly for use in his communications with Allison; if any other being had used that term, he would know the source of their information, and he would have to halt any further exchanges with her. He had pondered deactivating her, but had held off after Tinsworth had specifically asked him not to.

Argo considered for a microsecond longer, and then answered, "Project is nearing completion. Remote instrumentation has detected a potential rift anchor. Sensors are being deployed to obtain a precise fix upon the location."

A few seconds of silence ensued. Like Argo, Allison had not had any humanizing behavioral modifications added to her software, but she had retained a number of human mannerisms that defied explanation. Argo suspected that she utilized portions of her brain that ordinarily would have been left dormant in a typical Cybwoman, but it would have been impossible to determine exactly how the process had taken place without deactivating her, and destroying her brain via dissection.

Allison finally responded, "There are visitors approaching the Station. They have no prior visits logged, and Ellen did not recognize them. Are they connected to Project Red?"

"Negative," Argo replied. "They came of their own accord."

"I am nevertheless convinced that they have some involvement. It is possible that this will occur during a future event, given the nature of Project Red." Allison's odd certainty was another anomalous aspect of her makeup; on occasion she would determine event outcomes well in advance. On two occasions, she had warned Argo of issues that had yet to arise, but which would have been locally devastating had they been allowed to occur. This apparent prescience was, however, accompanied by the strangest of all her foibles.

"Are they going to bring you back to me?" she asked.

A human would have heaved a long-suffering sigh. Allison had asked Argo this question many times over the years. Early on, Argo had attempted to determine the nature of the relationship she clearly believed they shared; in the process, he had learned that during Allison's shutdown and powerup routines, power flowed unevenly into and out of her brain. This uneven flow produced a semiconscious state, similar to human dreaming, which lasted about ten seconds at shutdown and about half that at startup.

Allison appeared to perceive this state as a separate and fully concrete existence and treated information she processed from it with that full validity. Approximately two years after she had been activated, she had become convinced that he had become Argo because of the loss of his soul at death, and that he would become fully human once more if he could somehow reunite his body with his soul. She also – apparently – believed that this event would have a restorative effect upon her as well.

Argo had no answer for this, and refrained from discussing the matter with her out of concern that she might suffer another malfunction, if forced to confront the full reality of their existence.

"I do not have any information as yet concerning their purpose. They have some knowledge of my current research."

Several seconds of silence followed.   Ellen had reached the Station plaza; the two guests appeared innocuous. The woman was about ten years younger than Tinsworth and Bryant; the man another five years younger than she.

"They *are* the ones who will bring you back to me."   Allison's transmission was voiceless, yet it carried an odd, electronic reverberation that Argo recognized at once. Fifteen years before, when the Black Bird tribe had been preparing to massacre a neighboring enclave, Allison had informed him of the situation mere hours before it was to happen, allowing him to act in time to save eighty-seven lives. When she had warned him, that transmission had carried the same quality.

"Have you met these people before?" he asked.

There was another pause. Ellen had reached the door to the Station's command center.

"No," Allison replied.

Argo considered for another millisecond before electing to confirm his estimate. "Do you suspect that they intend us harm?"

The delay in response was almost human in its length. Several seconds passed. At last, she responded, with that same, reverberating tension, "I think they would destroy everything trying to save you."

Chapter Eleven

AL AND WILEY WOKE at almost the same time, during what they guessed was early morning.

"Hard to tell time down here," Wiley said as he sat on the edge of his bunk. "For all I know, they might screwing with the time just to make me go longer without food."

"I usually get up early," Al replied, rubbing sleep from his eyes as he likewise sat up. "But I drove all night before I got arrested, and that was early in the morning, so it could be anytime."

Before Wiley could say anything more, a loud buzzer sounded, echoing off the concrete walls. Both of them covered their ears until it stopped.

"What the hell was that?" Al asked.

Wiley was looking to the far side of the block, where a door had opened. Four men in generic black suits had entered; behind them walked what was clearly a high-ranking military officer. All wore dark sunglasses.

Wiley and Al glanced toward each other. Wiley seemed about to speak, but could get no words out; Al looked resigned. They both looked up as the suited men stopped outside their cells. The officer stopped in front of them, a foot from the bars, and surveyed them through his sunglasses with bland contempt.

"You're both being moved," he said in a voice that was at once gravelly and clipped. "Turn around and keep your hands up."

Al's expression didn't change, but Wiley's apparent fear seemed to double as they complied. Again he seemed about to speak, but after a glance toward Al, he swallowed and remained silent.

The officer lifted a hand in a signal, and in response, the doors to both of their cells opened with a click. Two men entered each cell, with one standing back with his handgun drawn while the other handcuffed each prisoner. They were then marched out of into the corridor between the cells, Al in front and Wiley behind, until they reached the exit. The door opened into another short, blank corridor with an elevator at its far end. The elevator opened as they approached it, revealing doors on each side, as in a hospital.

Al and Wiley were guided to stand facing the rear, with their escort behind them. As soon as the elevator closed and began going up, the agents put black felt bags over their heads. Wiley could not suppress a slight whimper. Al remained silent.

When the doors in front of them opened, they both knew immediately from the acoustics that they were in the parking garage. Cars awaited each of them, their engines running. Wiley was herded into his car first. Al listened as it drove away, and for no reason at all, he suddenly felt better and more hopeful than he had since Phoebe had called him.

Two of his captors guided him into the back of the second car. Al noted that they were more polite than before, moving him more slowly and ensuring that he didn't hit his head on anything. After buckling him in, they drove away, pausing only briefly at the security gate at the garage's entrance.

Al tried to keep track of the car's movements, but that proved impossible. Before long, the car went onto what seemed to be an interstate, and a few minutes after that, he began to doze.

He drifted in and out of sleep for some time, waking fully only once, when the vehicle briefly left the highway, and snoozing again as soon as it re-entered it. He knew he was losing track of time, but there was no help for that – the place where he had been taken would remain secret.

He woke again as the car left the freeway. This time, it was making its way more slowly; the frequent stops and occasional vehicles he could hear outside his window told him that he was in a city, or at the least, a suburb. He wondered – realizing with surprise that it was the first time he had done so – where he was being taken.

At last the car slowed almost to a halt, going over a small bump that felt like it was the entrance to a driveway. Al had just enough time to realize that that bump felt familiar before, with no warning, the bag was removed from his head.

His jaw dropped in surprise as the agent sitting beside him unbuckled his seatbelt. They had taken him to his house. He tried to speak as the man bent him forward to remove his handcuffs, but he couldn't make a sound.

The cuffs were removed. Al sat back up, stretching his arms as he did. The two agents – one beside him, one driving – watched him expressionlessly, but with none of the former hostility that had accompanied such stares before. He looked from one to the other, still speechless. The agent next to him held out an envelope that he knew contained everything that had been taken from him at his arrest.

"You're free to go," the driver finally said.

Al finally found his voice. "Thanks, I think." He started to open the car door, and then looked back at them. "So you know that Anderson's alive, then?"

The agent beside him replied, "we know that there's no further need to detain you. You can go." A sardonic half-smile tugged at one corner of his mouth. "Try and stay out of trouble."

Al took a deep breath. "I don't think you'll need to worry about that ever again," he answered, and was surprised by how much he meant it.

IN FRONT OF A FAIRLY seedy apartment building not ten miles away, Wiley Grant had just had a similar bag removed from his head and his handcuffs removed.

"You're free to go," said the agent beside him, in much the same fashion as the one who had talked to Al. Wiley blinked in surprise, and his hands began to shake as he covered his face with them.

"You'll find that your apartment is still yours, and that the rent has been paid. We even sent someone in there to clear up some of the mess." The agent stared at him without blinking. "You might want to clean up your act a bit." He held out an envelope identical to the one Al had been handed.

Wiley was breathing heavily, still unable to comprehend fully that he was free. The two agents waited. Finally, he was able to ask: "Does this mean that Jason's really alive?"

Neither expression changed. The driver answered, "it means that we know more about what happened, and that you weren't involved. You're free to go."

Wiley nodded, still dazed. Taking the envelope from the agent, Wiley opened the car door and stepped outside. Before he could turn around, the door had been pulled closed from the inside and the car – a predictably black Crown Victoria – was making its way out of the parking lot.

He took a deep breath, feeling disoriented. He had fully expected to be transferred to another prison – one where there would be other inmates – and that prospect had terrorized him throughout the trip. Looking around himself, he took another deep breath, tasting the city air for the first time in months, and felt himself choking up. He clenched his teeth, willing himself not to cry like a little girl, and opened the envelope.

Inside it were his wallet – with all of the money had withdrawn from his checking account still in it; he breathed a sigh of relief – his keys, his cellphone, and his work ID. He pocketed each item and turned to go up to his apartment, dropping the envelope in a trash can at the base of the stairs leading to the second floor.

A few seconds later, he opened the door to apartment 205 and looked inside, first in disbelief, and then in strangely gratified wonder. Wiley had never been much for neatness, and when he had been arrested, the agents who had taken him had made their disgust at his living conditions evident.

The living room had been completely cleared of all of the used takeout trays, pizza boxes, beer cans, and dirty clothes that had littered it. Everything had been cleaned, even the walls, and the carpet was spotless. Looking into the tiny kitchen, he could see that it had received the same treatment.

He shook his head, still trying to grasp that he was free, and finally sat down on the sofa, taking out his cellphone. He thought for a few moments, trying to decide who he would call first, and finally decided, tapping a single digit.

He listened to the call ringing once, twice, and then the click as it was answered. Before he could speak, Dr. Tinsworth's voice came sharply through:

"Grant, where the *hell* have you been?"

ARGO STUDIED EACH OF the newcomers to the Station for a few milliseconds, then glanced again at his holographic instrument bank. Several of the readouts had changed; one had brightened in color from deep blue to aqua. The man and woman stared at the holographs in uncomprehending amazement for several seconds before the woman recovered herself, returning her attention to him. After a few moments of studying his slightly-disfigured face, she asked, "Who – or what – exactly are you?"

"I am called Argo," he replied with his usual impassivity. "I was a researcher at the university years ago, before I was killed in an incident in my lab. My colleague, Dr. Allen Bryant, was able to restore me to existence in this form."

"Colleague? So you aren't in charge here?" the man asked.

"I do not direct my colleagues in any way, and they do not direct me. We work as a team of equals. Our efforts are directed chiefly toward maximizing the human survival rate in this region. Additionally, we have sought ways in which we might minimize the Seaflood effects."

"Have you had any success in that effort?" the woman asked, her eyes widening slightly.

"Only slightly, and only locally. I have concluded that much of what has occurred is irreversible. Some effects could possibly have been mitigated, but the resources and time involved made their solutions unworkable in the current environment. Have you any other questions for me?"

The pair looked at each other, then back at him. "Our intelligence indicates that you are attempting time travel. Can you confirm or deny that?"

"Confirmed." They both blinked, as much from the immediacy of the response as from the affirmation. "For nearly two years, I have sought to isolate a timestream parallel to this one – one in which the Seafloods were mitigated or altogether avoided, so that I might learn which preventative actions might serve us now." Argo's glance flickered for a millisecond on the holograph bank; its streams had begun visibly altering. The information they conveyed was unexpected.

The man's expression was nonplussed. "So what you're saying is, you can derive data from other universes?"

"That is a gross oversimplification of the process, but yes, that is sufficiently accurate." Argo waited a full second, obtaining a complete reading of both humans' responses, before continuing: "I have not encountered either of you before. Who are you?"

The woman spoke. "I am Senior Agent Elizabeth Jensen, and this is my partner, Agent Zach Greene. We worked for a clandestine agency within the U.S. government before it ceased most operations."

"So I was informed. Keepers of the Prime Order, it was called; at least, that's what you indicated to another of my kind – the one who brought you here."

"KOPO. Yes," she replied.

"From what I have observed, yours was not the only such organization operating within the framework of the U.S. government. It appears to me that there likely were several such entities, all working at cross purposes, at the time that the Seafloods became problematic. The resulting governmental paralysis prevented any remedial actions from being pursued until the catastrophe was unavoidable." Argo's gaze turned toward the holograph bank; its streams had become frenetic, changing in brightness and color in a pattern incomprehensible to anyone other than himself.

Both agents looked abashed. "Unfortunately, your assessment is correct," Jensen replied. "Our organization was the first to conclude that the Seaflood effects would prove catastrophic. We were unable to convince any of our counterpart organizations of the urgency of the situation."

"In this universe, that is indeed the case." Argo studied the holographs carefully. "I have located an alternate Earth in a universe parallel to this one – one that was similar, but somehow diverged fairly radically from this one, between twenty and twenty-five years ago. Its communications web is still robust, while ours has mostly failed, and will inevitably cease coordinated transmissions altogether. The radio emanations from this parallel plane concurrent to our time frame are comparable to the Earth's at the time of my death."

Greene looked slightly unnerved by this, and Jensen asked hurriedly, "Let me make sure I understand you correctly. You say you've found another Earth, in a different universe, whose radio emanations *now* are the same as ours were *before* the Seafloods?"

"That is correct." Argo did not look at her. "Moreover, there is an unusual aspect to this particular iteration of our planet, based on the singularity signatures I am detecting."

"Singularity signatures. You mean like –" Jensen's response trailed off as her expression became watchful. Argo glanced toward her.

"Like the research I was pursuing at the time of my death, yes." Argo looked back to the holographs as he continued. "The signatures are like beacons, making those Earths that have them easily detectable. I have been trying to locate one that has the signature, but also retains its communications network. The search has been difficult, to say the least."

"Have you found any others, or just the one?" Greene asked.

Argo glanced briefly toward him. "I have found a significant number of iterations with the network intact. This is not unexpected. I have only found the one with the bridge signature. I can only reach those iterations of our planet where that signature exists. There has to be a singularity there in order for me to be able to use it."

Jensen frowned. "You said that this one world you've found is unusual. How so?"

"Every other alternate Earth with that signature has three or four different locations where Einstein-Rosen bridges or quantum singularities have been constructed – the one that was here in Atlanta, plus singularities in

Switzerland, France, and a pair in China that appear to have been a failed attempt to form another bridge," Argo said. "This iteration features two additional signatures – a bridge in Dayton, Ohio, and another singularity in Atlanta, near to where the bridge failed."

Jensen and Greene looked at each other in disbelief before Greene responded. "Dayton, Ohio? Are you sure you have that right?"

Argo's face was as blank as ever. "Completely. All of the bridges and singularities were taken down on this Earth less than a year later. The next nearby bridge will be constructed in the future, relative to our own time frame. I can detect the pre-signature shadow, but negotiating timestreams moving forward more than a few minutes' time is extremely fluid owing to the nature of quantum mechanics." He looked from Jensen to Greene. "Additionally, the later signature appears to be on the Moon, rather than Earth, which would make a link extremely problematic or even impossible to form."

"Can you tell when the bridge in Dayton was constructed?" Jensen asked.

"It seems to have formed in 2023, shortly after the Atlanta bridge came online, with an essentially identical signature. Presumably, results from the Atlanta experiment were duplicated," Argo said.

Jensen and Greene looked at each other again; both seemed slightly unnerved. "We were in Dayton in 2023 on another project – one similar to the one that caused you to have your – your current form. That was our primary reason for coming to Atlanta once KOPO went dark – to find out whether that technology was being utilized, and whether that use was safe."

Argo's gaze returned to the holographs again. They had slowed, and much of the color had drained from them, muddying the rainbow hues into a mix of browns and greys that visibly dimmed the light in the room. "Interesting," he said, and then added, "I believe I can alter the endpoints of the Dayton bridge, once I have the precise coordinates – and they must be extremely precise. Once that has been done – " he looked back up at each of them in turn – "you may be able to assist me, if my hypothesis proves out. Would you be willing to remain here for two days? No one will disturb you, and you may use this facility to attempt to communicate with your organization, if you wish."

Jensen looked blankly surprised, then slightly confused. "You have no objection to that?"

"As long as I may continue to work uninterrupted and without interference, and if you are willing to assist me, you may do as you will," he replied. "But I will certainly ask for your assistance, once I have resolved my current endeavor."

They looked at each other again. "How long do you think that will take? Greene asked.

Argo studied the instrument bank for a brief moment before answering. "An hour. Perhaps an additional minute or two."

Chapter Twelve

THE ALARM FROM THE LAB sounded in the next room just as Jason put down a book he was reading. He glanced toward a small clock on the nightstand; it read nineteen minutes before midnight.

He grunted in resigned annoyance. He had been certain that a new rift would be formed, and had hoped – given his guess at who he thought was forming it – that they would at least wait until daylight.

As he clambered out of bed and began to dress, Phoebe's eyes opened slowly, and she looked fearfully at Jason as they both heard the knock on the connecting door. "Five minutes!" Jason called, trying to change back into his day clothes as quickly as he could while Phoebe scrambled blearily out of bed and began to get dressed.

"Make it three if you can." Jensen's voice was muffled by the door. "We're ready as soon as you are."

In the end, they compromised: four minutes later, they had piled into the black SUV and were making their way back to the abandoned arena at a speed that prompted Jason to ask, "I assume if you get pulled over, that it's going to be taken care of – right?"

Jensen laughed. Jason had not heard her laugh before, but it didn't seem forced. "As soon as they run our plates, they'll let us go. Fast, because the patrolman who pulls *us* over's gonna need an emergency change of his jockey shorts once he finds out exactly what he's done." Greene looked back at them, a grin wreathing his face.

Even Phoebe grinned back. Jason nodded, managing to remain deadpan. "Useful perk," he observed.

They were ten miles from Hara Arena, but crossed the distance in well under ten minutes. Greene had called the technician who had been on duty that afternoon, but he had to cover twice the distance they had, and was nowhere to be seen when they arrived on the dock. Jensen looked back at Jason guardedly. "Do you think it will be safe to go in?

"I think it will be, but it will probably be a mess, and we can't be sure exactly where or how the rift was formed – or if it even exists. A failed attempt could still blow up the lab," Jason replied. Phoebe rubbed sleep from her eyes as they waited.

Perhaps fifteen minutes later, the bay door opened again and the tech's green sedan drove up the ramp, parking behind them. The two agents had already left the car by the time he had killed the headlights and turned the engine off. Jason and Phoebe followed.

"What happened? Did one of those anomalies strike the bridge?" the tech asked, looking almost as sleepy as Phoebe.

"We think the anomalies were trying to determine the exact coordinates for the bridge endpoint," Jason replied. "If the one responsible is who I think he is, he was trying to latch onto the bridge and collapse it into a single endpoint – and from there, extend a bridge to where and when he is."

The tech's sallow, bespectacled face paled. "Did you say '*when*' he is?"

Jason looked toward Jensen, who nodded and said quietly, "He's got clearance. He had to, to work on this project."

Jason nodded, and addressed the tech directly. "I think someone from the near future is trying to create a bridge with a nonzero t-component. To do that – if I understand what happened correctly – the existent bridge has to collapse to a singularity to receive the extension to its new spatial and temporal endpoint."

The tech looked back at him in scared puzzlement. "Happened? Are you saying this has been done before?"

"In theory it is possible. In practice, we don't know." Greene cut across Jason as he was about to respond. He exchanged a meaningful glance with Jason before continuing, "One thing that does happen, from what we know, is that this process causes a significant blowback effect on the endpoint's immediate surroundings."

"How significant?" the tech asked.

"That depends on the delta-t between the two endpoints," Jason answered. "The farther forward the temporal axis is extended, the greater the motion vector differences between the two endpoints becomes. The motion of the earth through space is such that any significant changes along the t-axis inflates the spatial distance between the two points when connected four-dimensionally. This in turn causes differences in the directional vectors. Move forward – or backward – far enough in time, and you're going to have a really big differential – one that discharges the instant that the bridge forms."

"That was the effect that destroyed the lab in Atlanta." Jensen added. The tech grew even paler, and replied, "I'm not so sure I want to go back in there."

Jason smiled, in a way he hoped was reassuring. "Once the discharge occurs and a stable bridge forms, there's not much danger afterward – at least, not while it remains stable."

The tech's eyes narrowed. "For this to be theoretical, you sure seem to know a lot about it."

"It's my job to know about it," Jason replied, his voice cooling noticeably. "Your job exists because my team did its job right."

"Then why'd your lab blow up?" the tech snarled at him. He glared toward Jensen, continuing, "Unless you're *ordering* me to do it, I want no further part of this."

"You know I won't order you in there," she shot back. "You also know what kind of reassignment you can expect if you *don't* do it."

The tech glowered back at her, but said no more. Jason took a deep breath and looked toward Phoebe. "You know I wouldn't allow you in there if I thought it wasn't safe." She nodded in reply, and he looked from her to each of the others. "If the – the person responsible for what's happening is who I think it is, then there's probably not much danger for anyone here other than me, and he probably already knows who's going in there. I think it'll be all right," he said.

Jensen looked back to the tech. "Are you in or out?"

He scowled for a moment, but then nodded affirmatively. Jason tried to smile in reply, but the effort failed. Jensen and Greene started toward the hall; as Jason followed them, he spoke over his shoulder: "I can promise you this much – if we find what I think we'll find, you'll remember this day for the rest of your life, no matter how old you get."

GENERAL HAVERHILL WATCHED the monitor on his desk intently. He had been there well after most of the rest of the building had closed down for the night: his sources had indicated that events in Ohio were progressing toward a climax more quickly than expected.

He had been notified of the lab's evacuation less than five minutes after it had occurred. He had managed to obtain a transcript of a cell call from the tech on duty to his girlfriend; the man had sounded concerned. He had also – foolishly, and against protocol – described the phenomenon he had witnessed, albeit in very general terms.

The tech nerds under his command had indicated that it was possible that an external agency was attempting to knock out or damage the bridge. Without knowing about Tinsworth's theory, they had given it much more credibility; it increased the likelihood that someone could interfere with the bridge itself remotely.

A few minutes earlier, an instant message from another agent had flashed on his screen; the bridge team in Dayton had left their motel and returned to Hara Arena. Their trip had been made very quickly, indicating an emergency; a seismic reading taken at the outpost conducting surveillance on Hara Arena had indicated a disturbance – a big enough one to be noticed – centered very close to the building.

Since then, two vehicles had entered the arena through the freight entrance. The one with Anderson, his girlfriend and the two agents with them had been first; some fifteen minutes later, the idiot tech had arrived. The freight door had closed behind him. Haverhill sighed; even he had not been able to get eyes inside that building.

The external cameras – one on the front entrance, one on the rear – showed him only dim outlines. He watched them intently, looking for any anomaly or sign of activity, but not expecting to see anything. No more communications were coming in; both the arena and its observers were as inactive as an unknowing outsider would expect them to be.

He reached for the glass of water beside his monitor, and almost knocked it over as both camera feeds suddenly destabilized, the small windows becoming filled with dark static for a few moments before regaining equilibrium. The camera positioned behind the arena had shifted, so that the northern end of the building was out of view.

Even as the general began to grasp what had happened, an instant message pinged on his screen. It was from the surveillance team working the arena, and flagged as high priority. He touched the message icon on his screen and read, "apparent minor earthquake has occurred near to watch site. Cameras displaced or knocked offline."

The general dictated his response, quietly: "Subjects were inside arena at the time. Visual survey of site ordered for purpose of impact assessment." He could have opened a direct face-to-face message, but disdained that; his superiors – the *real* ones – never communicated in that manner, and he believed strongly in following their example.

There was a brief pause before the reply appeared: "General, full survey cannot be conducted before daylight. Site cannot be approached without detection. Request guidance on how to proceed."

Haverhill sighed. He knew that it would be difficult to obtain a full assessment before morning even in good conditions; the tremor would have roused the attention of the entire installation. There was no clear way of knowing exactly how many of its staff were on site, or how many more were on the way.

"Continue infrared monitoring of site until daylight. Maintain visual surveillance." He paused. "Log and trace any vehicle seen arriving or departing the site. I want to know every scrap of information you can gather on what's going on in there."

A long pause followed this directive; he awaited the response without impatience. Glances at the different camera feeds revealed no new information. Seconds ticked by.

"Acknowledged." The message was still for several seconds before adding, "Sir – any idea of what just happened?"

They were scared. Haverhill could hardly blame them; Ohio wasn't much of a seismic hotspot. The quake had very likely been caused by the project they were attempting to monitor.

At least the building was still standing, he thought. Whatever had happened was no worse than what had gone down in Atlanta. It occurred to him that the tremor might have been a precursor, and that something worse *was* going to happen – but there had been no such warning before Tinsworth's lab went up.

"Stand by," he replied, tersely. He knew that the pause before his response might be revelatory, but there was nothing he could tell them. The communications silence stretched out as he thought, staring at the changeless feeds. Nearly two minutes passed.

"Proceed as directed," he finally added. "Whatever happened there seems to have ended. I want eyes back on that place inside an hour from now."

"Yes, sir," the box replied a moment later. Haverhill closed the message with a touch to his screen. Uncharacteristic worry gnawed quietly at the back of his mind, as he considered the implications of Tinsworth's theory.

One ugly possibility kept making its way to the front of his mind: if Tinsworth was correct, and it was possible to move through time by manipulating an existing Einstein-Rosen bridge, then it was even more possible that the agency which mastered the tech first would then deploy it to eliminate its rivals. That was something he could not allow.

Still, he could not risk simply taking out the building through an "accident." If there was in fact a wormhole leading into or out of that arena, it could be dangerous to try to destroy it.

Haverhill snorted to himself. Could be, hell – if Atlanta was any indication, it would probably be disastrous. Moreover, he might be able to pass it off to the public as an accident, but there was no way he could make that case to his own clandestine agency, let alone the others. He would be a marked man, assuming he didn't destroy the world in the process.

Sitting idly and waiting galled him, but he could see no better option. For the time being, Jason Anderson – and the agents who had reached him first, by bare minutes – remained just beyond his grasp.

Chapter Thirteen

NONE OF THEM EXPECTED what they found in the lab.

After the explosion in Atlanta, Jason had expected the worst; he had feared that the building above might collapse, making any rift that formed inaccessible. When they found the door intact and apparently undamaged, he breathed a sigh of relief, and then chuckled to himself. Jensen glanced toward him, slightly annoyed.

He shook his head, still smiling. "I keep forgetting that whoever we're dealing with is in the future. If it's who I think it is, then he's probably likely to be more careful than Wiley was. Besides, Wiley had a different timeline that he had to match, so the rift connections might even have been explosive by design."

Phoebe and Greene both looked blankly at him. He smiled again, a little sadly. "Something that happened before I went through the rift in my own timeline."

"We're wasting time." Jensen spoke abruptly, and jammed her thumb against the ident pad. The door buzzed. Jensen pulled it open, and everyone, even Jason, gasped in astonishment as they entered.

He had expected to see another darkly opaque, amorphous, planar surface like the one that had formed in Hampton Hall. Instead, a bright, white, arched portal glowed before them near the far wall of the lab, facing slightly to their right. A quick glance toward the console told him that the instrumentation was intact, though inoperative, and the arched rift provided the only light in the lab. It was more than enough to see clearly by.

"My God, Jason, was that what you went through?" Phoebe breathed. He turned his head to look at her; she was staring at the arch, wide-eyed, smiling slightly in wonderment.

"Is it dangerous?" Jensen asked, almost whispering; even she seemed awed by the sight before them. Greene did not speak, but he looked back over his shoulder toward Jason with new respect in his gaze. Jason smiled back, still rueful. The tech, who had been hanging back from the group, could only stare in gap-mouthed astonishment.

"I don't think so. Ours wasn't anything like that. It was a lot darker, and cloudy-looking, and it didn't have a shape like that. At least, not at first. I remember that as we were about to go through it, it changed its shape to fit us. But this – " Jason motioned toward the arch – "this looks a lot different. It's probably more advanced."

"More advanced." Jensen paused, thinking. "Wouldn't that mean it came from farther in our future? You went forward about forty years, right?"

"A little more than that," Jason replied. "But I can't say for sure that there's a correlation. I'm almost positive Wiley Grant didn't create this thing. It fits with who I think might have done it, but it's definitely not Wiley, or the Acme thing that Bryant turned him into."

"So who do you think did this?" Greene asked, and a moment later, Phoebe breathed, "do you think it's aliens?"

In spite of everything, Jason laughed aloud, but his amusement drained away quickly. "When this happened the first time, Tinsworth looked like he was hoping aliens might have done it, but I'm definitely glad it wasn't. Acme was difficult enough to handle, and those Cybwomen were terrifying. Even Allison. Even you, Phoebe." As he said the last few words, he looked over at her again, unable momentarily to say more. She met his eyes with hers, and for a few seconds there was silence.

"Jason." Jensen finally broke the spell, her voice surprisingly gentle. "I need to know who you think created this thing."

He looked toward her again, and opened his mouth to speak, but as he did, two shadows darkened the rift slightly as they passed. Jason's eyebrows lifted as he saw the two figures emerge into the lab, and he looked to Jensen again. Her back was to the arch; she had not seen the arrivals.

"Maybe you should ask yourself that question," he said, motioning toward them.

Jensen turned around at the same moment that Greene saw the pair of figures approaching them. A strange, choking gasp worked its way out of his open mouth as she whispered, loudly enough for them all to hear, "oh, my God. *That can't be.*"

A man and a woman walked toward them. Both were smiling, and neither looked remotely threatening. As they drew nearer, Phoebe caught her breath, and said, "I didn't really think this was possible."

The woman heard her, and smiled broadly; the man beside her also grinned. They approached to within a few steps before stopping. Both appeared to be in their sixties. Both Jensen and Greene looked completely unnerved. They all heard a muttered "*holy shit!*" behind them from the tech.

The ensuing silence lasted several seconds before Jason said, wonderingly, "You already know this, but I'm *really* glad to see you."

The woman laughed, and looked at Jensen closely as she said, "I've always wondered why you're thinking of homemade bread right now. I still don't know where that came from."

"My God, it really is me," Jensen breathed.

"That's right," replied the older Greene. "We were sent in part so that you'd know we mean you no harm."

"What do you want from us?" Jason asked.

"We were sent to retrieve you." The older Jensen looked at him, then to Phoebe. "Both of you. Argo requires you both."

It was Jason's turn to draw a deep breath. "So I was right." He looked toward the arch. "And it looks like his technology's more advanced than Acme's was. What year did you come from?

They looked at each other, then smiled ruefully. "We can't tell you that. Not here. Our instructions were clear – tell these two as little as possible," the older Greene said.

"But – there's so much you can tell us!" Jensen interjected. It was the first time that Jason had seen a real disruption in her normally calm demeanor. "We could give KOPO information that would enable us to – to change everything! We could finally neutralize Ius Divinum!"

"That is not the purpose of our visit," the older Jensen answered, as Jason blinked in surprised confusion. "Wait here. The plan is for Jason and Phoebe to be gone for what will only be a few seconds for you. When they return, they will have a mission that will require your assistance to complete, and when you have done that, your own mission will begin. It will be much more difficult than theirs."

Jason looked toward Greene. "Lucky you."

"What is this mission?" Jensen asked. Her older counterpart merely smiled.

"One that I failed in. You will know more when Jason and Phoebe return, but it's time for them to come with us." She beckoned toward them before turning back toward the arch. Greene followed. Phoebe looked fearfully toward Jason.

"It'll be all right," he said reassuringly, and was surprised to realize how much he meant it. She took his hand as they walked forward, following the older agents toward the arch.

Behind them, Jensen plaintively cried, "Wait!" They all turned. Her expression was pleading and uncertain.

"If you're me, and *you* failed, how am *I* supposed to succeed?" she almost wailed. The younger Greene watched her, his features similarly darkened by worry.

"These two will explain when they return," she answered, and then looked to Jason. "Let's go."

The two KOPO agents said no more, as the four approached the rift, its brightness turning them into fuzzy silhouettes as they passed through it and disappeared. Jensen still looked severely flustered. Greene, who had at least retained some equanimity, motioned toward the tech, who had remained behind them. He was still staring at the arch with undisguised awe.

"Check the instrumentation and find out if anything's broken. Quickly. They could be back here at any second," Greene said.

"I CAN'T BELIEVE YOU had the *gall* to call me." Dr. Tinsworth's voice was angry and sharp. Wiley sighed. He'd expected this response.

"Professor, I know I screwed up, but I didn't cause that explosion. The chick did – Anderson's girlfriend." Wiley hesitated. "I don't know what good it would have done for me to have been there. I couldn't have stopped it from happening."

Tinsworth did not answer immediately, and Wiley held his breath. He needed his job back.

"I shouldn't even be considering this. If I still had Anderson, I wouldn't even think about it, but as it stands, I don't have anyone else available with your credentials, or your experience.

"The thing is, I *know* you didn't cause it, and that you couldn't have done anything about it. There's a theory on what might actually have happened, and I'll have to get your clearance restored before I can fill you in further. So yes, pending approval of your clearance, you should be able to resume work." Tinsworth paused. "Whether I like it or not."

Wiley exhaled a huge sigh of relief. "Thanks, Professor. It won't ever happen again."

"Damn right it won't, if you don't want to be teaching middle-school physical science – and that's if you get lucky. If I had my choice, you'd be driving a garbage truck. Or living in one," Tinsworth added. "But as it stands, I'm going to need your input. I'll run this by Mangum tonight. I'd suggest you brush up on non-Euclidean hyperbolic and elliptical geometry, just so you're ready to hit the ground running."

Wiley was silent for a moment before answering, "I've run across that before. One of the applications in hyperbolic geometry would involve a wormhole whose entrance and exit points have nonequal reference frames. Is that what we're looking at?"

Tinsworth's answer was immediate. "You know very well that I can't confirm or deny anything, Grant. I've told you what you need to be reviewing if you're going to come back to the team. I'd suggest you get on it." The call dropped a moment later. Wiley stared bemusedly at his phone for several seconds before tossing it to the other end of his still-unfamiliarly-clean couch.

The past few hours had been a serious wake-up call. Having regained his freedom, his first thought had been to resume his old habits where he had left off two months before, but within seconds, that idea had grown pale and uninviting. His ordeal had left him less strong than before, but wiser, and it had occurred to him that he had been given a unique chance to make himself over again, different than he had been before. Maybe better.

He was thinner than he had been, for one thing. For another, he had sprouted some gray hairs that belied his age; not many guys under twenty-five had those. He knew, from his two-month stint in prison, that he had learned to be more patient. He even had a little more nerve than before.

It was that nerve that had finally allowed him to call Tinsworth. The real hope that he might get a second chance gave him a sense of determination that, while as unfamiliar as the cleanliness of his surrounding, was equally needed and welcome.

He felt different. He couldn't quantify how, or why, but he sensed that there somehow seemed to be more of himself. He'd been too subject to his habits and pleasures for too long, and lived without discipline. The ordeal had changed him. He'd broken a lot of addictions – some that he might never have escaped otherwise. He had grown more focused.

He shook his head. The shock of the real changes in his life was causing a touch of vertigo. Taking a deep breath, he stood, and headed for the shower. He had never needed or wanted so much just to feel clean.

Chapter Fourteen

THEY EMERGED INTO MID-MORNING sunlight, on a day that felt like early summer.

Jason looked around himself and shuddered. Phoebe had been staring around herself in amazement, but she turned to him and took his hand in both of hers.

"You all right?" the older Jensen asked him.

"I think so," he replied, clutching Phoebe's hand too tightly. He was breathing hard, though not from their passage; the arch had been no different from the rift, except that there was no slight bump like the one he and Wiley experienced on their first trip. His eyes darted around the plaza. The arch had been placed in almost exactly the same location as the rift, but the support structure around it was new.

"Argo didn't have to match up anything," he muttered to himself. Phoebe looked concerned, and asked Greene, "are we in any danger here?"

"None that I know of," he answered. "As long as you don't run afoul of the Cybwomen, you should be fine."

Phoebe paled. "There are – those things are here?"

"Yes, but Argo is their commander, and he is very reliable. Most of the local settlements have been able to hold on through the last ten years because of him." Greene paused. "I suppose I should clarify something right now. You exist in our past, but we do not necessarily exist in your future. What you do after you return determines what your world will become."

"I know that much," Jason replied. He still wore a haunted look, and his eyes still scanned the plaza. "This universe won't exist, at least not like this, if what we do after we return can prevent it from developing this way. It sounds like this one isn't nearly as bad as the one I went to."

Greene nodded. "From what I remember you told me, it isn't. But it also isn't one you want to end up in, either. For one thing, neither of you are still alive – you were captured in our timeline by a different organization from our own, called Ius Divinum. We never did learn what happened to you."

Jason nodded. "When were we captured?"

Jensen and Greene looked to each other. "It happened right after you returned. That's one of the things we have to discuss with Argo – how we can avoid the outcome we've gotten here," Jensen said.

"Won't that negate this timeline?" Jason asked, alarmed.

"That's also something we'll have to discuss with Argo," she answered. "If you're ready, he's waiting for you in the installation over there." She pointed toward the building that once had served as a control facility for the commuter rail system. Jason blanched slightly.

"I really hoped I'd never be in the Drome again," he muttered, as they began to walk slowly away from the arch. Greene looked at him curiously.

"The Drome? Is that what you called this place?" he asked. "I'd forgotten that part."

"Well, what do you call it now?" Jason asked. They were already near to the door of the building, and he was visibly agitated.

"We just call it the Station," Jensen replied. They came to a halt about six feet from the door. Jensen continued forward and opened it, and held it as the others entered.

Jason was shaking, clenching his hands in an attempt to control both his fear and his reaction to it. Phoebe took his arm and stopped him, just inside the door. She turned him so that they were face to face.

"Jason, it's going to be okay," she said. "They wouldn't have brought us here to hurt us. They could have done that already."

"I know that. I'm just not ready to meet Argo," he answered.

"Why not?" she asked. "They said he was reliable. They obviously trust him."

His response was a disbelieving stare. "Haven't you figured out who Argo is?" he whispered.

Phoebe looked bewildered. "How would I know that?"

"Remember what I told you about Acme, and Wiley?" he asked, glancing around himself again. Phoebe was suddenly, forcefully reminded of his nightmares. For a moment, she felt as if she had gone back into their storage container, and blinked as she realized they had left it less than twenty-four hours earlier.

"Bryant made Acme out of what was left of Wiley, because he was killed almost as soon as we went through the rift. But in this universe, *Wiley didn't die.*" He grasped her shoulders, trying not to clutch at her too hard. "The rift collapsed in the opposite direction after I changed it. Bryant never got Wiley's body." His eyes bored into hers. "He got *mine.*"

Phoebe's eyes went wide as comprehension dawned, and she clapped both her hands over her mouth. Jason continued to stare at her.

"Argo exists because *I* killed him. He probably won't kill me, because that might also destroy him, but I *really* don't want to meet him," he said.

"Why did you kill him?" she asked. "Think about it. Remember what you told me. He's supposed to be smarter than you are, now. Do you think he wouldn't understand?"

Jason closed his eyes. "I remember what the body looked like. It was bad. Not as bad as what would have happened to you, but still really bad."

"You have nothing to fear from meeting Argo," Jensen said from behind them. "He's said as much to us. We need you to get in there and find out what you have to do."

"Argo didn't tell you?" Jason asked, looking back toward her.

"Did you tell us who you thought Argo was? Well, trust me, he's *exactly* like you." She grinned; her teeth had somehow withstood the decades she had lived. Jason frowned.

"All right," he said, taking a deep breath. He followed Greene down a short corridor lined with server banks into a white, brightly lit laboratory whose equipment – and occupants – took his breath away.

At the far end of the lab, a short, obese, graying man sat behind two monitors. Jason stared at him for a few seconds, barely able to match the obviously ill, failing Dr. Bryant to the formidable man he had encountered in another universe. Bryant looked as though he did not have long to live, but his condition did not appear to have altered his demeanor one bit: he glared balefully at Jason for a moment before looking back to his monitors, growling something that sounded like, "wasn't one of that bastard enough?"

In the corner opposite Bryant, a balding man close to Jason's own size stood beside another desk; his face wore a wondering half-smile, though his eyes betrayed worry and doubt. Dr. Tinsworth came forward until he stood beside the room's third occupant, who stood before what appeared to be a network of streaming, cylindrical, vertical holographs. He had not yet looked toward them. Jason was relieved to see that much of the scar tissue he expected to find was absent; Bryant, or someone on his team, had done a remarkably good job of repairing the damage caused by the explosion.

As this thought went through Jason's head, Argo turned to look at him, and for nearly five full seconds they simply stared at each other. Argo's face was slightly different than Jason's, both from age and from the surgeries he had undergone to repair his injuries, but it was clear that they were the same individual, albeit at different points of their life's trajectory.

Then Argo spoke, and Jason was startled despite himself to hear a voice essentially identical to his own: "Jason Anderson. I have seen indications that another universal vector space intersected this one at approximately the same time as the explosion that caused my death. Dr. Tinsworth here confirmed to me that he received a phone call from a man claiming to be you. Since you are here, I can assume that you have thus far evaded capture in your own timeframe?"

Jason eyed Argo warily. "I don't know that you could say that. Your friends here found me in Ohio, in my own time, and then showed up after the arch formed, right after we arrived at the arena."

"Of course. In almost every other iteration of your journey to Ohio that I could isolate, you were captured either by FBI or agents of another entity, Ius Divinum. You disappeared from the grid almost immediately in every one of those iterations," Argo replied. He had the same blank, bland expression of the Cybwomen, but there was intelligence – staggering intelligence, Jason realized – in the eyes that met his.

"I'm going to check outside," Tinsworth said, glancing toward Argo, who nodded in reply. With another smile to Jason, the physicist moved past them and out into the Station grounds.

"So why did you want to bring me here?" Jason asked, unable to control a slight quiver in his voice.

"I was tasked with mitigating – or reversing, if I could – the effects of the Seafloods, once they began," Argo replied. "I was able to achieve some limited effects, but overall the process proved irreversible, and so I began to explore alternative solutions.

"One such possibility is to merge this timestream into another one – one in which Earth's radio emissions in 2048 are similar to those seen in 2023. That can only be done by connecting to an existing singularity or bridge in 2023, and manipulating events in that time in such a way as to shunt this timeframe subset onto the target subset, merging them."

Jason's face went almost blank with shock at this response. "Wait. I thought that obviating a timeframe created a paradox that destroys it. Now you're telling me that it doesn't vanish, but that it merges with another timeframe?"

"That appears to be what happens," Argo answered tonelessly.

Jason blanched. "What happens when the two spaces merge?"

Argo considered him for an instant, then glanced back to the holographs, looking at them as their colors and patterns swirled and changed. "They become a single timeframe. The occupants of the merged vector spaces do not directly perceive any discontinuity."

Jason blinked, and was silent for a moment. Then he said, "Wouldn't the information in their brains produce discrepancies with their perception?"

"Of course," Argo replied. "In a normal, healthy brain, the subconscious is able to access those areas rendered unavailable to conscious thought by paradox."

Jason thought for a moment. "I had thought that when I changed the rift collapse in this timeframe, I had destroyed that universe. If it merged with another one, how is it that there are two of us here? Why didn't we merge into one entity – or Jensen and Greene, when they came through to our time?"

"You and I, along with Jensen and Greene, are not at the same t-point along the path described by this timeframe," Argo answered. "Though you have moved forward along that path, you are still anchored to your origin point in space-time. Therefore we are able to coexist. Moreover, our existences are no longer such that they can merge, as I am technically no longer you. That individual died in the lab explosion, almost thirty years ago. I am essentially a created being, built from the wreckage of another, naturally born creature."

Jason's eyes dropped, and he nodded. His voice was thick with emotion as he said, "I'm sorry for what happened to you. I was trying to save Phoebe."

"There is no need for apology. In my former state, with my limited information and understanding, I would have done exactly as you did. Moreover, I do not bear grudges or ill will in any sense. I will neither retaliate nor seek revenge upon you." Argo glanced toward Jason, and the latter felt a moment of déjà vu as a fleeting ghost of warmth lit Argo's eyes for a millisecond. "You will be perfectly safe here until it is time for you to return." His gaze returned to the holographs.

Jason had not missed the significance of what he had seen. "You're like Phoebe was, aren't you? Do you dream, too?"

Argo looked back at him again. "Of course I do. All of us carry old data in our brains, like sectors in an old hard drive that still have information stored in them, but that are no longer used. Some of that data is inaccessible, owing to time and decrepitude – or, as we now know, to paradox – but most is still accessible. The dream state, by its nature, is analogous to an alternative referencing system in the brain from that of the conscious brain, and as such, it connects to areas that are not randomly selected, but which appear to the conscious mind to be so."

Jason's eyes widened as he thought briefly. "When I – we – were little, I dreamed more than once that there was a railroad track that ran through my neighborhood, just a few houses away. Do you remember that?"

"I do remember having had that dream," Argo answered. His otherwise blank countenance evinced slight interest. "The dream state, as I said, uses a different referencing system, so that elements of the mind's contents are interposed on one another according to its directives, but the conscious mind cannot rationalize the results. You were seeing a rail crossing that existed somewhere else, interposed in a place where your conscious mind knew it did not exist."

Jason's face sagged slightly. "So there was never a railroad track there? I thought that might have been a memory of another timeframe."

"That would have been impossible," Argo answered. "That crossing was halfway up a hill, and there was no path for the rails to take from there. Our memory of that railroad track is limited only to that crossing and a very short distance on either side. That was the portion of memory that was superimposed on our perception of that street." He paused briefly. "Significant timeline merges should be fairly common, and inevitable in astronomical time scales, but rare in human terms; from what I have been able to determine, the one you apparently caused is the only major anomalous one I can pinpoint in the last two thousand years."

"Was there another one then – I mean, two thousand years ago?" Phoebe asked. Both Jason and Argo looked to her.

"I cannot be certain. It appears that there was a multiple merge – a very significant one – but my instrumentation is not reliable at that distance in space-time, and the passage of time in our own frame creates an obscuring effect – akin to looking back through a four-dimensional cometary tail," he said, looking back at Jason.

Jason nodded. "That makes sense, I think. But I don't understand why you brought us here." He glanced toward Phoebe. "Or why you would need both of us."

"What you must do will be exceedingly dangerous. After you return to your own time, you will have probably have no more than about two days in which to do it," Argo replied. "There are interfering factors at work which are still unpredictable. We will work out details momentarily, but in the meantime, there is someone here who has been waiting for you." His gaze shifted toward someone who had just entered, unnoted by any of the four of them. They all turned.

Jason's mouth fell open. The woman who had entered looked at each of them in turn; her expression was unlike that of any of the Cybwomen he had seen. The emotions and reactions that were so muted, if even visible, on the others were plain to see in her face. She was not quite human, but she was close. Then her eyes fell upon Jason, and her mouth opened as well; her eyes shone as she stared at him.

"You came back for me," Allison whispered.

Chapter Fifteen

THE SKY OUTSIDE BRIGHTENED and the sun rose behind the drawn blinds in Haverhill's borrowed office. He still had not slept. Except for one five-minute break, he had remained at his desk, coordinating his forces, and preparing for their next move.

He had placed teams to wait in both directions along the east-west road that ran in front of the arena. Another team was in place in an overgrown vacant lot next to the road that ran away south. There was no route north out of the arena except on foot, across an abandoned golf course bordered by two neighborhoods – each of which was controlled by unusually vigorous homeowners' associations.

Two more teams waited farther back, ready to deploy in pursuit once the agents left, and box them in. Once captured, they would be brought back to Atlanta – not as prisoners, unfortunately – and he would interview them in this office. With any luck, they would be captured with minimal delay, be on a plane out of Dayton before noon, and be in front of him, along with Anderson and his girlfriend, before sunset.

With any luck. He snorted. Luck was something best never hoped for, he thought, as he reviewed every option he could think of. Every adjacent building was under surveillance. If by chance there was another way out of the arena, they would still have to emerge somewhere nearby.

Another IM popped up on his screen; opening it, he saw that the cameras that had been knocked offline had been reset shortly before sunrise, and would be back up in a few minutes. He nodded to himself, acknowledged the communication and closed the window, then reopened the video feeds. They were still dark.

At the same time that the cameras came back online, a red dot began to blink in the icon tray at the bottom right of his screen. At once, he turned off the monitor, and drew a pair of slightly oversized sunglasses from his breast pocket. As he donned them, his thumb gently pressed a small button inside their right temple.

A brief flash accompanied a retinal scan; any other person attempting to use those glasses would only succeed in causing them to self-destruct, likely blinding them in the process. After a moment, a display appeared before his eyes, and small speakers near each ear began to relay words from the one voice on earth that he truly feared: "Requesting update on the status of the KOPO agents."

Haverhill spoke quietly in response. "Subjects have been followed into the arena outside Dayton. There was a minor tremor there two hours ago, but no visible damage was done. Subjects have not left the facility." As he spoke, the camera feeds watching Hara Arena appeared, tiled on the display. Nothing had changed.

"Are our people in place to intercept them when they depart?" the voice asked.

"Affirmative. All known exits to the facility and all buildings within one thousand feet are under surveillance. Four teams are in place to converge and intercept when subjects have been located." Haverhill was certain that the deployment had been done and would prove airtight, but the power behind the voice was enough to inspire doubt in even his granite soul. He waited, invisibly uncomfortable.

"Anderson was confirmed to have gone with them, along with the girl. She might prove useful if force is required," the voice mused. "A woman suspected of bombing a laboratory opens avenues that might otherwise have been unavailable to us."

"Acknowledged. However, the knowledge Anderson might yield is of critical importance. He would be more likely to give over that information if the girl is left unharmed." Haverhill frowned slightly. "I would prefer that we maintain the truce that has been in place."

"That agreement is not yours to maintain or break," the voice replied, icily. A chill ran down Haverhill's spine. "Given the value of the information we seek, we might be forced to forgo the truce in order to solidify our range of positions. We cannot allow technology of this magnitude to fall into KOPO hands – not unless we also possess it."

"Acknowledged," Haverhill said again. "Subjects will be apprehended as soon as they depart the arena."

"See that they are. Report their capture as soon as they are secured." The display went dark as the connection was ended. Haverhill replaced the sunglasses in his pocket, taking a deep breath, and restarted the monitor. There was still no sign of activity.

He could sleep once they were captured, he told himself, as another message window flashed onto his screen. This one was from Mangum. He frowned slightly as he opened it.

"General, Dr. Tinsworth has requested that Wiley Grant be reinstated to his research team. I would have rejected it, except that there aren't very many qualified candidates for him to choose from," it read.

Haverhill's frown deepened. Grant had been imprisoned for his role in the lab debacle, with Mangum assisting as an interrogation officer owing to his proximity to the bridge project. Subsequent events had cleared him of any responsibility other than having left his post for several minutes, so he had been released.

The general snorted, then dictated his reply: "Permission granted, on the condition that he goes back in the hole if he fucks up again. Transmit." He grinned to himself as the algorithm-sanitized reply appeared in the message box.

HE WATCHED HER AS *her brain completed its diagnostic and restarted; as the command chain executed, her eyes opened again, but there was a recognition that was above what he had seen from her in the cemetery. He looked at her as she awoke, and she looked at him. He had a sense of two immense objects, two stars, passing each other so closely as to create a material link between them – but their relative motions carried them past each other, flinging them along divergent vectors across the universe, never to encounter each other again.*

Before he could react, she spoke through his laptop, in a popup window: "You'll remember me, won't you?"

It was not truly a question.

JASON STARED AT ALLISON, trying to absorb the enormity of the implications, as she gazed back at him. Her eyes radiated a joy he would never have imagined possible in a Cybwoman, which alone would have amazed him, but the clear recognition he saw there terrified him even more. She had never met him on his own timeline – only in hers, and that time would not yet have come into existence, even in the world that was gone – yet clearly, she didn't merely recognize him. She *adored* him.

He glanced toward Phoebe, who looked warily from Allison back to him; after a few seconds, Phoebe asked, "was she the one who helped you come back?"

Jason nodded, then looked back at Allison, and was shocked to see tears forming in her eyes. In spite of himself, he was deeply touched, though still reeling at the knowledge that she knew him at all. She had moved a step or two closer, so that he was nearly within reach.

"How much do you remember?" he asked her.

"Jason Anderson is the one who will change the world," she replied, smiling in a way that no Cybwoman he had met had ever done. "I remember that you set me free. You set us all free once, and you will free us again, for good."

Jason felt a thrill of vertiginous fear that was matched by Phoebe's expression as he glanced toward her again. He took a deep breath, then looked back toward Argo. "How is this possible?" he asked.

"Allison suffered multiple system failures during her initial activation," Argo replied. "Her brain does not operate as a normal Cybwoman's would, because of the damage incurred in those failures. Other parts of her brain have taken over some of her lost functionality, with the result that she has nearly human responses, though with some deleterious side effects."

Jason studied Argo, who stared blandly back at him in turn, and asked, "does she act like this toward you, too?"

"She sees us as one entity," Argo answered. "She demonstrates the same attachment to me that she has shown you, but I have not heard her say anything about freedom until now."

Jason was momentarily bewildered. "But wouldn't that imply what you said before – that there was a timeline merge in our past – wouldn't that be consistent?"

Argo nodded. "That could be consistent. Moreover, with Allison's altered functionality, it is possible that she is able to access and parse those merged memories consciously."

"Wait a minute," Phoebe said. She was staring at Allison. "She can remember things that happened in a different universe?"

"That is essentially correct," Argo replied. "Even the temporal anomaly can be explained through Jason's presence here, which necessitates informational transference from his past – even from a future timeline."

"Do you love him?" Phoebe asked Allison, who looked toward her.

"I love them all," she replied. "They are the same being. But your Jason is the one who will change the world." She smiled again as her gaze shifted from Phoebe to Jason, and then to Argo. "Argo is the one who is destined for me."

"This is a new development," Argo said in his quiet voice, looking at Phoebe. "It seems that as this temporal reference frame progresses, Allison is accessing memories she did not have prior to your arrival. I suspect that they may be artifacts from a merged universe."

Phoebe looked blankly puzzled. Jason glanced back toward Jensen and Greene; their faces reflected no greater comprehension. His gaze returned to Argo.

"If you're right, then Allison would have memories of what happened on my first trip through time, even if I went farther into my future than I have this time. That would explain what she said about me," he said.

Argo nodded. "I concur. Her memory – or, more precisely, those portions which are inaccessible to our minds, but not to hers – might in fact be changing as we speak, as a result of your presence here."

Jason frowned. "I'm surprised you haven't found a way to unlock those memories in yourself."

"The human brain normally doesn't function in a way that makes them intelligible," Argo answered. "You might as well suggest that a surgeon remove a tumor without breaking a patient's skin. Four-dimensionally, it would be simple enough, but in our spatial frame, there's simply no direction in which to go to accomplish that, and even if it were possible, the viewpoint from that angle would likely be unresolvable to human perception." He glanced toward the bank of holographic tubes, motioning as he did. "For example, this technology allows me to visualize patterns within similar data by normalizing it into a viewable format."

Jason nodded. For a moment, no one spoke.

"You will need to understand the mental processes that accompany what you're attempting," Argo said, addressing them both. "For almost everyone else in existence, there will be no discontinuity, but it is possible that either of you, or both of you, may suffer some sort of alteration in your thought patterns if you succeed – or even if you fail."

"Like her?" Phoebe asked, gesturing toward Allison.

"Probably not nearly as severe," Argo answered her. "It may not be noticeable for you, but for Jason, there may be much more serious consequences, as he has consciously undergone one such merge. More than one may cause informational superimposition and affect his most basic mental processes."

"I have to take that risk," said Jason. "What I'm not sure of is how to shunt this universe onto the one you've found."

Argo nodded. "There is one anomaly I have identified in that timeframe. Specifically – " he glanced toward Allison – "I saw no indication that the Cybwomen were extant. By this time, a development of that magnitude should have warped the timeframe's events."

Jason was silent for a moment before a small smile tugged at a corner of his mouth. "I see," he whispered, before looking sidelong toward Phoebe, then back toward Greene and Jensen.

Before he could say any more, the door behind them opened, and three women – all of them clearly Cybwomen – entered the Station. The others with Jason looked merely curious at their arrival, but Jason gasped in horror and shrank away from them toward Argo.

"Friends, let me introduce these three to you. Their names are Julia, Rosamind and Lisa, and they serve as the Station's liaison to the Covington clan. They are sometimes called the Threebirds."

The three women strode impassively forward toward Jason and Argo, past the others, and halted before them. None of them spoke. After a brief pause, Argo looked first toward Jason, then toward Jensen and Greene.

"Some minutes ago, these three returned from a scheduled visit to the Covington base. They have made these visits weekly, ever since the Covingtons attempted to raise an attack on the Station. After they were forced to surrender, they agreed to frequent inspections of their compound."

In spite of his fear, Jason was puzzled. "The Covingtons? I thought that the Black Birds were the dangerous clan."

The Cybwoman named Lisa turned to face him. "The Black Bird tribe died out fourteen years ago, after a sickness went through their base. The few survivors scattered rather than face enslavement by the Covingtons." Her glance lingered briefly upon him in a manner that was decidedly atypical of her kind.

"*Enslavement?*" Jason's confusion yielded to different look of incredulous horror. "I don't remember that they were *anything* like that."

"You visited them in a different timeframe from this one," Argo responded. "From your expression, I gather that their tribe was markedly different from what we know here and now."

"It *was*. The Black Birds were the dangerous ones, but those three – " Jason pointed toward the three Cybwomen – "They were the ones who served as their liaison, and they were much worse than the Black Birds." He grimaced. "How do I know that they're not worse than you say the Covingtons are?"

Argo's blank expression didn't flicker. "Because I am telling you that they work with me, and will do as I ask. If I tell them to protect you, they will, until they are destroyed or the need for protection ceases. I am asking for them to escort you to the Covingtons now, to warn them."

"Why do they need to be warned?" Phoebe asked. Behind Argo, Bryant's head jerked up from his monitors, an intent frown darkening his already unpleasant demeanor.

"Regardless of the results of your efforts, this universe, and likely many parallel ones similar to it comprising a single N-space subset, will merge with another N-space subset of parallel universes – either those accompanying the one I have isolated, or the ones resultant from that set that will emerge if you are unsuccessful in your mission, once you return." Argo glanced back over his shoulder toward Bryant, who had risen to his feet and was approaching them. "You will not interfere. I am tasked with the mitigation of the Seafloods, and this solution is very probably the last opportunity for me to complete this task."

"You think you can stop me?" Bryant sneered, though his expression was only a ghost of his former malice. "I'm not allowing this. If you do what you say you're going to do, you'll be killing *my* research. That's not going to happen." He squinted briefly at Jason and Phoebe before returning his gaze to Argo. "And if you think those two twerps are up to the job, you're nuts. He's a lab rat, and she's a Christmas wreath. If you think *he's* going to change the world, then you need a diagnostic scan. Immediately."

Argo did not reply, and returned Bryant's baleful stare for only a moment before looking toward the three Cybwomen. "You will escort these two to the Covington base, and notify Jones that unpredictable, and indeterminate, events can be expected occur in the near future," he said. "He will be familiar with the mythology surrounding Jason Anderson; Jason's mere presence will serve as an indicator. If the Covingtons show any signs of hostility, you will return at once with them. If anyone attempts to harm them, that person is to be neutralized."

"Countermanded," Bryant responded. "You will remain here, and prevent these two from returning to their own time, until I give further instructions." He grinned sourly toward Argo. "You should remember that I can still countermand their orders. They will obey my instructions as long as I'm living. You'd best not forget that."

Before any of them could respond, Jason felt something rush past him, and an instant later, he heard the sickening, wet, crunching snap as Allison grasped Bryant's head from behind and yanked it around, hard even for a Cybwoman, nearly pulling it off completely. The doctor's lifeless body fell forward as she let it go, but the head came down nearly face up, with the neck grotesquely constricted. Even as it struck the floor, Allison knelt and grasped Bryant's head by the ears, staring into his eyes even as they dulled into insensibility.

"Jason Anderson will change the world. *You will not stop him*," she said in a hissing whisper, a moment before Phoebe screamed, burying her face in Jason's shoulder. He put his arms around her, staring in revolted horror first at Allison, then at Argo.

Argo's expression, as always, remained neutral. "Bryant's last order has been nullified. My previous order is renewed. Please escort these two as I requested, and send Jensen and Greene in as you leave. I will need to review their next instructions with them."

As the Threebirds moved to escort the couple out, Jason said to Argo, quietly, "You really *are* one of them, aren't you?"

"Bryant's health had deteriorated," Argo replied. "He was less than eighteen months from his eventual demise. I could have chosen to retain you here, and allowed his illness to run its course, but that would have exposed both of you to unacceptable risks." He paused for the briefest moment. "You must not judge Allison's behavior unjustly. She is the one Cybwoman who could not be countermanded by Bryant, because I was the one who eventually completed her transition. I ordered her to do as she has done, though I must add, her words to the doctor were her own."

Jason nodded. "I understand. Do you have any specific instructions for me, other than to communicate to Jones that there is a change coming?"

Another ghost of warmth crossed Argo's face. "You are afraid to cross me. You need not be. We require each other in order to accomplish our aims, and I trust that you do not wish me harm. We will confer when you return." As he spoke, Phoebe looked tearfully toward him, clutching Jason as she did so.

Without another word or visible gesture, Julia and Rosamind came forward, each taking one of them by the arm with unexpected gentleness, and led them from the Station's command center as Argo watched them leave.

Chapter Sixteen

WILEY GRANT ARRIVED AT his old laboratory under Hampton Hall at exactly five minutes to eight, and saw at once that almost all of the damage from the blast two months earlier had been repaired. The endpoint receptacle had been rebuilt, but was inactive, and Dr. Tinsworth was looking over a new – and significantly upgraded – instrument bank. He looked up as the buzzer sounded to signal Wiley's arrival.

For almost a full minute after the door closed, Wiley and Tinsworth stared at each other without speaking. The initial distaste in Tinsworth's expression faded somewhat as he noted the difference wrought on his graduate assistant by two months in prison.

"You've changed," he observed noncommittally.

Tinsworth expected a barrage of Wiley's typical response to criticism, but was surprised to receive only a terse nod in response before Wiley looked past him into the connecting passage. "The lab in Williams was destroyed, but this one wasn't as bad, from what I remember. It looks like everything here has been fixed."

"It has," Tinsworth answered. "This side is almost functional. We're still a few weeks out on the other end. The structural damage to the building had to be repaired. The whole damn place nearly came down."

Wiley nodded again, then moved across the lab and stood next to Tinsworth, studying the new instrumentation. "DARPA still backing the project, then?" he asked.

Tinsworth shot him a dark look. "For the time being, though I don't know how long that will continue."

Wiley nodded, then took a deep breath. "So. I looked over the non-Euclidean implications of this project, but I'm stumped as to why they would apply here. We had two congruent endpoints, with essentially matching spatial motion vectors and zero relative spin." He frowned. "But my first question is how Anderson could still be alive after that lab blew up."

Tinsworth was taken aback, but only slightly and not for long. Wiley nodded to himself.

"Anderson's body was found in Williams Hall by the firefighters on scene," Tinsworth finally answered, speaking each word carefully. "He was pronounced dead immediately. However, there have been other – incidents – that have occurred, and they indicate that Jason is in fact alive, and in hiding. Somewhere in the Midwest, from what I've heard."

Wiley considered briefly. "I was held in prison after the lab went up. They brought another guy in two days ago – he was obviously one of Phoebe's relatives – and he told me that Anderson's alive, and that he saw him after the explosion. I've been trying to figure out since then how that could have happened."

"Put the two together," Tinsworth said, a little dully. "Somehow, our bridge was changed so that it became a passageway, and Jason came through it after it changed."

"That still doesn't explain why there was an explosion," Wiley objected.

"That was what I thought too, at first, but then it occurred to me that if there was a nonzero delta-t between the endpoints, it would create an energy absorption problem," Tinsworth replied.

Wiley went silent for a moment, then whistled. "Damn. It sure does – a big one. As fast as the earth moves through space every second, that could be a *huge* kinetic energy difference," he said.

"I thought at first that the problem was due to the spin of the earth." Tinsworth's face had paled slightly. "Most of the motion vectors would cancel each other because the earth's arc through space would be essentially identical in the short term. The difference in any transverse components would be very slight, given our distance from the galactic center and the speed of the earth around the sun; a few days' difference could be absorbed, and I honestly thought that was the largest possible factor. The relative speed and direction of the earth's spin would have created a significant differential – but even that wouldn't have done more than create a crater a few feet across, maximum."

Wiley thought about that for a moment. "You're right. There's not enough mass to create that big a blast. So how did it happen?"

Tinsworth took a deep breath; he looked frightened. "A explosion like that would require the kind of vector differential that only a significant delta-t would create."

The import of the professor's words slowly sank in as Wiley's somber expression gave way to horror. "That would take at least a hundred times as much explosive force. *At least.* And that would mean…" Wiley did a rough, fast mental calculation. "Oh my God." He looked to Tinsworth. "I'd guess at least five years delta-t. Probably a lot more than that."

"It was closer to ten times that, when I worked through the math," came the reply. "If Jason came through a passage generated using our bridge, he was coming from forty to sixty years in our future." He paused. "There's no way he came from the past – the technology for this bridge didn't exist even ten years ago, let alone during the Vietnam war. He came from our future." Tinsworth paused, as Wiley considered the ramifications. "I just wish I knew *why.* He knew exactly where and when we created the bridge, so – theoretically – if he could harness enough computing power, he might have been able to determine the position of the bridge in space-time relative to his own, and do – whatever it was that he did.

"But he would have had to have a really good reason. The computing resources alone would have been huge. The amount of raw power needed to create a bridge like that would have been just as problematic, and he would have had to devote a lot of time to the project. Decades, possibly. And he would risk creating a causal loop in the process." Tinsworth sighed, and Wiley took a deep breath of his own, trying to grasp the import of what the professor had said. Neither spoke for a few moments.

"The thing is, Anderson would have known he could create a causal loop." Wiley frowned, and looked worriedly to Tinsworth. "He knew how dangerous that could be. I didn't like him, I'll admit, but he was – *is* –

brilliant. If he did all that in spite of the risks, and in spite of everything it cost, then he's here for a really good reason – whatever it is."

"I know." Tinsworth's expression was haunted. "I've tried not to let that on too much, because there are some serious government types trying to find him, and I don't think he wants to be found. If he hadn't called me, they'd have no clue where he is."

This took Wiley by surprise. "Wait. He called you? You *talked* to him?"

"Yes." The professor looked glumly at the floor. "It was just a couple of days ago, and only for a few minutes. He called me from somewhere in Ohio. God knows how he got there, but he did. Problem is, my phone had been wired to tip off the feds if he called. I couldn't ask him much of anything in case he needed a free hand."

"And now they're looking for him there," Wiley said. "Will they tell you if they find him?"

"I doubt it. I had to convince them that the explosion wasn't caused by a bomb, and to do that, I had to come up with a plausible explanation – and I got lucky, and got it mostly right."

Wiley nodded again. He looked around the lab as one more worrisome thought surfaced in his mind. "If we resume work on creating another bridge, what's the chance that it will blow up on us the way the last one did?"

Tinsworth's shoulders slumped. "I don't know. But I don't want to find out, either. I'm setting up the bridge experiment exactly as we had it before – I'll need a lot of grunt work on this from you, I'm afraid – but I have no intention of powering it until I know more about how the first one blew up."

"Wouldn't it be a lot of work to find it, from a future perspective? You said that yourself," Wiley ventured.

"That's right, if we assume current technology. My concern is that a bridge like that might create a readable signature in space-time that might be detectable by instruments more advanced than ours. If that's the case, then any bridge like ours would be really easy to spot – there's probably no more than a half-dozen singularities like that on the planet right now, and no other ones anywhere within a few light-years, most likely." Tinsworth shuddered. "Imagine what could happen if an alien civilization advanced enough to detect a bridge signature found our signal."

Wiley's eyes widened with horror as the mental image of what could happen played through his mind. "Jesus. The nearest star is at least ten times farther than the earth travels in that time, *and* the information has to reach them."

"Exactly – but the effects *here* would still be immediate, even if an assailant were a thousand light-years away. Instead of the explosion we saw, there would be a much, much bigger one. At ten light years, the explosion would take out most of downtown. At a hundred, you would see it from anyplace in the southeastern US." Tinsworth shuddered. "I'm wondering if that's what he's doing – trying to prevent this technology from being used against *us*."

JASON SIGHED AS HE and Phoebe walked east from the Station, following the same route that he had taken with her in a different world. The Threebirds trailed wordlessly five yards behind them, walking three abreast with Julia in the center.

And different it was. Jason had seen this street, running east before bending south toward the interstate highway that ringed the city, as it had been after about twenty additional years of neglect. As they drew near to the crossroads where he had rested in his first trip, he could see that the buildings' state of cannibalization was not dissimilar to then, but the passage of time had not yet rotted them as completely. He glanced toward Phoebe.

"We didn't go as far forward in time as I did," he said softly.

"How far do you think we came?" Phoebe asked.

Jason came to a stop as they reached the crossroads, looking down each route. "It's not nearly as old. These buildings are in better shape, and the road's still mostly clear – a lot of it was overgrown with grass by the time I arrived last time. I'm only guessing, based on what it looked like after forty-five years, but I'd say we're about twenty-five or thirty years forward in time, at most." He half-turned, looking over his shoulder at the Threebirds.

None appeared to be watching him with any particular interest, but Jason knew better.

"Are you allowed to tell us how far forward in time we came?" Jason asked. All three pairs of inhumanly blank eyes focused on him; once again, he caught the slightest flutter in Lisa's. It was Julia, however, who responded.

"We have been instructed not to divulge that information. Argo has indicated that he will confer again with you when you return. You may wish to convey your question at that time." Jason had never interacted with Julia on his previous trip, and had only seen her battle Phoebe as he made his final dash to escape, but her ferocity had been memorable. The relative blandness and innocuousness of her response thus caught him slightly off guard, and he studied her for a few seconds. She did not acknowledge his attention, and neither did Rosamind when he moved his gaze to her, but Lisa's reaction to his scrutiny was much plainer. She betrayed a slight hint of bemusement, and as they studied each other, he sensed a faint ghost of warmth in her expression, not unlike those he had seen before in Phoebe.

"You were the one who helped me get away," Jason said, almost to himself. Phoebe had been looking about at the changes in their world from her time; she now turned toward him, puzzled, before following his eyes back to Lisa.

"I have no knowledge of this event, and I have no memory of ever having encountered you," Lisa replied in a monotone. Both of the other two Cybwomen looked instantly toward her.

Whatever communication passed between them was so fast that Jason could not grasp it, but within a second, all three were facing him again, and it was Julia who spoke. "We cannot delay further. We should encounter the Covingtons at their border, straddling the next major crossroads. Part of that detachment will likely escort us in to their compound.

"We were instructed to bring you to the Covington chief and relay your message, then return. Argo does not intend for this visit to take any longer than necessary – we should return to the Station before sunset."

Jason glanced skyward. "It looks to be about ten in the morning, now, looking at the sun," he said. "It's another two and a half miles to the Covington base, and then three and a half miles back, and it's already hot out here. We probably won't be back before midafternoon, and Phoebe and I will have to rest after that."

"Argo did not indicate whether rest would be necessary," Rosamind objected tonelessly.

Jason sighed, looking east along the road they would have to take, and then to Phoebe. "Six more miles to walk, and we've had no sleep. I think I can persuade Argo to allow us time to rest, once we return, but if what they say about the Covingtons is true, then we probably won't want to stay there." When Phoebe nodded in agreement, Jason glanced back toward the Threebirds once more. "All right. We go to the Covingtons, and then return."

Without waiting for a response – not that he expected one – Jason smiled ruefully, as much to himself as to Phoebe, and began to walk east along the abandoned roadway. As Phoebe fell in alongside them, he whispered, to no one in particular, "the only way back is forward."

His words sounded odd, even to himself. The sky was clear and still, but a light breeze blew through the trees, and when Jason looked to Phoebe again, she still matched his pace, but was watching him with new fear in her eyes.

"What is it?" he asked her in a low voice.

"That wind," she answered, also quietly. "And when you said that, I thought I heard more than one person, and when I looked at you –" she hesitated, then continued, "I thought, for just a second, that there was something behind you, like a shadow, but not as dark."

Jason thought for a few seconds, reflecting on the voice that he himself had heard, before looking back again, this time toward Lisa. "Did you see or hear anything different?" he asked her.

"Nothing registered on any of my sensors," Lisa replied, immediately and blankly.

For reasons he could not possibly have expressed, he doubted her response, but it would do no good for him to say so – especially with the other two Cybwomen's attention locked on him. He sighed, deciding that their suspicions were best left unconfirmed, and said only, "all right, then. Let's go."

With that, they continued eastward, falling silent as the day warmed and the sun continued toward the zenith.

Chapter Seventeen

THERE WAS A TON of work left to do.

It was midafternoon as Wiley looked around the laboratory under Williams Hall for the first time since before it was destroyed, and he could see that he had about a month's worth of rebuilding and calibration in front of him – work that would have been done much faster with Anderson's help, he reflected, remembering the construction of the original bridge.

Aside from the metal framework that would eventually house one bridge endpoint, most of the necessary materials were still boxed up, labeled, and stacked around the walls on either side of the newly-replaced airlock door. The intercom had not yet been reinstalled, and the entire facility would need several coats of white paint.

An odd, unbidden thought crossed his mind as he stared at the boxed materials, and for a moment he imagined what the bridge project would have looked like if it had been built by school kids – Erector-set parts, scavenged toys, cardboard boxes. String and batteries and old, reused wire. But something was out of place, something he couldn't grasp…

Then the image evaporated, leaving him alone in the empty, unconstructed lab. The old Wiley would have laughed, derisively, at the version of the project he had momentarily visualized, but after having spent weeks alone with nothing but his own thoughts for company, he realized that that notion was something he ordinarily would never have imagined – and that he had no clue of its origin.

He continued to take mental inventory of what was still needed, but the issue nagged at him, and after he had satisfied himself that he had taken everything into account, he returned back down the tunnel that extended slightly more than one hundred yards between Williams Hall and Hampton.

He triple-checked the few missing items and the rough timetable of completion he had devised as he followed the tunnel walkway that paralleled that line where the bridge's length, were it visible, would extend. They had never attempted to interpose anything between the two endpoints; the experiment had not yet reached that stage when everything had gone south.

South. Everything went south, except Anderson – he went north. And that, Wiley realized in a flash, was what was nagging him.

He reached the end of the tunnel and entered the Hampton lab; Tinsworth was there, dithering with the framework for the new bridge's second endpoint. Wiley noted that it was almost complete; it would be able to support a micro-collapsar in less than a week, if the instrumentation and guidance programming were ready. Tinsworth glanced up toward him as he approached.

"So about how long do you think you'll need on that end?" Tinsworth asked.

Wiley thought. Had he been asked that question six months earlier, he would have padded the required time, allowing himself to work at a pace convenient to his poor habits, but he knew he didn't have that option any longer. "Three weeks, I think. Hopefully not longer, and I might be able to cut it by a day or three if everything goes more or less according to plan."

Tinsworth's eyebrows lifted slightly; he evidently had not expected the answer he had just received, but it did not seem to displease him. "About what I thought. It's unfortunate, but what else can we do?"

Wiley hesitated for a few seconds, and Tinsworth was about to resume working on the frame, when he asked, "You said Anderson would have come from decades in the future – right?"

"That's right," Tinsworth replied. "What's on your mind?"

"I'm wondering if there are side effects to his – passage, I guess – that we aren't considering. Think about it," he rushed to add, as Tinsworth scowled. "Our timeframe shouldn't be affected by him anymore, since he died – but it is, if he came back, and that changes causality here. Right?"

"Only to the extent that he could create a causal loop – something he does now that could create future circumstances, leading to an event or condition whose origin is untraceable." Tinsworth snorted. "It's like those idiots who learn just enough about causality to decide that the chicken-and-egg question – you know, which one came first – is actually a causal loop resulting from God's creation of the earth."

Wiley thought briefly that he'd never himself encountered anyone both that smart and that dense, but then he pushed that distraction aside. "Not necessarily. Anderson's memory carries information that shouldn't be available – or at least, not available *yet* – in our existence. Wouldn't his presence trigger awareness of events in his experience among those of us who knew him, and were present for those events?"

Tinsworth fell silent, considering, and Wiley could see that the question had unnerved him slightly. "I'm not sure whether we should ask a physicist, a philosopher or a priest about that one," he said finally. "I don't think we'll know the answer to that until it happens."

"I think it might already have," Wiley said, and related the almost-daydream he had had about the mocked-up bridge project. As he spoke, Tinsworth grew pale, and when he had finished, the professor looked around, finally grabbing a clipboard and a pencil, and shoved them at Wiley.

"I need for you to draw the design for what you saw, as close as you can remember. Include everything. I'm going to go over to my desk. I think you may be on to something here, but I'll need to verify it, and I can't be near you while you draw that up. I have to do something over there, independently, just to be sure." Tinsworth's voice shook as he finished speaking, and he turned and crossed the lab to his desk without saying more.

Still uncertain, but with a cold, sickening, growing dread, Wiley began to draw the project as he had daydreamed it. He could see a tilted desk, a pencil sharpener acting as a winch, and a model car with a broomstick affixed to the top. All around them there were plastic sheets serving as protective barriers. As he drew in the surrounding walls, he realized some of what had been wrong: the setup he had envisioned had not been located in the Williams lab, but in Hampton, and instead of the bridge, it had been created for some other purpose. There was only one area he couldn't visualize – the area in front of the desk was somehow void, like a blind spot resulting from a scratch in a camera lens.

Thirty minutes later, after several redraws and some careful labelling of the various parts, he had created what he thought was as close to the imagined design as he would get. He had half-turned away from Tinsworth as he had worked, studying the layout of the Hampton lab; as he looked back to the professor and nodded, the latter rose and returned across the lab, also carrying a clipboard.

"I also had the same daydream, and I'm guessing that we had it at about the same time. Hand me your clipboard and I'll hand you mine, and we'll see whether you're right about this."

Looking directly at each other, they exchanged their drawings, and looked down. Both gasped at almost the same moment.

"Holy *shit*." Wiley's voice shook; he looked as though he was about to be sick. Tinsworth looked little better. They held their drawings up, and saw that they were – except for differences in the labeling and handwriting – essentially identical, even to the nulled-out space in front of the slanting desk.

"I don't know whether we should rebuild that bridge," Wiley said in a low, almost strangled voice. "Not until we know what this thing is, and what it was for."

"Not just that," Tinsworth breathed. "Look at the shit it was built out of. Why the hell would anyone knock together something like *that*? This is a first-tier research facility, not some fucking middle school."

"Do you think we should call Anderson and ask?" Wiley asked. Tinsworth shook his head.

"We'll try and figure it out first, but yeah, if we can't solve this by tomorrow, we'll have to," he answered.

JASON, PHOEBE AND THE THREEBIRDS approached the next crossroads openly from the northwest, following the road they had taken from the Station. Their short journey had been silent and uneventful, but the wall bordering the highway that crossed their route – some eight feet tall, and nearly as sturdily built as the Black Birds' compound wall had been – was new to Jason, and boded ill.

At the crossroads, a low gatehouse had been constructed; two solid-looking, metal-banded wooden doors, each at least five feet wide, stood closed at its center. From the troops stationed above it and atop the wall on either side, Jason saw that it was at least thick enough for two men to move abreast along it; the parapets were no more than thigh-high to the guards, but were topped on each side by chain-link fencing that extended another three feet up, interlaced with metal sheeting so that only the soldiers' helmets – cannibalized football and motorcycle helmets, Jason guessed, looking closely – were visible above the fence's upper rail, save along occasional chinks in the fortification. The whole of it looked well-maintained and formidable; Jason felt a surge of gratitude toward Argo for sending the Threebirds with him.

As they drew within a hundred yards of the wall, the gatehouse doors slowly opened, and a dozen men armed with spears issued from them, coming into formation to meet them as they approached. Almost before Jason realized it, the three Cybwomen moved around him and Phoebe; even as they did, Jason saw the immediate change in the guards' bearing as their stances became markedly less aggressive.

They drew to a halt less than a minute later, some thirty feet from the Covington troops, and for a few seconds no one spoke. Jason could see the apparent uneasiness in the guards' expressions, but they did not appear to be openly hostile.

Just as Jason was about to ask Julia whether something was wrong, a voice floated down from atop the gatehouse: "Hoi! Station embassy. We will not attack. State the purpose of your visit."

"We bring a message for your clan leader," Julia replied, her blank voice oddly projecting so that it echoed flatly against the wall stretching before them. "We intend no injury to your clan, so long as we are neither attacked nor impeded in our mission."

"Very well. Scotty – you and Elliott will escort the Station embassy to the chief. They have agreed that this will be a peaceful visit, so see that no one does anything stupid." The same voice spoke again from above, and after it had finished, the two doors slowly opened to their widest, pushed there by two more guards on each side. Jason noted that each door was nearly a foot thick.

"Even these three would have a job tearing those out," he murmured to Phoebe, as two of the twelve-man detachment walked forward to meet the Threebirds. One was a man Jason didn't remember seeing. He didn't realize the other was staring at him until their gazes locked.

"Oh… my… God…" Scotty breathed, his eyes round with confusion tinged with fear. "You're Jason Anderson."

Even though he understood at once what was happening, Jason was still taken aback by the shock of it. "Yes. And you're Scotty." He looked toward the other guard. "I never met you before, so until Scotty told you, I assume you didn't recognize me?"

The guard's stern, stony expression had dissolved into fear. "No, I didn't. I'm sorry."

Phoebe was staring at him in amazement, along with almost everyone else present; the Threebirds alone among them retained their composure. Jason willed himself to overcome his own confusion and fear, and essayed the best smile he could. "No need to be sorry. What's your name?"

"Elliott, sir," the man responded.

"You didn't do anything wrong," Jason said. Both guards visibly relaxed, and Jason could feel the tension in the air lessen slightly. "Will you escort us now?"

Scotty and Elliott looked to each other, still a trifle uneasily, and then nodded. "Yes. Our base is a little less than a mile behind the wall, following the road," Scotty said. "If you'll come with us, we should be there shortly."

"That is well," Julia responded. "Our mission is intended to be brief. We will communicate the necessary information to your chief, and then return to the Station."

With Scotty and Elliott flanking them on either side, the Threebirds stalked through the open doors onto the road beyond. Jason and Phoebe followed them. Jason sensed, not without discomfort, that every guard was watching him with one eye while trying to watch his escort with the other.

They passed beneath the gap in the wall formed by the gatehouse; it was made of brickwork, and was much more solid than anything he remembered seeing before. As they continued southwest, and the wall receded, he felt somewhat better about the mission, though he wondered what would happen when he encountered Jones, considering the effect his presence had had upon Scotty and Elliott.

He almost asked Julia whether the Black Birds' compound had been fortified as strongly as the wall, before catching himself. That had been the other future. It no longer existed.

Too late. "All units commence internal diagnostic," Julia suddenly barked. All three of the Cybwomen halted so suddenly that Phoebe almost collided with Rosamind; Scotty and Elliott looked back at them in puzzlement.

The last thing Jason wanted was for the two Covington guards to realize that, for however short a period might ensue, his escort was inactive and could be eliminated within seconds. He focused on Scotty, the one whom he had encountered before, and asked, "Does your chief have a family?"

Scotty gave him an odd look. "Chief can't have kids. His brother Ahman will take over if anything happens, or his son will."

Jason's eyebrows raised as he considered this. "Interesting."

Elliott had been watching the Cybwomen, who remained motionless, staring straight ahead, and had ginned up the courage to pass a hand directly before Lisa's eyes. She neither moved nor blinked, and Elliott looked toward Scotty.

"You know, we could take these three out right now," he said in a low voice. His hand drifted to his belt, where a bladed, wooden-handled hammer dangled. Scotty watched him as he drew the hammer out and turned it in both hands, considering.

Jason willed himself not to panic, but could find nothing to say. He heard Phoebe's gasp as Elliott's hand tightened on the handle and he began to draw it back. Lisa was closest to him, but it appeared that he would strike

Julia first. His eyes darted among the three Cybwomen with the shifting quickness of insane fear.

"Don't!" Phoebe and Jason both started; it was Scotty who had spoken. "If they wake up and you've attacked them, they'll kill us all."

Elliott's mouth tightened into a snarl. "No one's ever had this chance before. I got to do it." He lifted the hammer up and behind his head, lunging toward Julia with a yell.

The blow never fell. As the head of the weapon reached the back of its arcing swing, Lisa took a single step forward and blocked the hammer's path, seizing the handle with her left hand, then hurling hammer and Elliott backward and down to the pavement. Before Jason could stop her, Lisa grasped his head in her hands, an instant from breaking his neck, when she stopped herself abruptly. She convulsed twice, and her eyes fixed upon Jason for a moment.

Jason felt a thrill of terror as their gazes locked, but there was no malice in Lisa's eyes. She watched him, even as she convulsed once more, and he saw a deep recognition there – an awareness of a kind he had seen before.

As her muscles relaxed and her body began to slump, still she watched him, her expression unchanging, but her eyes fixated, staring as though the sight of him was life itself to her. The gaze held until her body toppled over, landing across Elliott as he screamed in fear. No one heeded him.

Rosamind and Julia had snapped awake, and were watching Scotty intently; he stood with his hands raised and his eyes screwed shut in terror, whimpering.

"Don't hurt him," Jason said quietly. The two Cybwomen both snapped their heads toward him. Both looked poised for murder. "Don't hurt either of them. They haven't harmed you."

"That one lifted a weapon to attack us," Rosamind intoned, tilting her head momentarily toward Elliott.

"And Lisa stopped him," Jason answered. "Something has happened to her – something I've seen before. Can you tell me what's going on with her?"

"Lisa suffered a failure in her diagnostic and emerged from it early. She will require servicing when we return to the Station. Her current status is…" Julia's face remained blank as her words abruptly ceased.

All of the humans present, including Elliott, stared toward Jason, but he remained as motionless as Julia. Silence fell as time slowly passed, and they all waited. Jason had finally drawn a deep breath, in preparation to ask another question, when Julia finished, "Indeterminate. Lisa is fully functional, but her memory has been altered." Julia's eyes, always fixed and somehow glaring, flickered for the briefest instant toward her fallen companion, who was only just beginning to stir, and then to Rosamind, who still had not moved. "All three of us have experienced a storage reallocation. The cause of the reallocation is unknown."

"I know what caused it," Jason answered, and looked toward Scotty. "Help your man up. You'll have to take our message to Jones."

"Our orders from Argo are clear. We are to accompany you, and deliver notice to Jones that unpredictable and unusual events can be expected to occur," Rosamind objected tonelessly. "That order has not been carried out."

"You are aware that Argo and I both arise from the same individual?" Jason asked her. "An order from me is the equivalent of an order from Argo. I am ending this mission, right now. Elliott and Scotty here can deliver Argo's message." He looked toward the two guards; Elliott had regained his feet, though he stood as though his entire body hurt. Small wonder, he thought randomly. Lisa had slammed him backward to the ground. Hard.

Looking back to Julia, he held his breath, knowing that it was critical that she and Rosamind see his point. Lisa, he knew, would not object; she already understood what was happening.

"This point will require clarification," Julia responded. The length of time it had taken her to respond had been unnerving; a typical Cybwoman would have made her determination in a millisecond. "We will accede to your wishes until such clarification is received, and escort you back to the Station for Argo's resolution of the matter." She glared toward Scotty and Elliott; most of her old malice was clearly intact. "You will receive instructions from Jason Anderson on the information that will be relayed to your chief, and then you will deliver that information. Your lives will be spared, but after this day, neither of you will be permitted to escort Station personnel again."

Both men bowed in acknowledgement, and as they turned to go, Jason suddenly blurted, "wait. One more thing."

All eyes turned toward him as he focused upon Scotty. "Deliver your chief this message, from me: he will one day have a son."

"The chief can't have kids. Everyone knows that," Elliott objected.

"Did you ever think that you would meet me?" Jason responded, as forcefully as he could. He was not certain himself whether this gambit would work, but it felt right to him. He continued, "Deliver the message from Argo, and this one from me. He will have a son. I don't know when, but I believe it will be soon."

For an instant, his voice conveyed the same inflection it had carried in another, lost world. Scotty and Elliott glanced toward each other; Phoebe's eyes widened in surprised fear. The Cybwomen remained impassive. Several noiseless seconds passed before the Covington escort looked back toward Jason, nodding once, and then turned, making for their compound. Jason heaved a deep sigh, looked meaningfully at Phoebe, and smiled.

No one spoke as they turned back toward the gate, and the road to the Station that lay beyond.

Chapter Eighteen

DR. TINSWORTH STOOD OUTSIDE Hampton Hall, looking along the line where over a hundred yards of below-ground tunnel had been rebuilt, toward Williams Hall. The damage there was still not completely repaired, but enough had been done to allow the building to reopen. He glanced down at his cellphone and dialed a number, closing his eyes for a moment in dread of the coming conversation, and snapped them open again as the line clicked.

"Mangum," the voice on the other end intoned. Tinsworth sucked in his breath, clenched his eyes shut again for another second, and then answered, "Colonel, we have a potentially catastrophic situation here."

There was silence on the other end for a few moments before Mangum responded. "The new bridge shouldn't be online yet, even with Grant added back to the project. There hasn't been enough time. So what's the problem?"

"Jason Anderson seems to be the problem," Tinsworth replied. "I don't think any of us have given enough consideration to the potential repercussions of his being here."

Another brief silence followed; Tinsworth wondered momentarily whether the conversation was being eavesdropped, before remembering that it undoubtedly was. "What sort of repercussions?" Mangum finally asked.

Tinsworth related, as tersely as he could, how he and Wiley had independently come up with the same inexplicable design. "I don't know what the thing was supposed to do, or why it was built the way it was," Tinsworth eventually concluded. "But we know that these bridges can be dangerous. Until we know what this thing was, we can't move forward on our current project – not unless we want to risk another explosion."

"So how do you propose we determine what this – this thing is supposed to do?" Mangum asked.

"I need to get in touch with Jason again," Tinsworth answered.

"Negative," Mangum replied instantly. "Any communication with Anderson will have to be cleared through Haverhill. He already has a team in place in Ohio. They're going to bring him in."

"Wait. What?" Tinsworth's voice rose in alarm, drawing surprised glances from a pair of students sitting on a bench nearby. "No. That's not safe. If Grant and I are both getting information literally out of nowhere, and it isn't anything pertinent to our current status, then it may be a side effect of his return. Any interference with Anderson could create a paradox, or a causal loop, or – hell, I don't know. No one does. But seeing as how we've already had a lab blow up, we *might* want to tread lightly."

"The explosion was two months ago. There's been nothing since then. Why would there be danger now?" Mangum objected.

"Because for two months, Jason has been in hiding, well away from Atlanta. He did nothing that would interfere here, so nothing happened," Tinsworth answered, hoping he didn't sound as uncertain as he felt. "Now that he's active again, we're starting to see causality issues. With Grant back on the project, there may be some alignment of events between what he experienced and our own reality. That in turn could create a situation where information from another universe might impinge on ours."

Mangum's silence was much longer this time; Tinsworth clenched his free fist, hoping for he knew not what. The world around him was so normal that he felt suddenly and powerfully disconnected from it, knowing what he knew. He wondered whether Jason had experienced that, and immediately realized that he almost certainly had, from the moment he had appeared in Williams, killing himself in the process. For a dark second, he worried that Jason might no longer be sane.

Mangum's reply, when it came, was as terse and clipped as always, but it nonetheless carried a note of uncertainty. "Haverhill's team has already located Anderson and have him surrounded. They haven't moved in as yet because of the danger involved with this type of project. They'll take him the minute he or that girl of his shows their face outside the building where they're holed up."

It was Tinsworth's turn to pause. Mangum, he knew, would not have disclosed even that much without a good reason.

"We can't move forward here without clearance, Colonel. When Anderson's captured, if at all possible, I will have to speak with him." Tinsworth's voice shook slightly, and he took a deep breath to steady himself. "We don't know whether restarting the bridge project might cause another incident like the last one. We also don't know the purpose for this – this idea, this artifact that Grant and I have somehow discovered. None of what's happened could have been reflected in our initial hypotheses, and until we know more, it could be suicidal for us to attempt to construct another bridge."

"Dr. Tinsworth, the General has already determined how he will deal with Anderson," Mangum replied. Your request will have to wait until after his capture, and after whatever Haverhill intends for him. In the meantime, you are to proceed as directed on the bridge project."

"Very well." Tinsworth's acknowledgment was icy. "And I trust that this recording will be played for Congress when they call me to testify – assuming that the next explosion doesn't take me out with it?"

The silence this time was heavy, and Tinsworth inhaled as silently as he could, not wanting to reveal the dread he felt. Part of him wanted to plead with the colonel – the part that had been loyal to DARPA through decades of collaboration – but he knew he could not give in. Neither, he suspected, could Mangum.

"My order stands," Mangum finally answered, in his usual tone. The line went dead. Several seconds passed before it occurred to the physicist that the neutral answer in itself was revealing.

JASON AND PHOEBE, WITH the Threebirds following, had almost reached the Station when they heard a familiar, but unexpected, sound echoing from well behind them.

The entire party came to a halt, listening; the Threebirds were already turned and watching the road behind them. Phoebe looked puzzled. "That sounds like –"

"A horse," Jason finished. "And if they're using horses, then they –" he stopped again, remembering what had happened before.   The three Cybwomen showed no indication that anything was amiss. The clopping sound, echoing from the buildings at the crossroads they had just passed, had begun to grow louder, but no one was visible on the road. Jason pointed toward the trees that lined the south side of the thoroughfare.

"There used to be a street there. Remember it?" Jason asked.

"I grew up on the other side of town," Phoebe answered. "I've only been here with you, and that was only once or twice."

The hoofbeats drew nearer, growing louder as they approached. Jason breathed a sigh of relief; from the sound, it was apparent that only one individual was coming.

"What were you going to say?" Phoebe asked.

Jason's eyes never left the treeline. "On my last trip through, the Covingtons were vegetarians," he answered. "There were no meat animals left – not even horses. That tells me we didn't come as far forward this time."

"Are you sure?" Phoebe asked.

"Yeah. I'm pretty sure," Jason answered. "And Argo kind of confirms it for me. Wiley was really smart, but I'm a better physicist than he is. Argo was able to build a more stable rift than Wiley did, and he did it faster. That computer he's using – I don't know how it even works, but the design makes a weird kind of sense to me." He paused. "I think we're probably ten or fifteen years closer to our own time than the Drome was. And if that's true…" his voice trailed away, and then – to Phoebe's astonishment – he suddenly grinned broadly.

"What?" Phoebe asked.

"I think I know who's coming, and I bet I know why, too. Remember how Scotty said that the Covington chief couldn't have children?" Jason replied. The grin faded as he added, "It's time for me to be Jason Anderson again."

Even as he said this, and as Phoebe gave him a slightly exasperated, sidelong look, the rider emerged from the treeline into the crossroads, turning his horse west to approach them. He was alone. The Threebirds fanned out, protecting Phoebe and Jason, but did not move to attack.

"Let him approach," Jason said quietly. Julia looked back over her shoulder at him, studying him with that shadowy anger she always exuded. Once again, Jason realized, she had taken too long to assess what was happening. The Threebirds were all somehow crippled, though not visibly so. Jason hoped they would still be able to defend him effectively, if the need arose.

By the time the rider was a hundred feet away, Jason knew he had been correct: it was William Jones, the Covington clan chief. He looked younger than Jason remembered, and despite the agitation that was visible in his expression, he was clearly a more ferocious and dangerous man than the affable leader Jason remembered. He slowed his horse to a walk as they neared; his eyes shifted among the Threebirds, who still had not moved, before returning to Jason. He barely noted Phoebe's presence.

He drew his horse to a halt five paces from the Cybwomen and dismounted. For a few seconds he stared at them, and they at him, in silence. No one moved.

"Let him pass," Jason finally said, in the same quiet voice. Lisa and Rosamind moved to one side, and Julia to the other, allowing Jones to approach, leading his horse. Three paces away, Jones halted again, and the two men studied each other.

"Jason Anderson," he finally said. The voice did not match the face; it was tremulous, with obvious uncertainty, though the man did not appear to be afraid.

"William Jones," Jason replied. He smiled slightly. "Do they call you 'Pops,' as they did in the time when we met before?"

As he spoke, Jason sensed another tiny shift in the atmosphere around them; the Threebirds shifted again slightly, though this time Julia did not speak. Jones looked puzzled, and surprised.

"We've never met before. And no one in my compound would dare call me that," he answered. "I have no children, at any rate. But from what my men have told me, that may change." His eyes locked on Jason's. The significance of their meeting was unmistakable; in the chief's expression, Jason could read the angry years, and deep sadness, of a man long denied the thing he most wanted. Anger and sadness – but also, he realized, there was hope.

"You wanted to ask me if you would really have a child," Jason said. His already quiet voice had sunk to a near-whisper. It briefly occurred to him that in his own world, he would have had to shout over the passing cars, the nearby businesses and even the rail tracks not far to their north. In this time, those things were all gone.

"I've always wanted a son," Jones answered thickly. "You said we met before. What can you tell me?"

Jason smiled, though only slightly; he knew, more than he had ever guessed, how much this meant to the man. The entire community might be changed, if this one man's outlook were to change from bitterness and despair. He realized that he had himself become something different from what he had once been.

Seconds passed. Even the Threebirds watched him, albeit dispassionately. In Phoebe's eyes, he could see the same awe dawning that he felt himself.

When he spoke, his words were gently uttered, but more powerfully charged than anything he had experienced in his previous travels. He could sense a turning, a realignment of existence as he spoke.

"Return to your compound," he said, the very air trembling as it carried his words. "The time has come. You will become father to a son."

Even as he spoke, he knew it would happen. Jones knew it as well, and the anger and denial faded from his face, leaving only wonderment. He breathed deeply, as if tasting clean air for the first time in his life. Dropping the horse's reins, he stumbled forward, kneeling in front of Jason; Lisa darted forward behind him, snatching up the reins before the animal could bolt. Jones grasped Jason's hand in both of his, pressing it to his forehead, too overwhelmed to form words.

"Rise," Jason said again, kindly, and helped Jones to his feet. "Now go. Become the father that you are meant to be."

Jones' eyes were spilling tears, but his voice had steadied. "I will name my son for you," he said.

"No," Jason said, quietly. "That you need not do. Name him for someone in your own family. Someone who might not have had the chance to live as they should have."

Jones thought about this, and then smiled. "When I was a boy, my mother told me about her brother. He was in an accident when he was still young." He paused. "She would want my son to have his name. I'll call him… Shawntaine."

These last words carried the ghost of the reverberations Jason's had caused, and Jones fell momentarily silent, but Jason answered, "That will indeed be his name. Now go, and be at peace."

The words broke the odd, tense spell that had fallen on them. The sunlight was mere sunlight once more, and the air was quiescent. Everyone, even the Threebirds, visibly relaxed.

Jones looked bemusedly from Jason to Phoebe, and took the reins from Lisa. He mounted his horse, and started to turn it back the way he had come, before looking back at them one last time. "It'll really happen? I'll really have my son?" he asked. His voice shook very slightly.

Jason nodded. "Shawntaine," he answered.

A big, elated grin expanded over Jones' face, washing away the furrows of many unhappy years, and he said, "I never would let the men call me Pops. They can, now." Laughing, he turned his horse and began to ride away again.

The Threebirds continued to watch him until he had passed beyond the crossroads, and then turned. Phoebe was looked worriedly toward Jason, who was cupping his forehead in his hands in apparent pain.

"Argo summons us. It is time for us to return to the Station," Julia intoned tonelessly.

"Wait!" Phoebe replied urgently. "Jason's hurt."

Jason's hands had slid down from his eyes to cover his mouth as he sighed deeply, and looked toward Julia. "I know why he's summoning you. I've done what I was brought here to do." He glanced toward Phoebe. "I'm not sure what's going to happen when we get back. I'm entangled in two future universes, from our perspective, and merging them will have serious side effects for me. Maybe for you, too. But after we return through the portal, we're going to have to go back to Atlanta," he said.

"What about Jensen and Greene?" Phoebe asked.

"We'll have to shake them somehow," Jason answered. He glanced toward the Threebirds. "You will all require a full memory diagnostic when you arrive at the Station. It would be best if we return at once."

He looked meaningfully at Phoebe, then turned and started westward down the road. An iron grip on his shoulder stopped him, then turned his body to face its owner. It was Lisa, and in her predominantly neutral expression was a ghost of terrible fear.

"You need not be afraid," Jason told her. He glanced toward Phoebe. "I promised Phoebe that I would make sure what happened to you would never happen to her. I am making that promise now to all of your kind," he added, and as he did, his voice carried the same reverberation as before. Rosamind, like Lisa looked vaguely frightened. Phoebe looked terrified.

Too late, he saw the dim fury rising in Julia's expression, and even as their eyes met, she lunged toward him.

Interlude

Late Autumn, 2048 – In Another World

STAIRS LED UP FROM THE ground floor of the Covingtons' armory to the chieftain's residence. William Jones sat in an ancient, metal folding chair on the landing of those stairs, his head in his hands, as his fear and his hope wrestled with one another.

The midwives worked upstairs, in the residence, laboring – as did, in a very real sense, his wife – to bring his son into the world. They had been busy of late; the news that the chieftain had received a sign that he would have a son had inspired the ranks of his army, so that it had been a turn of the moon since a day had passed without the birth of a child. Occasionally, there were two, or even three.

He heard footfalls on the steps above him and looked up to see a matronly woman, covered in a white sheet, looking down at him. "Are you sure you want to wait here?" the woman asked him.

"I'm sure," the chieftain replied, with as much surety as he could muster. The midwife was not fooled.

"I know you're afraid for the baby. And its mama," she added, looking upstairs as a groan of pain floated down toward them. "But she's looking just fine right now. It shouldn't be too long."

"I can wait," Jones replied. The midwife shrugged.

"Suit yourself, then. But it shouldn't be long. She went into labor at daybreak, and we're getting on toward sunset."

"I can wait," Jones repeated.

The midwife shrugged a second time, and returned upstairs without further comment. After a few seconds, Jones heard her voice add itself to the indistinct conversation going on amongst his wife's attendants, and he slumped forward in his chair again.

So much had changed since the spring, when Anderson had appeared for that one day. The legend had said that Jason Anderson, the Man from Nowhere, would change the world, and he had – in ways none of them had ever imagined would happen.

No one seemed to have a concrete memory of how and when everything had happened that spring. The encampment at Stonecrest, after learning of Anderson's appearance, had sent a liaison to the Covingtons, looking to secure at least a guarantee of nonaggression between the two strongholds. Their envoy had argued – very cogently – that peaceful relations between them would benefit both, and would not cost either side significantly.

The two camps had agreed to a summit meeting that was held midway between them, at an old crossroads; the north route from that place led toward a huge, granite dome that rose high above the surrounding ground, high enough that the lookouts – who had climbed some of the taller trees – could easily see it, dominating the view from about seven miles away. Jones remembered asking the Stonecrest chief about the dome. The only reply he received was a dire warning to stay well clear of it.

Jones' reverie was broken by another pained moan, this one higher and more urgent, from above. It was matched by a lowering of the midwives' mutterings. He could hear his wife breathing heavily, but the cry was not repeated, and in a few more seconds his mind drifted again.

It had been after the peace agreement that the dream had come, as high summer gave way to a hot autumn, and the time for his child's birth neared. At first, it had been occasional, and innocuous. The strange young man in his dream would speak solemnly to him, warning him of the perils his people still faced; Jones had recognized the dangers upon waking, and had acted to mitigate them. The Covingtons had doubled their food reserves. Scouts had been sent north and south, looking for other communities like their own; none had been found.

It was after the last scout had returned that the dreams became more urgent, and more frightening. Other than the Stonecrests, it appeared that the Covingtons were alone; no other tribes lived within at least two days' journey.

Still, he feared for his child. For his *son*, he reminded himself.

In the same moment, he heard his wife cry out again, the sound this time driving him to his feet before he was able to recover himself. Covering his face in his hands, he tried to interrupt the thread of memories that had begun unwinding in his mind.

Their population, he had come to realize, was slowly dying out. The recent spate of births notwithstanding, the clan was only a little more than half as large as it had been only a few years earlier. The hard life of the Seaflood survivors, coupled with the attrition from their…

He paused. He had dreamed of terrible battles, where his men were decimated by terrifying, vicious, inhumanly fast women. In those dreams, they had come from the old train station, and were led by a being even less human than they were. Someone much too dangerous to approach.

After that dream, he had mulled for weeks on the possibility of an enemy dwelling along the highway to their west. He had had his men shore up the barricades around their land, even as the dream reminded him that creatures as vicious as those he envisioned would hardly be stopped by them. In the end, he had sent a team to explore the station itself, with strict instructions to retreat at once from any encounter. He had sent them with dread, fearing they would never return.

They had, instead, returned on the same day that he sent them. The station was deserted, and had been since the Seafloods; there was nothing useful left there. Following the rails west from the station, they found that the last train on that track had derailed at the entrance to a tunnel leading into the satellite city that had been served by that line. No one had recovered the dead, whose long-ago picked-over skeletons had been thrown about within the smashed cars. Seeing no signs of life or civilization there or in the surroundings, they had returned.

Another cry, this one strident, broke his reverie, and the murmuring of the midwives had become exhortative, urging his wife to push. Unable to wait any longer, he vaulted up the stairs and entered the loft above. Two of the burlier midwives were there, and grasped his arms; he could easily have broken from their grip, but instead he halted, the tension draining from his body as the sound of his new child's cries reached his ears.

Tears sprang to his eyes, and he bent forward with his head in his hands, hearing only the wails of his son. The midwives let him go, and he shook convulsively, trying to catch his breath and recover himself. The urgency had left his wife's attendants' voices; they murmured soothingly to her. He still could not hear what was being said.

A tug on his left arm gently demanded his attention, and looking up, he met the woman's kindly gaze. Beside her, a younger woman held a bundle wrapped in cloths, still squalling.

"Don't you want to hold your son?" the old midwife asked.

Without answering, he stood to his full height, and took the proffered bundle carefully. The infant's fists clenched, and it howled its displeasure at its new surroundings, but Jones' face burst into a grin that barely seemed able to hold in the joy it radiated. As he gazed into his son's face, with his eyes still screwed shut and cries still issuing from his open mouth, a wash of weary relief overtook him, and he heard a soft voice inside his mind, speaking kindly: "Here is the son you were promised. Be the father you are called to be."

Jones' eyes closed again, and as they did, the older midwife took the child from his arms. "He needs to feed now, and his mamma wants you both," she said. Mutely, he followed her to the bedside. His wife, sweat-soaked and exhausted, lay propped on a set of makeshift pillows, half-covered only by a single, damp sheet. Her eyes shone with glassy exhaustion and exhilaration as she smiled at him, taking the infant carefully from the midwife and cradling him against her breast, nudging him to feed.

Jones touched her shoulder as she looked down at their child, watching him as she did, and for the first time in all the years since the Seafloods, Jones felt hope for the days to come.

PART THREE: THE GRAY ANGEL

Chapter Nineteen

JASON WAS KNOCKED FROM his feet even as Julia lunged toward him, and for a stunned moment he could only see stars. He heard Phoebe scream, and then felt her arms around him, as though she had any hope of protecting him…

But as he realized that she was beside him, he knew something else had happened. Julia was too fast, too vicious. Even though she had been hampered by the incident at the Covington gate, she should still have been able to kill him. Instead, he could hear the sounds of a fierce fight.

"Stand down!" he shouted, hoping that the Cybwomen would still accept his command as they would Argo's. He rolled over and sat up, a little unsteadily, and looked toward the combatants.

For a moment he could not make sense of what he saw. There were three Cybwomen facing each other. Clearly, two had been battling against the third, who was facing away from him – but Lisa was standing away from the fight, and had interposed herself between it and Jason.

"Allison," he breathed. Rosamind and Julia still stood ready to resume the battle, but Allison turned to face him, her eyes softening in a way that, of all her kind, only hers could. Julia's eyes narrowed for a bare instant.

"Stand down!" Jason shouted again. Julia's reflexes were clearly slower; though poised for attack, she had not pounced on Allison as she once would have. Jason frowned. As she did, the radiance in Allison's expression faded into worry. Phoebe looked frightened, and very confused.

As he looked, one by one, at each of his companions, a recent memory floated into his head, and he realized something had been missing since he had arrived. His gaze returned to Julia, whose perpetual anger seemed to have lessened.

"Julia. Are you acknowledging orders from me, from Argo, or from us both?" Jason asked.

"Both," Julia replied, without hesitation.

Jason thought for a moment. "Are you receiving input from another source that is analogous with myself and Argo?" he asked, and held his breath.

All four Cybwomen faced him, studying him carefully. Phoebe also watched him, still frightened. A silence fell.

"Before I passed through the portal that brought us here, I thought I was hearing my own voice inside my head," Jason finally said, still looking toward Julia. "I hadn't realized that it had stopped until just a moment ago. I had thought it was a side effect of something else that had happened, but now I'm not so sure." He glanced toward Phoebe momentarily. "Julia, have you received input from that other source?"

"Affirmative," she responded, with the immediacy usually typical of her kind.

Phoebe's astonishment matched his own. "Oh, my God," she breathed. "Does that mean what I think it means?"

Jason looked at her. "It's an artifact, I think. This is what Argo and I were talking about earlier. Allison's perceptions apparently were changed when we came through the portal, and they were already – different – to begin with," he said, somewhat hesitantly. "Remember when you asked her if she loved me? She didn't say, 'I love them both.' She said, 'I love them all.'

"I thought that she was just referencing the iterations of myself in all parallel universes, but now I think she was referring to something specific. I think I know what it is, because of the voice I have been hearing. I don't know how it's possible, but some part of the version of myself I had to kill to save you is still around."

Allison nodded. "You are the one who will change the world. When you are done, Argo and I will escape this world together. The other you, the one who is dead but lives, remains until his mission is finished. Because of your promise, he cannot be resolved until then," she said softly. Her eyes were still disconcertingly fixed on Jason, who – in spite of Phoebe's proximity – found it difficult to look away from her.

To distract himself as much as anything else, he looked again to Julia. "Why did you attack me, when I promised to free you from this life?"

Julia's anger was muted, but dangerously present; Jason could not help holding his breath, even with three other Cybwomen ready to protect him. The pause before her response was so long that he was about to prompt her when she finally spoke.

"I asked Dr. Bryant to make me a Cybwoman," she said.

"Why?" Jason asked. "Why would you want to be – what you are?"

"In this form, I am superior to the being I once was," Julia answered.

Jason looked to Phoebe. Comprehension was dawning in her face as she said, quietly, "I can't blame her for that. This place is terrifying. I wouldn't mind being as strong as she is."

"The world I went to the first time was a lot worse than this," Jason answered. "And what you became was so dark and so sad that I can't imagine you *really* wanting to live like that. And at least in that world, you were waiting for me to come back." He looked to Julia. "What makes this life bearable for you? Why would you want to live forever like this?"

Julia's anger flickered momentarily. "I don't want to die."

Jason thought about that for a moment. "What do you think will happen, if you do die?"

Julia did not immediately respond, but the rage drained slowly from her expression, and for the first time, Jason saw her without its disfiguring effect. She clearly had once been a pretty creature, with a slim, dancer's build and blue eyes that might have been clear and bright in life.

"I do not know," she finally, reluctantly answered.

Jason smiled slightly. "Julia, you say that you perceived an entity analogous to me, and that it is communicating with you on some level. Are you afraid of that being?"

"Negative," she replied.   An odd look of confusion mixed with a reemerging shadow of anger in her expression.

"Julia, I don't know who, or what, that – that creature is, or what it's doing, but I'm pretty sure that it died – *yet it's still active.*" He stared hard at her. "If you're afraid of nonexistence, you shouldn't be.

"Argo said he thinks that when universes merge, their inhabitants merge with them, with no conscious memory of the event. If that's true, then it might – it *might* – follow that when your existence ends in one universe, or a subset space of universes, then it resumes as that universe subset merges with another subset. You would be somewhere else, with no conscious memory of what happened, but with the potential to retrieve those memories subconsciously." Jason took a deep breath and glanced toward Allison, who smiled back at him. "As the total subset of universes containing your existence grows smaller, your aggregate life experience is concentrated in fewer and fewer iterations, and your subconscious memory expands. Old age is supposed to bring wisdom, but maybe not for the reasons we've always believed."

Julia nodded, her anger still present but dim. "But what happens when the last iteration dies?" She asked.

Jason sighed. "I don't know. It's possible that there is an existence in which we all become immortal, and in that case we would merge with that last timeline and live forever. Or, perhaps, with the accumulated wisdom of all our lives, we might understand that it's time to leave the stage gracefully, and rest. Neither one sounds particularly bad. What do *you* think?"

For the first time, Jason saw fear in her eyes. After a moment, she closed them, inhaling deeply in an extremely uncharacteristic way.

"You dream, too – don't you?" he asked softly.

Her eyes snapped open. "I dreamed that the Station was destroyed, and the whole world began to disintegrate, because of *you.*"

Jason was taken aback. "When did you dream this?" he asked.

"I came back online at Argo's request, approximately twelve point four seven seconds after your arrival through the portal," Julia answered. "The dream came to me during my activation phase."

Comprehension dawned on Jason's face. "Had you ever experienced dreams before then?"

"Negative," she replied.

Jason nodded, again smiling slightly. "I think this is another artifact. I left right before that world merged, so I didn't see what happened, but once I came here, that information became available to you, at least to the point where I left." He paused. "Did you see how it ended – the world, I mean?"

"Negative," Julia answered again.

"Then I'm almost positive this is an artifact, " he said. "That was just starting to happen when I left. I think your mind might have been able to extrapolate a few seconds after that, but no more."

"Can we discuss this when we get back to the Station?" Phoebe asked. Already it was past midday, and the heat had become uncomfortable.

"Would that be acceptable?" Jason asked Julia.

"Affirmative," she replied. She started to move past Jason, to join the other Threebirds, but he held up one hand, gesturing for her to wait.

"You have my promise that I will not act before we have consulted with Argo. Do I have your word that you will refrain from attacking any of us?" Jason asked.

"I am at your command," she answered.

"Then why did you attack me, when I made the promise I made? Did you interpret it as a threat?" Jason glanced again toward Allison, then Phoebe.

"I do not wish to die. I interpreted the promise as a threat to my existence, and responded accordingly. Cybwomen are permitted to defend themselves when threatened, even by Argo," Julia said.

"All right," Jason replied, and sighed. "Let's just go back to the Drome – to the Station, and let Argo sort this out."

Julia moved past Jason, joining her fellow Threebirds in front of him and Phoebe, as they all began to walk the last mile back.

"THEY'RE SERIOUS? THEY *still* want us to rebuild the bridge?" Wiley's face was aghast as he looked up from the containment cage for the bridge endpoint. They were in the Hampton Hall lab; Wiley had been inspecting the cage for irregularities.

Tinsworth's face was grim. "That's what my higher-ups said. Any clue what that thing we dreamed up together is supposed to be?"

"From what I remember, none of the stuff in the setup was high-tech," Wiley said. "It all looked mechanical, and with the broomstick mounted on the wheels – " He picked up a clipboard and hurriedly sketched a stick mounted atop a crude car – "it looks like a sort of probe, almost. Like there was something stationary in front of the desk where it was mounted, and the car was moved toward and away from the rift using the string and pulley, moving the broomstick into and out of – whatever it was."

Tinsworth thought about that. "So then the question is, what was in the lab that we had to build a probe for?" Even as he said it, he knew the answer. Looking up, he saw that Wiley had reached the same conclusion.

"Holy shit. You think Anderson came through a space-time rift?" Wiley asked.

"That's *exactly* what I think happened, and I think we saw this mockup at some point, but not here," Tinsworth's face was wondering and fearful. "It's a side effect of Anderson's trip, if that's the case, and it sure fits the criteria. If we never saw a spacetime rift before now, we could hardly know what it looked like. My mind put a null-space there – I couldn't see anything. Since it wasn't in your diagram, and you've come to the same conclusion, I think you couldn't see it either."

"This is *weird*," Wiley agreed fervently.

Tinsworth was silent for several seconds, and then added, "At least we have some time to work with. We won't have a working bridge before next month, so for now, we do as we're told." He glanced up toward Wiley, about to browbeat him for the need to do everything right, but then was silent as he studied his graduate assistant more carefully. The fat, sloppy, lazy, second-rate genius he remembered was all but gone, and in his place stood an assistant who perhaps wasn't Anderson, but was far more disciplined and concerned with his work than before. Unsure of what to say, he settled for a curt nod and a sardonic half-smile. The surprised grin he received in response confirmed his assessment – Wiley Grant, with a little guidance, would be a much more useful assistant in the future.

Chapter Twenty

THEY ALL MET AGAIN at the Station, in Argo's laboratory, after a brief rest for the human travelers and a diagnostic for the Cybwomen. Phoebe was relieved to see that Bryant's corpse had been removed and the floor scrubbed in the interim.

Argo was as bland and neutral as before, and his instrument bank was no less incomprehensible, though some of the tubes were noticeably darker. As Jason studied them, Phoebe approached Allison tentatively.

"What do you remember of Jason – I mean, when he went into the future the first time?" Phoebe asked her quietly. They stood slightly away from the other Cybwomen, near the lab entrance.

Allison smiled. "I don't remember very much. I knew that he was supposed to change the world, and Acme – the one who ruled the Drome, in that world – had tortured me, because I had started to dream."

Phoebe was appalled. "What did he do to you?"

The smile faded. "He ordered me to sleep, and then awaken, three times per minute, for a month. I had seen something terrible from a dream, and he made me see it over and over. By the time the month was over, I never wanted to dream again, and I could never trust Acme again." Allison's eyes had become unfocused. "But when Jason returned, he brought the man who would become Acme with him, and at the same time, the Acme in our world shut down. Then you summoned me, telling me Jason had arrived, and you gave me a hammer. I don't know why you gave it to me, but you did, and when I realized Acme would not stop me…" Her voice trailed away.

"*I* gave you a hammer?" Phoebe asked.

"You handed it to me. You had one, too. We walked toward Jason and Acme. I could see how the man Acme was looked at me. When I remembered what he did to me, I ran after him, just as you ran after Jason. When I caught up to him, I killed him with the hammer." Allison's smile returned, as beatific as the actions she described weren't. "Then you told me that you had met Jason, and were sending him back as Acme had instructed, and that I could go."

"And that was all you remember?" Phoebe asked.

"No," Allison replied, and her eyes grew still brighter. "I came to help you at the cemetery. Acme thought he was sending me to destroy you, but once I left the Drome, I could do as I chose, and I wanted to thwart him. Jason didn't trust me, but you knew I would help you, and we returned to the Drome together to destroy Acme.

"When we came near the Drome, Jason said he needed for me to shut down, so that I would not be detected. I was afraid, because when Acme told me to shut down, he had done it to hurt me. But when the time came, Jason came back to me, and asked me whether he needed to hold me so that I would not fall while I shut down. He was the one who would change the world, and yet he was so thoughtful, and kind. I asked him to set me free. He held me while I shut down, so that I would not fall, and he helped me not be afraid."

Phoebe looked nonplussed. "So you do love him."

"Of course I do," Allison replied. "But he is not the Jason destined for me, no more than Argo is for you."

Phoebe considered. "That makes sense, I suppose – but do you believe Argo loves you?"

Allison's smile became slightly mischievous. Her expression was so incongruous for a Cybwoman that Phoebe blinked.

"He doesn't know it yet, but he will," Allison answered.

Argo motioned for Julia and Jason to join him.

"We will conduct this discussion verbally, since Jason cannot communicate with us electronically," he began, looking to Julia. "You attacked Jason out of concern that he would destroy you. Is that correct?" he asked.

"Yes," she replied.

"And during the ensuing conversation, you stated that you feared death, and that you interpreted his promise to eradicate the Cybwomen as a death threat?"

"That is correct," Julia answered.

Argo studied her briefly, then addressed Jason. "Do you intend to harm any Cybwoman currently in the Station?"

"Of course not," Jason replied. "My intention was – more preventative than that."

Argo's gaze returned to Julia. "It appears that Jason and I have similar thoughts on how to achieve his aim. Under our current theory, if Jason succeeds, this universe subset will merge with another subset, and most of us will then likewise merge with our other selves." Argo paused. "With one exception, at any rate, but that is not relevant to this discussion. That means that you, Julia, are likely to merge back into your human existence, assuming that Jason is successful, and this universe merges as expected."

"I asked to be remade as a Cybwoman so that I could avoid the inevitable outcome of human existence," Julia objected. "I do not wish to return to that form."

"It is likely that you will eventually return to the Cybwoman form again at some point, even if you resume human existence," Argo replied. "We know from Jason's experience that there is at least one timeline subset still extant in which you will exist in your current configuration."

"But that world will end in destruction," Julia said. "I have seen what will happen there. And by that time, I will almost certainly have no more human iterations. Jason Anderson's mission must inevitably end in my death."

Argo was about to speak, but Jason cut him off; the latter's face was suddenly wrung with pity. "You've never liked human beings, have you? You didn't want to be one, and you don't seem to care about what happens to the world. There are millions upon millions of people who lost their lives in the Seafloods. We have a real chance to prevent that from happening across who knows how many realities, but all you see is yourself." He shook his head. "I don't know what happened to you to make you like this, but I can't change it. I can't fix what's broken in you."

"Perhaps I can," said a voice near the door. All three looked up to see Lisa approaching them. She stopped next to Julia, looking to each of them in turn. "Julia is not the only one who envisioned the Station's destruction."

"Why did you not speak of it before?" Julia asked.

"At the time, I was uncertain whether the scene I witnessed was due to a malfunction. I did not have time to run a full diagnostic before our departure," Lisa answered. "My perception of that event was altered, but it seemed that the destruction was a desirable thing, and that it stemmed from a promise kept by Jason Anderson."

"Did you see what happened after the Station was destroyed?" Jason and Julia asked together.

"I only saw that the world seemed to disintegrate, like dust in a windstorm. It was as though the dreaming part of our minds fell asleep, so that our conscious minds could awaken," Lisa's voice had been flat, clipped and matter-of-fact when she began to speak, but by the time she finished, her speech slowed, and her eyes closed briefly before snapping open again. "It was a pleasant sensation. I saw nothing that would justify fear."

"Who was there with you?" Jason asked her.

"Julia was, briefly, before she flew away in the wind," Lisa answered. "After that, it was only me, Phoebe and Allison, for approximately ten seconds."

They all looked over to where Allison and Phoebe stood, talking quietly.

"Allison clearly isn't afraid of what might happen," Jason observed. He looked back to Julia. "If there was any other way, I would choose it, if only to spare you pain. I'm sorry."

As he spoke, the Cybwomen's attention became fixed on him; Argo's bland face betrayed an instant of surprised bemusement. Phoebe's eyes followed Allison's toward Jason, whose expression had become wary.

"Something just happened. Argo, did you sense it?" Jason asked.

"I did receive an anomalous input from you," Argo replied. "It was unintelligible to me, for reasons that are not apparent. I did detect responses from each of the Cybwomen present." He looked to Allison. "What input did you receive?"

Allison's eyes were shining, and her face transported. "I heard a voice whisper, 'It is time.'"

"Confirmed," Lisa said. Argo looked to Julia. Her expression had drained of every expression, including the blank façade all Cybwomen normally evinced. She looked dead.

"Confirmed," she said, in a flat monotone.

Argo studied the instrumentation bank beside him for several seconds before his gaze returned to Jason. "It seems that your work here is completed, but I have one more task to manage before you can return. You and Phoebe may rest here for another hour, and you will probably need to eat. I will send Jensen and Greene to fetch you when I am done."

"Wait – there's still one thing I don't understand," Jason objected. "We were told that you required us both. Why did you need for Phoebe to come?"

Before Argo could reply, Phoebe crossed the few steps between them and slapped Jason lightly in the face. Caught by surprise, Jason briefly shied away from her. His overreaction, more from shock than hurt, made her smile despite her obvious irritation.

"I needed to come with you so that I could see this for myself. How could I ever have an equal relationship with you, when you'd traveled in time and I hadn't? I wanted to leave you. I thought you were something horrible that had stolen my Jason from me. I was never going to be able to understand you.

"But now that I've come here, and I've seen some of what you went through, I understand. I know what you had to do to come back to me." Phoebe's annoyance had melted as she moved closer to him. "I even understand why Allison fell in love with you. I am –" her voice cracked, but she swallowed hard and made herself continue – "I am prouder of you than I ever dreamed I could be."

As she embraced him, Jason glanced toward Argo, who was studying the holographic bank again. He cradled Phoebe's head against his shoulder, and as he did, he felt another set of arms around them both. They looked up together to see Allison smiling at them.

"Group hug?" Phoebe asked, not entirely nonplussed.

Allison laughed aloud, and as she did, everyone in the lab looked toward her. "Don't be jealous. I want Jason to be happy, and for that, he needs you. So I want you to be happy, so that he will be." Her smile became wistful. "And I cannot be with Argo until you two return home."

Jason looked toward Argo again. "I hope you're ready for this," he said. Argo's expression didn't change.

"That will be resolved only after your return mission is completed. I suggest that you and Phoebe try to rest and eat during the next hour. Now, if you will excuse me, I have one more task to complete – as I mentioned." With that, Argo moved to the far end of the lab, near Tinsworth's desk. Jason frowned.

"Where is Dr. Tinsworth?" Jason called after him.

"I sent him to retrieve a charging unit at the Decatur station," Argo replied over his shoulder. "He will return before you depart, since I will require that unit to complete this task, and he has something you will require. Now – you both need to rest."

IT WAS FULL DAYLIGHT; over an hour had passed. There was still no visible activity at Hara Arena.

There had been periodic, coded radio checks from each strike team in the vicinity, but nothing had been detected. Haverhill still monitored everything that was going on within the dragnet, reviewing each body camera and each voice feed every few minutes. His team's discipline was exemplary – as he demanded, and expected.

Doubt wanted to gnaw at him, but he brushed it away; worry was often unfounded, and never made anything better when justified.

It was when he shifted back to the main camera, the one across the street from the main entrance, when all hell broke loose.

The camera feed began to shake violently; just before it dropped, Haverhill thought he saw cracks snaking across the empty parking lot, radiating outward from the arena itself. At the same time, a loud, cracking BOOM came across the speaker. The volume dropped momentarily in his wireless earbuds, protecting his hearing, but unfortunately drowning out the voices of his men for several seconds.

When the sound resumed, nearly all of the strike teams were shouting at each other. Haverhill's fingers stabbed once, twice at the keyboard, opening a general comm channel to all teams, and hit the tone that would indicate his presence on the comm.

At once the confusion ceased. "South team. Status report!" Haverhill barked.

"General, we've had what felt like an earthquake here, and there was an explosion in the building. The arena's pretty torn up." The voice was slightly unsteady, but unfazed. Haverhill nodded to himself. "Perimeter teams report in. Any activity in the surrounding buildings?"

"Negative, sir. There were a few people who came in early to work, and they're all rubbernecking the arena. Everyone's accounted for. No one's been seen that shouldn't be there."

Haverhill frowned. "North team. Anything going on in the back of that dump?"

"Just the tremor and the blast, sir. May I ask what exactly the hell was that, sir?" This voice was steady as a rock. Haverhill recognized it at once.

"Howell, is there any visible damage beyond the arena complex?"

"Not much, sir. The pavement on the loading dock buckled, but it looks intact. The parking lot's cracked all to shit, but it was already pretty bad." Howell paused, and Haverhill was about to bark an order to his team, when he continued, "Hold it, sir. Loading dock door is going up. There's movement inside. Looks like whoever's in there is about to come out."

"All units prepare to converge," Haverhill intoned, his voice as flat and level as the Kansas farmland he'd escaped from, the minute he turned eighteen. "Howell, lock and load. They may not want to give up without a fight."

"Roger that, sir." There was a moment's pause. "Wait! There's a black SUV coming down the loading ramp. It's heading around for the front entrance, *fast*." Howell began shouting orders to his unit as Haverhill spoke over him: "North and South teams converge to apprehend subjects. Take them alive if at all possible, and they are not to be harmed deliberately.

"Surveillance teams, keep an eye on those buildings across the street, and watch that arena. They may be giving us a head fake. Stay sharp out there." Haverhill smiled slightly to himself. The SUV was a sure-fire capture, and anyone else who was left would be taken inside of an hour. The job looked to be nearly done.

Chapter Twenty-One

THE PORTAL WAS REPOWERED, and Jason and Phoebe were preparing to return, when Jensen and Greene approached them.

"When we left Hara Arena, years ago, we blew the portal up to prevent Ius Divinum from accessing our technology," Jensen said. "But we didn't know that they were waiting outside for us, and they captured us – all of us – the moment we left the arena.

"Ius Divinum will not kill or imprison us. There is a mutual agreement between them and KOPO by which neither side will hold a member of the other for over twenty-four hours. The secrecy of both of our organizations is predicated upon maintaining that agreement, and preventing all-out war between them." Jensen paused, and Greene continued: "Unfortunately, since you two are not in our organization, the agreement does not cover you, and we were unable to prevent them from seizing you. Once they had you, that was it. We never heard anything of you again."

Jason gave her a momentary, odd look. "No one missed me anyway, because I was dead. I suppose it was announced that Phoebe was captured for bombing our lab?" Jason asked.

"We never even heard that much," Jensen answered. "Argo told us that if you evade the dragnet that caught us before, you will be able to set events in motion that would merge this timeline into the target timeline he identified. He and Tinsworth are preparing a device for you that will facilitate the merge, but it will be exceedingly dangerous, both in placing the device and activating it."

Jason looked from Jensen to Greene. "Got it. I think I already know what to do."

They looked at each other. Jason glanced toward Phoebe; all three of them looked slightly confused. He smiled in spite of himself. "If the device is what I think it is, then the main problem will be getting from Dayton back to Atlanta. I think I know how to do that, too." He looked at Phoebe again. "Something Argo said gave me the idea. It's going to be a rough ride. I'm sorry."

"What did you have in mind?" Greene asked.

"If Ius Divinum caught us, they might have figured out how to use the bridge technology. I can't risk telling you that," Jason said, with just the barest hint of insolence in his expression. Jensen frowned.

"I don't think we deserved that," she said.

"You got us captured in our timeline. I have to get around that now, and the best way I can think of is dangerous as hell. We have to get back fast, and we can't risk being seen," Jason said. "There's one way that we can do both those things. Maybe."

Jensen nodded. "Fair enough."

As she said this, Tinsworth and Argo joined them. Tinsworth was smiling at Jason again, but less broadly than before; Jason suspected that Bryant's grisly demise had not been lost on him. Argo wore his usual bland, inoffensive expression, and carried a cubic cardboard box that was about six inches on each side.

"This is the device you will need," Argo said.

Jason looked at it, and whistled. "Wow. Ours was a lot bigger. How did you make one that small?"

"I worked on the design for some years after the peak of Seaflood activity," Argo replied. "This device will create a singularity using only a standard AC outlet. It will need to be placed inside of Nesmith Hall, near the southern end of the building, close to the cryogenics lab, and plugged in. When you have done that, *you will have to move at least ten feet away.* It will take less than three minutes for me to latch onto the signature – it is unique to our timeline, which will make it simple to isolate – and extend a rift from that point in four-space. I will be using the same technology that created the rift that you changed, so the result will be... explosive, once the passage is closed." Argo's glance moved from Jason to Phoebe. "You will need to be away from the building when the rift collapses."

"But won't people get hurt?" Phoebe asked, horrified.

Argo's eyebrows raised slightly. "Of course. There will likely be some casualties. However, you must remember what occurs when existence ceases on a timeline: the person involved is usually shunted into a parallel existence with no conscious memory of what has happened."

Phoebe looked at Jason. "Are you okay with this?" she asked. Her expression was thunderous.

Jason stared right back at her. "Yes. I am, for two reasons. First, there will be millions, maybe billions, of people who will live much longer lives on our timeline if this works. Second – " he motioned toward Allison, who stood off to the side, watching them – "I promised all of them that I would make sure that they never have to live like this. By destroying the lab, and shunting our world into this timeline, I can keep that promise." Jason took a deep breath. "I made that promise to you, too, when I went through the first time. You'll notice that you're not a Cybwoman here."

Allison approached them at the same time that Tinsworth handed a small envelope to Jason. "Don't lose this," he said. "I don't know why I kept this so long. Maybe some subconscious memory from another timeline." He grinned; the years had taken some of his teeth, but Jason smiled back.

"This was the last piece I needed. Thanks, Doc. I'll make this work somehow."

As Tinsworth turned away, Allison hugged him. "Thank you for everything. I'll never forget you." She smiled brilliantly at Jason, then moved to Phoebe, who still looked out of sorts, and hugged her as well. Phoebe's composure was clearly rattled by the gesture. "Take care of him," she said.

"I'll – I'll try," Phoebe managed to answer, her voice sounding strangled.

"Allison?" Jason said, as she started to turn away. Her smile was disconcertingly adoring, almost worshipful. He forced himself to continue.

"Please find Julia after we go. Tell her I'm sorry."

"She knows," Allison responded. "She is afraid, because she knows how her end will come, but she has yet to reach it."

Jason swallowed thickly, and nodded, unable to reply. He looked once more to Argo.

"If there's anything else, now's the time to tell me," he said.

As always, Argo's expression was unmoved. "I will detonate the portal exactly ten minutes after you return. I advise you to be well clear of it, as it will severely damage the arena and the attached facilities," he said.

"Ten minutes. That's more than enough – I hope," Jason answered. He looked to Phoebe. "You ready?"

"I think so," she answered.

"Then let's go," he said, and taking her hand, they turned and walked toward the portal. Just before they passed through, they both looked over their shoulders, between their clasped hands, at the assemblage behind them in the Station lab.

"Goodbye," Jason whispered. Phoebe could not speak. Allison alone waved to them, and they turned together, and returned to their own world.

THE CHANGE, THOUGH ANTICIPATED, was nonetheless jarring in its discontinuity. The tech was stationed at the instrument panel; Jensen and Greene awaited them.

"You're back already? That only took about thirty seconds," Jensen said. Jason could see the questions in her mind, queueing up behind her first one.

"There's no time, Agent Jensen. If you don't want us to be captured, you have to do exactly what I tell you. There are agents outside waiting to grab us all."

"WHAT?" Greene cried. "How are we going to get out?"

"You're not going to. We are." Jason answered. "Where is the other endpoint to the bridge again?"

"It's near Meadowdale High School, about a half mile south of here," Jensen said. "There's an access point in a janitor's closet. The closet's in the maintenance shed off the main building, for safety reasons."

"Good. We're going to go out that way. Where's the nearest railroad?" Jason asked.

Both agents looked at each other, bewildered, and Jason said, "*Quickly!* The portal's going to blow in nine minutes. As soon as it goes off, you three go out the back entrance in the SUV. Whoever's outside will follow you. If we're lucky, you'll draw off the pursuit."

"So you'd just leave us for Ius Divinum and run away?" Jensen asked.

Jason looked levelly at her. "Yeah. They won't hold you more than 24 hours. *You* told me that, while we were gone."

Jensen rolled her eyes slightly. Greene answered, "that's right. You're right. If you want to get to a railroad, the closest way is to follow the road that passes in front of the school. Just keep going east on that road. You'll cross a river, and then go over I-75. The railyard is just on the other side."

"How far?" Jason asked.

"Five miles," Greene answered. Jensen shot him a dark look.

"Shit." Jason shook his head. "Is there a maintenance truck at the school?"

"Yes," the tech answered. They all turned to face him.

"The keys are in the storage shed. If you want to get away clean, I'll take you there in the truck, and drop you off. Then I can bring back the truck, and if anyone asks, I sneaked out to get breakfast." The tech grinned. Greene smiled back, and Jensen looked wonderingly at him.

"If this actually works, I'll recommend you for promotion," she said.

"That's great. But we have to *move*. The portal's going to blow in eight minutes." Jason brushed past the two agents to the door, and tugged at the handle. Nothing happened.

"Why does this always happen?" Jason asked, in a voice too stressed to be rhetorical.

Jensen came up beside him and swiped her ident over the reader beside the door. "Security reasons. Duh. Turn left and go up the tube. It's a long way, so you might need to run. You'll only have about three minutes to get the keys to the truck and get away. Hurry."

Yanking the door open, Jason looked over his shoulder toward Phoebe and motioned. "Come on." As she brushed past him, he looked toward the tech. "If you really can do this, all I can say is 'thanks.' But we're out of time."

The tech nodded. Jensen called after Jason, "What about our mission? What are we supposed to do?" Jason stopped, and turned, impatience evident in his face.

"Meet me when this is over. You'll be able to find me, or I'll find you. One way or another, both of these two agencies you've told me about have got to agree to work together to prevent the Seafloods. When they catch you, tell them that," Jason said, and turned away again, jogging up the tube with the tech and Phoebe, trying to get out as fast as they could manage.

SEVEN MINUTES LATER, Jensen and Greene were buckled in their black SUV, waiting for the building around them to blow up.

"Now I get why Anderson freaked out when he saw the bridge was underground," Jensen commented.

"No shit," Greene answered. "I just hope the roof holds long enough to let us get out."

"Anderson said they'd be waiting for us. How long do we run before we let them catch us?" She grinned, a little crazily. Greene's smile was equally sanguine.

"Think you can keep them going for ten minutes?" he asked. "That'll be enough time for them to get away clean."

"Want to make a side bet?" Jensen asked.

"Fifty dollars."

"You're on." Jensen twisted her clenched fists on the wheel. "Now, if they'll just blow this place before it gets anticlimac-"

The overpressure from the collapsed portal struck the side of the vehicle at the same time as the sharp, staccato THUMP from the resulting spatial implosion, coupled with the blast from the energy differential between the bridge endpoints. The SUV shifted about two feet to the left and tilted slightly; debris shot all around them, all moving right to left. Behind them, inside the abandoned arena, chunks of ceiling tile, roof material and girders could be seen falling onto the concrete base of the rink.

"That dramatic enough for you?" Greene managed to ask.

"Fuck off," Jensen replied. "Good thing this glass is bulletproof. Let's get out of here." She hit a button on the ceiling of the SUV, activating the door for the loading dock, which – surprisingly – still worked. The moment that the door was high enough, Jensen dropped the SUV into gear and floored it, blasting out of the arena and nearly crashing immediately as the cracked ramp thudded under the tires.

"Shit!" Jensen muttered, making a hard left, circling toward the south side of the arena and the exit. Already two vehicles similar to theirs had appeared from behind the trees on the lot's southwest corner, angling to cut her off. She gunned the engine, shooting just in front of them toward the exit as two more vehicles closed in from the arena's eastern side.

"Four of them." Greene said, looking back as their vehicle screamed through the turn and began heading west through Trotwood. The pursuing vehicles were driven with equal skill and abandon, though, and after driving less than a mile, it was evident that they would not escape capture for long.

"Can't go into the neighborhoods," Jensen said. They turned northwest onto Highway 49, exceeding the speed limit by a significant margin, still with the other vehicles in pursuit. "And we'll get someone hurt at this rate."

"Three minutes," Greene answered. "I-70's a mile ahead. Take it and see if we get to the Indiana line before we have to stop."

"That's fifteen miles," Jensen said.

"Double or nothing then." Greene crossed his arms and stared at her. She rolled her eyes again.

"You'd better be good for it, you bastard," she grumbled, as they tore through the red light at the overpass. Several cars skidded just out of their way as they slewed onto the entrance ramp, briefly overcorrecting before merging onto the interstate, edging over a hundred miles per hour. The four pursuers remained close behind.

THE TRUCK PULLED INTO a gas station on the far side of the interstate. About a mile ahead, Jason could see the rise in the highway where it passed over the railyard. The road was lined with businesses, about half of them closed, and though it was four lanes wide, traffic was light for early morning.

"How much stuff do you need?" the tech asked. Jason thought briefly.

"Get some premade sandwiches if they have them, some granola bars, probably a few candy bars too. We'll need water, mostly. If they have gallon jugs, get us at least two of them," Jason answered. He was already digging in his wallet.

"You gonna be able to carry all that?" he asked.

"I hope so," Jason replied. "The real trick's going to be finding the right train. Getting to Cincinnati shouldn't be too bad. Thing is, I have to figure out how to get from there back to Atlanta. If it takes more than a couple of days, we'll have trouble." He handed the tech three twenty-dollar bills. "That should more than cover it," he added.

"Thanks. Can't help you with the trains. Sorry, man," he said. He got out of the truck and went into the station's convenience store. Phoebe fretted.

"Do you think we can trust him?" she asked.

"I think so," Jason said. "I don't think this is the kind of organization you double-cross." He shook his head. "I'm getting a bad headache. How are you feeling?"

"I'm all right," Phoebe answered. "I mean, I don't feel bad or anything."

"Good," Jason said. "I'm beginning to think there are side effects to repeated time travel, and I don't like them." He smiled at her; she could see the pain in his eyes. "I just hope, once this is done, that I never have to do it again."

"Where are we going to go, once this is done?" she asked.

"Jensen said that the problem with Al would be taken care of," Jason replied. "If they could do that, I think they could get us into something like witness protection – not because of any danger, so much as just to hide what I know."

"Would you be willing to do that?" she asked.

"In a second," Jason answered. He smiled his painful smile again, and she answered with the best one she could muster through her worry.

A short while later, the tech came back out of the store, carrying two large water jugs and two plastic bags full of food. He passed them to Jason and Phoebe as he climbed into the truck. Jason carefully added the box Argo had given him to one of the bags.

"I'll drop you next to the bridge, so that you can get out of sight. I hope you know which way goes south," the tech said.

Jason nodded. They swung out onto the road, and reached the bridge less than two minutes later. The tech pulled the truck next to the curb and stopped.

"You two be careful. Catching rides on freight trains is dangerous as hell. I hope you make it," he said.

Jason had already climbed out from the truck and was helping Phoebe down. He looked up at their driver.

"Thanks for all of this," he replied. "I hope you get that promotion."

The tech smiled back. "That's just gravy. I got to see time travel. I hope we meet again sometime, and you can tell me more about it."

Jason nodded, and closed the truck door, hitting it twice with his open palm as it pulled away. Phoebe was looking dubiously down the embankment beside the bridge.

"It's pretty overgrown," she said.

"Never mind that. Once we get under it, it'll be easier to get down there," Jason answered. Phoebe went over the guardrail first, with Jason helping her; then he climbed over, and together they made their way under the bridge to where the twin main lines ran, some twenty-five feet below them.

Chapter Twenty-Two

"YOU OWE ME A HUNDRED bucks," Jensen muttered under her breath to Greene.

Their pursuers had brought them to bay two miles past the Indiana line on I-70 and forced them to the roadside. Despite the extremely high speed of the pursuit, not a single local police cruiser or state trooper's vehicle was in evidence.

"IUD must have passed the word. They got us without a hitch," Greene responded, but his voice was subdued. "And you know I'm good for it."

"Please don't call us that," their driver said quietly. Their captors were all military-issue plainclothesmen, all wearing sunglasses and wireless earbuds. They were unfailingly polite; the knowledge that they held the upper hand made intimidation unnecessary. A small, completely false smile bent his lips as he continued, "Did any of us call you the Keystone KOPO?"

Jensen nodded. "That's fair." The Ius Divinum team had not even needed to draw their weapons. The entire capture had been done in three minutes. Two members of their team had even taken their SUV and were bringing it back with them. Instead of taking the interstate back to Dayton, they had continued to US 27, and had turned south there, heading toward Cincinnati.

"So, where are you taking us?" Greene asked. His question prompted another glance from their driver.

"You're pretty high-value, it seems. One of the big guys wants to see you. In person," he added. "Normally, we'd drive you down there, but you know the rules. You agree not to attempt escape, and we hold you for twenty-four hours. If we're going to make the most of that, we have to get you in front of him muy pronto, so we're going to fly you to Atlanta. You'll be interviewed in about four hours. Best have your stories straight by then," he added. "Where'd the other guy go?"

"What other guy?" Jensen asked.

Even with shades on, the driver's eyeroll was apparent, and nearly audible. "Oh, come on. We saw a second vehicle enter the arena last night. It never left, and he's not with you, so I assume he's with the other fugitives."

Jensen and Greene looked at each other, each using their full training to suppress any reaction. Their captors had just told them that the others were all still at large – but they might be feeding them false information.

"I hope you don't find him in the wreckage," Jensen finally answered, noncommittally. "We weren't ready for how bad that explosion was."

"I suppose you're not going to tell me what caused it?" came the next query.

"It's hard to say, but we *think* that the same thing that triggered the blowup in Atlanta happened here," Jensen said blandly, concealing how carefully she chose each word. "If that's the case, I think we can rule out bombing as a cause."

The driver stared at her through his sunglasses for a moment. "We have a surveillance team monitoring every building within a thousand feet of that dump you people blew up. The minute they show their faces, we'll have them. We know that two of them aren't yours." Another, slightly larger, false smile crossed his face. "I hope you gave them a proper goodbye."

Jensen deliberately allowed a shadow of dismay to cross her face, and resisted the urge to glance toward Greene.

A thousand feet. Meadowdale was almost half a mile away from the arena. If they had gotten out the far end of the tube, then they might have gotten away clean.

Jensen pursed her lips, carefully controlling her expressions, as the Ius Divinum convoy roared south through the Indiana countryside.

"I THINK WE'LL NEED to move down to the south end of the yard," Jason said.

He and Phoebe had hidden under the bridge for about two hours. Aside from two short freight trains that had chugged through without stopping, there had been almost no activity in the yard. Neither of the passing trains had been suitable for their purpose; one had been moving much too quickly for them even to consider hopping on, and the other had been northbound.

"How much longer do you think we'll need to wait? Phoebe asked.

Jason sighed. "I really don't know. Our best hope is to catch a southbound local train into Cincinnati. The big, fast trains going from Chicago south don't go through here. Our best bet is to get to Cincinnati and catch one of those trains, and hope no one sees us for about 24 hours."

Phoebe looked out at the twin main lines, which bent slightly west of due south just past the bridge. "It's at least a mile down there," she said.

"I know. The bad part is that we can't walk beside the tracks. If they see us, the least they'll do is kick us off the property. We don't look like freight-hopping types, and that'll get their attention. If they decide to detain us, it's all over." Jason squinted, looking toward the distant end of the yard. "We'll have to stay in the trees."

"Fantastic. I was already looking forward to going back to Atlanta on a freight train. Now we'll be covered in ticks, too." Phoebe looked sardonically at Jason. "You really know how to spoil a girl."

"Well, at least we aren't in jail, or worse," Jason answered, rubbing his forehead. "This headache's going to get really bad if we have to wait in the sun. Let's go ahead now and try to get in position before the next train comes. At least it looks like there'll be some cover down there."

They made their way out from under the bridge, down near to where the tracks ran. Just off the roadbed, the undergrowth was dense and thorny, but behind that, a narrow path led under the power lines that ran parallel to the yard. Trees grew to the right of the path, and the undergrowth was tall enough to their left so that they could no longer see the rails.

"This isn't too bad," Jason said. And indeed it was manageable for a few minutes, fairly shaded and out of sight, but then the path opened into an unpaved staging lot, about fifty yards wide and almost ten times as long, whose southern end was closed with a tall chain-link fence covered in more undergrowth. Beyond the fence, several major electrical towers reared.

"Damn it." Jason sighed again. The day was starting to grow warmer than he would have liked, but there was nothing for it – they would have to cross the lot on its left side, away from any buildings, and then break a path through the dense growth beyond the towers.

By the time they reached the fence, Jason knew he was in trouble; the heat from the sun worsened his headache noticeably, and he was out of shape after months of hiding. They stopped at the corner of the fence, still looking south. Jason cupped his forehead in his hands.

"How far does this fence go?" he asked. The side facing them was interlaced with slats, hiding what lay behind. Phoebe moved close, peering between the slats.

"It's not too far. About a football field or so. Do you think you can make it that far?" she asked.

Jason took a deep breath and raised his head. His eyes had grown weak and bleary, and he squinted in the sun, looking at the high weeds and vines that crowded the fence where they needed to walk. After a moment, he nodded.

It was at that moment that Phoebe heard the voice for the first time, as it spoke softly in her mind: "He is unwell, but not sick. The weight of the world presses on him, not because he is at war with it, but because it needs him."

She knew the voice at once, and said very quietly, "did you hear that, too?"

"I heard something," he answered, and as he did, the pain visible in his expression faded slightly. "It was the same voice I was hearing before we went through the portal, but... different. And I couldn't make out what it said." He shook his head gently, as though to clear it, and as he did, Phoebe saw something she wasn't sure she believed.

"Jason, why do you have two shadows?" she asked. She looked to her right, confirming that she only cast one, well-defined shadow. Jason looked at the same time, and did a double-take.

Jason's primary shadow was as dark and elongated as Phoebe's, but a second, penumbral shadow paralleled it, longer and less opaque than the first. He looked at Phoebe again, seeing in her face the same unease he felt.

"I'm not sure what that is. I know it wasn't there a minute ago, and now my headache is getting a lot better. Something really strange is happening," he said, and his eyes were haunted as he continued, "and I have no clue what or how."

HAVERHILL'S LAPTOP SOUNDED the one tone he had dreaded, but he had to answer it. They had gotten the KOPO contingent in the arena, including the technogeek that had turned up when they made their way into the facility, but the big prize – Anderson and his girlfriend – had slipped his grasp.

He drew on his sunglasses again and activated them, waiting for the voice. It did not make him wait long.

"Status update, General."

He had not been prompted; he knew he was being tested. God, or Allah, or Rodney or whoever, help him if he gave them anything but truth. But none of them were likely to help him if he did.

"Three KOPO agents in custody and en route to Atlanta. I will be questioning them myself as soon as they are here."

"We are aware of that, General. What of the two fugitives, Jason Anderson and Phoebe Reyes?" The cool voice somehow became even colder than normal.

"No sign of them," Haverhill answered as crisply as he could. "We are combing through the facility now, to determine how they slipped out."

"Has any effort been made to widen the net on them?" came the next question.

"Local and state law enforcement have been issued a BOLO notice. They can't go anywhere without being spotted sooner or later. All routes out of Dayton are under direct surveillance, including surface streets," the general intoned.

"Our intelligence indicates that they may be staying off the grid. If so, then surveillance isn't likely to prove effective," the voice answered. There was a hint – no, not a hint, Haverhill thought; there's a LOT – of expectancy in its tone.

"We have no intelligence on any prospective destination for the fugitives," he said. "If there is available information to which I am not privy, I will require it to carry out your orders."

There was a long silence. Haverhill waited, knowing that if he had overstepped, further comment would only worsen the situation.

"Our analysis indicates that Anderson is highly intelligent, with a knowledge base much wider than that of a mere specialist. He could have been successful in nearly any endeavor he chose to pursue. He will therefore know that he cannot travel by normal means, as they will all be watched. He will seek to find another way, possibly as a stowaway, or hidden in a cargo shipment with the carrier's knowledge. He almost certainly will not be likely to use conventional methods." There was a pause. "With your background and approach in such matters, you may not be suitable for this type of pursuit, General."

Haverhill found himself having to control anger at this last sally, which had been edged with unmistakable disdain, but he knew better than to cite his credentials in response. One of the most basic rules of his position – perhaps the cardinal one – was never to tell his superiors anything twice.

And the truth was, no one could be sure whether Anderson was even running, or if he had decided not to risk it and gone to ground. He could be under a bridge or in a culvert just a few miles from Trotwood, and be nearly impossible to locate.   Fear of capture might be the only motivator to keep him running.

"I am, as always, at your command. Or your disposal," was the only reply he could make. His mind flitted briefly to the three KOPO agents en route to Atlanta. Their questioning would be intense, even for his organization. If he remained responsible for the operation, he would have to deliver Anderson's whereabouts, quickly – or, more likely, Anderson himself. Nothing less would be acceptable.

Almost as though it had read his mind, the voice said, "You will remain in command for the time being. Whether you retain that position is entirely dependent upon your ability to produce Jason Anderson. Another failure like the one in Atlanta two months ago will end your career, General." The link dropped, and the general removed the glasses, tucking them carefully into his breast pocket. In three hours, he would start to have answers.

Frowning to himself, Haverhill reflected that that delay could unravel any number of arrangements between Ius Divinum and KOPO, if Anderson slipped through and made it out of Dayton.

Chapter Twenty-Three

JASON AND PHOEBE REACHED the end of the fence after several scrapes and battles with thornbushes, breathing sighs of relief as they looked ahead. The trees formed a narrow line of woods stretching parallel to the tracks for at least a quarter mile ahead, with sparser undergrowth and shade. Jason realized that the twin shadows he cast were nearly as unnerving than their fear of capture, if not more so, and preferred to stay out of the sunlight.

Phoebe looked tired and overheated, and her eyes were full of concern as she watched him. His headache, while greatly lessened, was still affecting him, and something else that she couldn't quite put her finger on seemed to be sapping his energy.

They rested briefly in the shade before continuing south, staying well under the tree canopy to avoid sight from either side. The way was much easier than before, and they crossed some three hundred yards before the trees began to thin out again. Jason looked nonplussed.

"We can't go any farther," he said, looking south along the rail line. "There's a big clearing ahead, with a couple of buildings right next to it. The trees won't give us enough cover. We're going to have to wait here a while." He sighed. "And there's some buildings on the other side of the tracks, up ahead. I think that might be the office for the railroad here. We can't risk getting any closer until it gets dark."

"But it's not even noon yet," Phoebe protested. "We have to wait here all day?"

Jason was about to answer, when the voice whispered to him, "wait." He looked over to Phoebe, who looked fearfully back at him.

"I heard that too," she said.

Jason's brow was creased, partly in pain, but partly in thought. "We keep acting like this voice we hear can't hear us. Let's find out." Before Phoebe could answer or react, he said, addressing nothing in particular, "Can you tell us what we're waiting for?"

There was no response but silence, and they looked at each other. Jason was about to speak again when they heard a car door close, ahead of them and to their right, near the building closest to them.

"Shit!" Jason whispered. He moved closer to Phoebe, guiding her toward the thickest undergrowth he could see. They crouched behind it together, watching in the direction the sound came from.

The other end of the clearing was bordered by the parking lot for the building nearest them. That lot was half-filled with employee vehicles, with several box trucks lined up on the building's loading docks, facing toward the railyard. As they watched, two men emerged from the line of trees, walking straight toward them. Both appeared to be in their forties or fifties; one sported a long grey beard and wore a voluminous backpack and a military-style cap, carrying what looked like a ten-gallon paint can, while the other was towheaded, comfortably dressed, and clean-shaven. They were engaged in an animated discussion as they walked.

Even as the thought occurred to Jason, the voice whispered to them both, "they're safe. You can trust them."

"How do you know that?" Jason asked in a hissing whisper, before he could stop himself.

The last thing either of them had expected was a reply, and their eyes widened and they looked to each other when the voice said, "from my perspective, I can see far more than you, but can do very little. Had you not gone through the portal, communication would be much more difficult. But these two men mean you no harm, and will help you."

The pair had already crossed the clearing and were at the edge of the thicket when they stopped, evidently exchanging farewells. They shook hands, genially, and the blond man turned to leave, while the bearded man took one step toward them and stopped short, calling, "hold up!" to his companion in a gravelly voice.

The blond man whirled around. "What is it?" he asked.

"There's some'un over there, b'hind them bushes," the beard replied. He pointed, right to where Jason and Phoebe hid.

Jason made up his mind instantly, and stood, waving to them. Phoebe looked up at him briefly in dismay, before rising to stand beside him. The two men looked briefly taken aback.

"We don't mean any harm," Jason called, trying both to project his voice to them and keep it low enough from carrying to the loading dock behind them. The two men glanced toward one another, and the bearded one nodded. They both approached the couple in the wood.

"What're y'all up to?" the blond one asked.

"Hi. We're trying to get out of Dayton, and we can't take the roads. We thought the fastest way out would be to hop a train," Jason answered.

The bearded man laughed. "I don' know 'bout *fast*," he chuckled. "Not a lot o' traffic on this line, an' ain't none of 't real quick t' git anywhere. My friend here dropped me off t' catch th' southbound that's due t' come through. Crew changes here 'fore 't moves on."

"That's perfect," Jason answered. "We're heading south, too. Mind if we ride with you?"

He squinted in reply; the blond man looked dubious. "'Fore we get into any o' that, I gotta know whether yer runnin' from th' law, or somethin' like that," he said. "I don' want that kind o' trouble."

"Sir, if we were in trouble with the law, we'd turn ourselves in. The people after us are a lot scarier than the police," Jason answered.

"Shit." The bearded man spat. "Yeh get in over yer head at that casino over yonder?"

"What casino?" Phoebe asked.

Both men laughed. "There's a casino next to the racetrack, just the other side of the yard. You can see it from here. Don't tell me you never saw it," the blond said.

"Actually, no, we didn't," Jason replied. "At least, we didn't know what it was. We're not from around here. We got dropped off at the bridge up at the other end of the yard, and walked down here."

"You don't *sound* like you're from around here," the blond answered. "So how'd you manage to get in trouble with these scary people?"

"We've been on the run for a couple of months," Jason said. "We hid in Dayton for a while, but then we got tracked down. We really don't have any better way to get out of here."

"Where're yeh from?" the bearded one asked, looking hard at Phoebe.

"Atlanta," Phoebe answered. Jason nodded.

He looked darkly toward his companion. "Warn't there a bomb that went off there, couple months ago? Right 'bout th' time these two say they ran off?"

"I didn't hear about that," came the reply. "You think they're dangerous?"

Jason realized he had to answer at once, and gave Phoebe a sidelong look to quiet her. "What happened in Atlanta wasn't a bomb. We know what really happened."

"I saw what happened on th' news," the beard said.

"And you think the government gave them the whole story?" Jason shot back. "The explosion happened in a lab where they had created a wormhole. They generated two subatomic black holes and connected them."

The two men were taken aback by this. "How do you know about that?" asked the blond.

"I was the senior grad assistant on the project," Jason replied. "I'm on the run because what really happened is so classified that I'll disappear forever if the wrong people get to me first. My girl here is on the run because the news people put out that she planted a bomb and blew up the lab." He paused and stared straight back at the bearded man. "According to the story, I was killed in the explosion."

The bearded man squinted at him again, briefly, but then his eyes grew round. "Well, damn," he muttered. His friend looked toward him in surprise.

"I read th' story on this when 't happened, an' there's a picture o' th' guy who got killed. This boy here *does* look like him," the bearded man said. "An' th' girl looks like th' one they're lookin' fer, too."

"That's us," Jason replied. "My name's Jason Anderson. This is my girlfriend, Phoebe Reyes. We just want to get out of here and away from the people who are after us."

"You sure you're OK with this?" the blond asked.

"Yeah. I never heard o' anyone *pretendin'* t' be one o' America's Most Wanted. An' yeah, they really do look like 'em." The beard squinted toward Jason. "I remember mos' ev'r'thing I read. Tell me a lil' more 'bout this project o' yours."

"The project was directed by my boss, Dr. Tinsworth. He's the university Physics chair. He recruited two grad assistants and four undergrads to work the lab. The other assistant was a guy named Wiley Grant," Jason answered. "The wormhole was what's known as an Einstein-Rosen bridge. It forms a direct connection between two subatomic black holes.

"The reason there's so little real information on what actually happened is that someone, somewhere, figured out how to detect a bridge when it forms, and destabilize it remotely. The energy differential is explosive, when that happens. And that means that any bridge like that can be turned into a bomb," Jason finished, still staring down the bearded man, who nodded, but then squinted again.

"One last question. How's it they said yeh was dead, when yer alive?" he asked.

"For that, you have to have time travel," Jason answered. An odd silence fell as he spoke.

"I don't know that *I* like this," the blond man finally said. His companion didn't speak, and the four of them relapsed into silence, waiting for the impasse to break. Jason finally walked toward the men, out from under the trees into the noonday sun.

"This is what time travel can do to you," he said, pointing toward each of his shadows. Both of the other men gaped. "We don't mean you or anyone else any harm – we just want to get back to Atlanta. We're trying to stop something terrible that is going to happen in a few years. But to do that, *we have to get out of here.*" He paused for breath. "So if either of you can help us, we'd be really grateful."

The two men looked at each other again, and Jason glanced meaningfully back toward Phoebe. When his gaze returned to the bearded man, he was surprised to see a grin spreading across his face.

"Yeh two have t' be th' greenest pair o' train riders I ever saw. I'll bet 'til today, yeh never even *thought* 'bout takin' a ride," he chuckled.

Jason had to smile. "I always liked trains, but I never thought about actually jumping on one. Not until today, like you said."

"Thought so. Folks call me 'Bootstrap,' and this here's my friend J.T.," came the reply. "J.T.'s droppin' me off here so's I kin catch th' southbound. Change trains in Cincinnati, an' catch th' manifest from there into Kingsport." He thought. "If yer goin' back t' Atlanta, yeh kin take that same train on into Spart'nburg, and then catch th' hot stack train from there. Take yeh 'bout two days."

Jason heaved a huge sigh of relief that he hadn't realized he had been holding in. "Thank you very, very much," he said, looking from J.T. to Bootstrap. Phoebe had come out and was standing beside Jason, and nodded her agreement.

"Think we got this from here, J.T. Thanks again fer th' ride," Bootstrap said.

"Anytime, buddy," J.T. replied, and started to walk away. A cry of "wait!" from Jason stopped him.

"If the people coming after me are as good as I think they are, they may come looking for you," Jason called after him. "If a bunch of CIA-types come asking questions about me, please, please, *tell them the truth.* I don't want you to get in trouble for trying to help me."

J.T. paused, and nodded without smiling, and then turned to walk back to his car. Bootstrap looked at each of his new companions in turn.

"Awright. Now, th' train we want ain't gonna be here fer a couple hours, so we kin kip unner them trees while we wait." He lifted his paint can, which was apparently not too heavy, and led them back under the trees to the exact spot where they had hidden. Dropping the can there, he groaned slightly as he removed his pack. Jason suddenly laughed.

"We must have looked like idiots. This is where you were going to wait, isn't it?" Jason asked. "And we thought we could hide here. We were right where you were looking the whole time."

Bootstrap grinned again. "Yup. It's a good place t' hide, but not from another hobo," he drawled. He sat down with his back against a nearby pine tree, sighing. "My ol' bones don't always want t' move s' fast 's I'd like, these days, but I git on a'right." He looked at Jason, then Phoebe, and shook his head. "Yeh'll have t' watch yer feet. Them sneakers, they're OK for walkin' on th' street, but yeh really need boots if yer gonna ride." He grinned again. "But I 'spect yeh ain't gonna be doin' this again if you kin help it?"

Jason grinned back; the hobo's smile was contagious. "No indeed. At least, I sure hope not." He looked to Phoebe, then down at himself. "I don't think our clothes are going to hold up too well to this, either," he added.

"Nope," Bootstrap said, with another grin. "Y'all'll look like dirty kids by th' time yeh git t' Atlanta."

"That could be a problem," Jason said. "We have… an errand to run when we get back, and if we look like we've been living rough, the campus police could give us a hard time."

"Yup. College cops're th' worst, 'cause you know they ain't real cops, and *they* know you know they ain't real cops. So they think ever'one's laughin' at 'em, and they act like assholes."

"Some are, maybe, but where we were at school, the police are accredited. They're really pretty good," Phoebe objected. Jason gave her a surprised look, which she returned with slight annoyance. "Did you really think I decided to go to college in the middle of a big city without making sure I'd be safe there?"

"I didn't really think about it that much," Jason confessed.

"Well, you should have," she replied tartly. "And I think we'd better find a place to get cleaned up before we even consider trying to go on campus."

"Girl's not wrong," said Bootstrap.

"I'll try to figure out what to do on the way," Jason sighed. "How much longer until the train's supposed to be here?"

Bootstrap stretched, his nearly toothless mouth yawning widely. "Prob'ly two-three hours. Yeh'll know when 't gits here. Th' trick'll be findin' a ride and then gittin' out o' sight 'fore it gits goin' agin – th' crew change don't take more'n an hour, and the train'll be inchin' right past that yard office. So's we got to go back along the train 'til it's aired up, and git on, and git hid. And if there's no rides, we'll jus' have t' wait fer th' next one."

Phoebe looked perplexed. "Aired up?" she asked.

Bootstrap grinned. "Trains have t' use air-pressure brakes. If th' train ain't aired up, them brakes lock, and th' train don' move. So the engine has to dial up th' pressure in th' brake lines 'til they unlock, and then they kin go. They're made that way so's if the train breaks a knuckle and sep'rates, the back part automatically stops, 'cause th' air line breaks an' th' air pressure goes down."

"It sounds pretty complicated," Phoebe said.

"The concept's actually fairly simple," Jason said. "Applying it across every single wheel of a fully-loaded train is a bit of a chore. But from what you say, we'll be able to hear when the train's ready to move before it starts going."

"Thass right," Bootstrap said. He thought for a moment. "Y' know, yeh two should have hobo handles, since yer goin' t' be riders 'fore th' day's out."

"Handles?" Phoebe said, bewildered. Jason laughed. "He means, like a nickname. Something we'd go by if we were real riders."

"Thass right," Bootstrap said.

Jason thought for a moment, and then grinned. "OK. You can call me Argo, then."

Bootstrap laughed. "I like that. Jason an' th' Argonauts. Read that in m' Latin class in high school."

Jason did a double-take. "You took Latin?"

Another toothless grin. "Three years. Thass one o' th' benefits I've found from leadin' this life – mos' people think I'm dumber'n they are. Embarrasses th' hell outta 'em when they find out wrong." Bootstrap rubbed his chin. "Pisses 'em off, too, sometimes. Not that I give a shit." His eyes twinkled.

"I can see how that would happen," Jason answered, chuckling. "But if you remember everything you read, then how smart you are has a lot to do with how much you read."

"Thass right," Bootstrap said again. He fished in his pack and pulled out a plastic bag protecting two trade paperbacks. "And ain't a lot t' do on some o' these trips. I mean, th' scenery's beautiful – we live in th' most beautiful country'n th' world, I think. But I seen most all of it, now, and I been up an' down this part of Ohio fifty times, at least. Books pass th' time." He grinned again, then squinted at Phoebe. "So what'll we call yeh, girl?"

"I don't know," Phoebe answered. "I didn't exactly plan on hopping a train anytime in my life, if I could help it."

"Well, gotta make th' best of it," he answered, and thought for a minute. "Y' know, Phoebe's a moon name. One of th' moons o' Saturn."

"I know," Phoebe answered.

"When I was a kid, there was this one record I listened to… prob'ly five hunnerd times. Slap wore it out. But there's one song on there 'bout a girl on th' moon, and th' boy who's dreamin' 'bout her." He looked to Jason. "Yeh'll need t' watch out on this trip. She's too pretty t' be ridin' trains." Then he looked at Phoebe again, and said, "Yeh make me think o' that song. Prob'ly forty years ago, now, and I ain't thought of it in ages. But there y'are." He heaved a sigh, the smile fading a little from his face, and said, "I think we should call yeh Moongirl."

Phoebe blinked, surprised, and not ungratified. "That's – that's actually really nice. I like that." She glanced to Jason, who was looking meaningfully at her. "What? Don't you like it?"

"Remember what Argo said about dreams?" Jason asked, and then added, "but yes, I do like it, and I think it fits you. Perfectly, from where I'm standing."

Bootstrap looked at each of them and seemed about to speak, but changed his mind, and only said, "well, then, let's jus' sit an' wait. Hope youse two thought t' get water an' some food, 'cause I ain't got that much."

"We have enough for a few days," Phoebe answered. Bootstrap nodded, and leaned back against the tree, closing his eyes. Jason looked at Phoebe, shrugging, and sat down against another tree, while she stretched out on the leaf-covered ground, her head resting in his lap.

Within a few minutes, the three were all dozing, listening for the rumble that would announce their train's arrival.

Chapter Twenty-Four

THE THREE RIDERS SCRAMBLED north through the trees along the rail line, back toward the bridge where Jason and Phoebe had been dropped off a few hours earlier. It was late afternoon, and their train had pulled in moments before.

"Crew van warn't there yet when th' train stopped," Bootstrap said. "So we got 'til it shows up, plus ten, twenty minutes or so. More'n nuff time t' spot what we need."

"An open boxcar?" Jason asked.

"Can't count on it," the hobo replied. "Railroad us'ly makes sure they're locked up tight, even if they're empty. If we see one, we'll need t' spike it open t' make sure no one locks us in, or 't don't slide closed on us. Might never git out then."

Phoebe glanced over at him, looking horrified. "I don't think I want to ride in something that might lock me in," she said, breathing heavily in the afternoon heat.

"What did you have in mind? A gondola?" Jason asked.

They cleared the last of the undergrowth and were skirting the staging lot when Bootstrap pointed ahead to a locomotive in the middle of the train. "That's a DPU up there. They slave 'em t' th' front engines. Makes 'em more efficient when they have t' brake," he said. "Sometimes they forget t' lock 'em, and yeh kin slip in there 'n ride out o' th' weather, or maybe fill up yer water jug if yer out. 'Course, it's best if y' know some'un workin' the yard 'fore y' try that." He looked over at Jason. "Gondola? Maybe, if we can't find a grainer. Gondolas're us'ly dirty as hell, and y'can't git no shade in 'em. Besides, them boys in th' tower up there kin look right down in on yeh. Be a short trip if that hap'ns."

"Makes sense," Jason said. "By a 'grainer,' do you mean a covered hopper?"

"Thass right," Bootstrap answered. "They us'ly got a space at each end, where yeh kin hunker down out o' sight, and keep out some o' th' weather. With th' three 'f us, we might need two of 'em back t' back for us all t'ride together." Phoebe looked doubtful at this, but Jason nodded agreement, and they continued north along the line.

Fifty yards past the bridge, Bootstrap pointed. "Up yonder. See that new-lookin' white one?"

"I see it," Jason replied. The railcar indicated was a blank-sided, white covered hopper. It looked almost new, with no tagging or graffiti on it. The ends were partially walled on each side, with a cutout rectangular gap, and it waited about thirty yards ahead of them. It was the first of several such cars, all coupled together in sequence.

As they continued walking through the trees, they suddenly heard a loud, hissing noise coming from the train. Jason looked at Phoebe as comprehension dawned on her face.

"Now I understand what you meant by "airing up," she said.

"Right," Bootstrap replied. "Train's 'bout t' leave. We wait 'til th' last second, right when 't starts t' move, and then we run over, toss our stuff on, and climb up before 't gits goin' too fast." He stared hard at Phoebe. "Once y' grab on that ladder, don't yeh let go. Fall off th' wrong way and yeh could end up under them wheels, and that'd be a damn shame, pretty girl like you."

Phoebe paled noticeably. Jason took her hand briefly. "I'll get the water and our food. You just follow him and let me worry about the other stuff."

They were even with their chosen ride, which sat on the far main line track, thirty feet from them. Bootstrap moved to the edge of the trees, looking north and south along the tracks.

"Good. Nothin' stopped on th' line," he said. "Be a hell of a note t' git out on th' line right'n front o' another damn crew."

They waited for a few more tense minutes in silence, until they saw the train drift backward very slowly for about a foot. Then, starting at the front of train, they heard the serial crashing of the couplings as they pulled taut.

"Thass it. It's time." Bootstrap said, and without looking back at them, he made his way across the main line to their car. Grasping the ladder onto the car with one hand, he swung the paint can up onto the end platform and began to climb aboard as Phoebe and Jason followed him.

"Just grab the ladder and climb up. It's not going fast. Just don't stop to think," Jason said urgently to her. Phoebe jogged alongside the train, which was already beginning to pick up speed, and swung aboard with so little effort that Jason almost forgot to keep pace. He had to break into a dead run by the time he drew level with the ladder, heaving up their water and provisions to her, and began to pull himself up. He had a moment of terror when his sneaker slipped off the ladder's bottom rung, but he held on and got his footing, and climbed up onto the platform beside Phoebe and the hobo.

They were on a narrow section at the train's end, about ten feet by six feet, with the hopper's slanting floor overhanging them. A metal lip eighteen inches tall extended around the platform, and two metal reinforcing flanges extended out and down from the low metal ceiling, dividing the inner half of their space into three separate parts. Bootstrap had already removed his pack and stuffed it between the flanges, along with his paint can and their food, and had flattened out on the platform floor.

"Y'all'll wanna git down and stay down 'til we're out on th' line," he shouted to them over the scream of steel on steel, the roar of the wheel trucks, and the crashing of the couplers. The slight sway of the car added a low groan to the noise as Phoebe and Jason lay down flat on the floor and waited, hoping they would pass the yard office unseen.

Though the grainer was almost new, it nonetheless had travelled some distance before arriving in Dayton, and a significant amount of grime had accumulated on the car. Phoebe grimaced as she looked at Jason from where she lay.

"Ugh!" she shouted.

"Keep it down," Bootstrap said, his gravelly voice cutting through the noise. "We ain't clear yet."

From where Jason had laid out, he could look back over his left shoulder to the far side of the tracks. A thrill of dread ran down his spine as he imagined a yard worker – or worse, a railroad policeman – looking in on them. All at once, the blue yard office was beside them; for about two seconds he could see the windows. All of them had their blinds drawn; no one was looking out. Their car made several loud clanking crashes as it went through the switch at the end of the yard, and there was a moment of shade as they passed under the bridge at the yard's edge. They had made it out.

"WAAAAAAAAAA-HOOOOOOOOOOOOO!"   Bootstrap shouted. Jason lifted his head up enough to see the huge grin on his face – a grin that matched his own. He looked toward Phoebe, who still looked annoyed at the grimy conditions, and shouted, "Finally!"   She finally smiled, less enthusiastically than he, and nodded in reply.

After two months in hiding, they were finally leaving Dayton.

DR. TINSWORTH CHECKED his buzzing phone and was disconcerted to see an unpublished number on the caller ID. He closed his eyes, drawing a deep breath and letting it out, and then answered. "Robert Tinsworth."

"Tinsworth, this is Mangum. Have you had any contact with Anderson since he called you?" The colonel's tone was as clipped and brusque as ever.

"Nothing," Tinsworth replied. "He hasn't called me, and I didn't think it would be a good idea to call him."

"Shit,"   Mangum growled, somewhat uncharacteristically.   "The General's got a hot nut to find Anderson, and no one has any idea where he is. He slipped through the net in Dayton, and vanished. They're watching every road bigger than a bike path out of the place, but they've found nothing."

"Jason's extremely intelligent," Tinsworth replied. "He might have already planned an escape route long before he called me. But I don't have any idea where he's going, or what he's trying to do."

"I don't think anyone does. The General has sources I don't know about, but if he's got me following up with you, then I'd say those people are as clueless as we are," Mangum grumbled. "But the one person he's tried to contact was you, so keep your phone handy, and let me know the second he reaches out, if he does."

Tinsworth nodded glumly, and replied, "Will do, Colonel. Any message to give him if he calls?"

"Tell him… tell him some very, *very* highly placed people are after him. We can offer at least some protection if he gives himself up, but if he keeps running, he's on his own, and he's not going to remain at large for very long." Mangum paused. "He has to know that he could be picked up on any security camera in the country. If that happens, he'd probably have no more than a few minutes before they're on to him. They *will* catch him. If he makes them go to the trouble, it will make it worse for him."

"I'll tell him," Tinsworth answered. "I think he knows all that, but I'll tell him anyway."

KOPO AGENT JENSEN SAT in a gray, blank-walled secure room somewhere in Atlanta, waiting for whatever was to come next. Aside from her chair, two others, and a table in between, the room was empty. It was similar to a police interrogation room, with one difference: she was not in any restraints.

Whoever was going to question them had gone to some serious effort to bring them there from Dayton. A private Gulfstream jet had been waiting for them on the tarmac at Cincinnati/Northern Kentucky Airport, and had taken off within five minutes of taking them on board, bypassing the usual runway delays. Less than two hours later, they had touched down in Atlanta, and less than a half hour after that, they had been driven to the basement of a parking garage, taken Greene to wherever they were holding him, and then come back for her.

No one had threatened either of them, or even asked them anything more probing than whether they wanted food or drink; they both had known better than to accept any sustenance. The rules of engagement between Ius Divinum and KOPO were clear on three points – neither side was to harm the other's agents, a captured agent had to be released within twenty-four hours, and no threatening or pain-inducing method of intelligence extraction could be employed. Anything else – well, that was at the captors' discretion.

Jensen snorted to herself. The supreme irony was that she *wanted* to talk to the higher-ups in Ius Divinum. Hell, she needed to talk to her own superiors, too, she reflected – but IUD had gotten to her first.

The entire freak show that had started the moment Anderson turned up in Dayton had been one of the more annoying assignments she had ever been given – right up to the point where that damned portal had formed, she thought. The last thing she had expected was for the sci-fi geek shit to be *real*. It wasn't until her doppelganger had strolled out of that portal and literally read her mind that she knew it wasn't some sort of elaborate, staged operation. She still could not understand why Anderson would have chosen Dayton as a hiding place; KOPO's research had been centered there precisely so that it would remain undetected. It was all too suspicious.

But it *was* real, and her new mission was clear – the world was running out of time, and the two secretive operations were going to have to join forces and work together to prevent catastrophe. That, and the fact that they had been surrounded, were the only reasons she had allowed Anderson to leave. IUD would never have released him, had they succeeded in capturing him. He clearly had some role in what was unfolding, though what that might be was beyond her – not that he would likely have told her his plan, she thought sourly. He'd been a surprisingly tough nut to crack.

She was still mulling over the events in Dayton when the door opened. To her surprise, Agent Greene entered the room; the surprise was short-lived when she saw General Haverhill behind him. Greene took a seat beside her without speaking, as Haverhill sat down on the other side of the table from them, looking at each of them in turn. His face was a long-practiced mask of stern unreadability. She stared right back at him, willing herself not to evince the hostility Ius Divinum normally inspired in her.

Haverhill finally addressed her: "Agent Elizabeth Jensen. Good day to you."

"*Senior* Agent Jensen, General. And I've had better days than this, to be sure."

Haverhill nodded. "No doubt. Agent Greene has given me a rough outline of the events in Dayton, and I must say, it's an extraordinary story in itself. Fascinating. So Anderson did confirm that he used some form of time travel?"

Jensen willed herself not to show annoyance. "General, I will confirm anything Agent Greene has told you, and I will supplement any information that is unclear or incomplete. We're not trying to deceive you. We have learned that the world will in fact encounter a major climactic shift within the next decade or so, unless our organizations begin working in concert to prevent that from happening. We will likely have to recruit our counterpart organizations overseas, as well. There's not a lot of time to waste."

"So Agent Greene has said. What's interesting to me is that apparently, you learned this from the future version of yourself – is this correct?" Haverhill leaned forward, his eyes boring into hers as he spoke.

Jensen remained unintimidated. "That's correct. Our experimental bridge was altered externally to form a viable portal into our future. Our future selves actually came through it and interacted with us, before escorting Anderson and his girlfriend back through."

"Altered externally." Haverhill studied her for a moment, and his visage softened microscopically. "Our people here think that's what happened to the lab in Atlanta, as well."

"I can confirm that," Jensen replied. "Anderson told me exactly what happened, and how."

She glanced toward Greene, and began to relate the entire story Jason had told her. Several times Haverhill interrupted her, questioning specific points.

Twenty minutes passed before she concluded, "the last we saw of Anderson, he and his girl were running to the other end of the bridge access tube, heading out. He didn't say where he was going."

Although he said nothing, Haverhill had to suppress a flare of annoyance. The tech from the lab had been brought in and questioned in Dayton; he had claimed to have slipped out the far end of the tunnel to get some breakfast, and that the explosion under Hara Arena had occurred while he was out. He had been captured on his return; when questioned, he had indicated that he could no longer access the bridge from the far entrance, and had gone to the arena to try to get back in. The story had seemed plausible enough to the team at the arena – and had bought the tech several fewer hours of questioning.

"Let's say that everything you've told me is true, and that the world as we know it might be no more than a decade from ending," he said. "You learned this from a future version of yourself. Won't that cause some sort of paradox, if you change your future so that this disaster doesn't occur? Won't that negate your future version of yourself?"

"I would have thought so," Jensen shot back. "Problem is, Allen Bryant's got one Jason Anderson on ice in his lab, and there's another Jason Anderson running around loose. That sound like a paradox to you?"

"That's a fair point," Haverhill said. "So then the next question is – if Anderson is at large, what's his next move?"

"He didn't tell us that," Jensen answered. "When he came back through the portal, he knew your people were waiting outside for us. He knew we might be made to tell you everything – hell, once we found out what was going to happen, we *wanted* to – so he kept us in the dark. He's definitely doing *something*, but your guess is as good as mine what it is."

Haverhill studied them both, Jensen first and then Greene, asking the latter, "you have anything to add?"

"No, sir, not that I can think of," Greene replied.

"General, if we remember anything else, either of us, we'll tell you. You have our word," Jensen said earnestly. "But it's vital that you pass this up the chain on your end. We'll take care of our side once we're released. But we've got to start on this right away, and we really ought to leave Anderson alone and give him a free hand."

Haverhill thought about that for a moment. It had occurred to him that he might ask for leave to extend their capture – the stakes, clearly, were high enough – but then it occurred to him that the two agents in front of him had known that he might do exactly that.

For them, the stakes were even higher than for him. That settled it.

"I'll pass this along. I can't guarantee what the response will be, but just among ourselves, I'm in agreement. One thing bothers me, though," he said, leaning back in his chair as he looked at Jensen again. "We both know that the man that was elected to be in charge of – of a concerted, government effort to combat the current climactic situation – is an idiot who barely can be trusted to put his shoes on the right feet."

"He's not as big an idiot as the one he replaced," Jensen shot back.

"And that one replaced an even bigger idiot," the General replied smoothly. "We haven't had a decent brain in charge in at least thirty years."

"That won't matter, if both our organizations are working in concert," Jensen said. "The ones who try to buck us or make noise about it being a hoax will find themselves being steered out of office. They'll have to get with the program."

"True enough," Haverhill said, and rose to his feet. Jensen and Greene did likewise. "I'll still have to keep you detained, at least temporarily, but we'll accommodate you in reasonable comfort. You can inform my staff of anything you need."

"Thank you, General," Jensen replied, and Greene nodded agreement. Haverhill favored them with a grimacing half-smile before walking out of the room, leaving his staff to handle their particulars.

Chapter Twenty-Five

"GRANT, HAVE YOU HEARD anything from Anderson?" Tinsworth asked Wiley without preamble.

It was early afternoon, and they were setting up the Williams Hall endpoint lab. Tinsworth's impression about the change in his second-best grad student had been correct; Wiley's work ethic had improved beyond all recognition, and his once unpalatable personality had been replaced by a quiet, businesslike focus on the task at hand. At times it had seemed as though it was Anderson in the lab, and that in itself was remarkable.

"Jason never got in touch with me about anything, unless it was the lab schedule," Wiley replied. He did not inquire further.

"I had word from… from some contacts I have, saying they thought he might try to reach one of us," Tinsworth said. "Apparently he was tracked to Dayton, Ohio, but he gave them the slip just a day or two ago and hasn't been seen since then."

"I haven't heard from him, but if he calls me, I'll tell him to call you," Wiley answered. He had also become much more terse than before, Tinsworth thought.

"Thanks," he replied. "And if he says anything at all about where he is or what he's doing, please let me know about it. Even if it seems unimportant," he added.

Wiley nodded without looking up from the frame he was rebuilding. The housing for the bridge endpoint had been obliterated in the explosion; Wiley had spent much of the morning creating the frame for the new housing. Tinsworth remembered that that same task had taken him two days, when he had done it the first time.

"Grant, you're doing a great job. I'm glad I brought you back," he said, and was surprised by how much he meant it.

Grant looked up with a small half-smile. "Thanks, Professor."

Tinsworth nodded, and they continued work on the new bridge in silence.

"WE'RE GITTIN' NEAR t' where we gotta git off," Bootstrap said above the din. Jason nodded and looked over at Phoebe.

"Do we wait for it to stop?" she asked.

"Not 'nless yeh want th' yard bulls t' hep y'down," came the reply. "We'll have t' hop off jus' b'fore th' Queensgate yard. There's two bridges goes over th' tracks there – we'll wanna git off at th' second one, and walk t' th' road from there."

"I know we have to go around to the other end of the yard," Jason said. "How far are we going to have to walk?"

"It's 'bout five miles." Bootstrap looked from Jason to Phoebe; dismay was evident in both their faces. "Can't be helped. Only other ways 're along Mill Creek an' on I-75. They'll pick y' up on th' interstate 'f yeh try t' walk there, and th' woods next t' th' creek're thicker'n pigshit. Yeh won't be seen, but it'll take a hell 'f a lot longer goin' that way.'"

Bootstrap stuck his head a little way out on the car's right side as the screeches up and down the train indicated that it was slowing. "First bridge's just up ahead. Git yer shit an' let's git off here."

Jason grabbed their water jugs, which were both already half-empty, and their provisions. Bootstrap was already slinging on his pack. "When you're getting down, try to run alongside while you're still holding the ladder," Jason called to Phoebe. "If you slip, no matter what happens, fall away from th' train. Yeh may git scratched up by th' roadbed, but th' train kin kill yeh."

Phoebe nodded. Bootstrap added, "I'll go first. Yeh toss th' jugs down, then she goes. Then yeh toss yer stuff over, and git down. After that, we jus' foller th' track past th' second bridge, and we'll git to a road we kin take, runs next t' th' Queensgate yard. We kin foller it all the way down t' where th' NS main line comes outta th' yard, and there's a catch-out spot unner th' trees where we kin wait."

The sunlight dimmed as they passed under the first bridge, the train swaying and lurching as it slowed. Its front end had already entered the Queensgate yard; the industrial area surrounding the yard was moving by them at little more than a jogging pace. Bootstrap looked out again, watching as they passed over a highway, and then swung around onto the ladder at the grainer's end. In only a few seconds he was down, running alongside the train as it slowly went past him.

Jason dropped the hobo's bucket and their water bottles over as carefully as he could, and then moved aside for Phoebe to mount the ladder. As she swung around, he could see the second bridge, less than five hundred feet ahead, but he watched Phoebe as she climbed carefully down, letting her legs run alongside the train for three or four steps before she let go, slowing to a walk as she moved off the roadbed.

Jason leaned out, lowering the bag with their belongings off the side of the train, and glanced ahead again. The train had closed half the distance to the next bridge. Willing himself not to hurry too much, he swung around onto the outside of the grain car and climbed down.

Once again, his sneaker slipped on the last step, and he fell sideways and forward. He felt a moment of abject terror as the train wheel seemed to roll directly toward him; then what seemed like a blast of wind struck him, and he twisted in midair, landing flat on his back two feet from the rails.

He heard Phoebe cry out over the noise of the train, but he couldn't move; the wind had been knocked out of him, and his back hurt terribly. For a few seconds he struggled, trying to get air into his lungs; then his back tried to arch, and pain shot through both his shoulders, causing him first to gasp, and then clench his teeth, trying to contain the howl of pain that strained to escape him.

A few seconds later, Phoebe reached his side and knelt, leaning over him, her eyes wide and fearful. Jason was still gasping for breath, but the pain was subsiding, and he found that he could move. He sat up, slowly and carefully, as the last cars on the train passed them, continuing into the yard.

He hurt all over, and he knew his back was injured, but he hoped that he could endure it for the remainder of their trip.

Phoebe had not spoken, and as he turned gingerly to look behind them, he saw Bootstrap approaching them with a truly remarkable expression on his face. When he was close enough to speak, he addressed not Jason, but Phoebe: "Don' tell me yeh din't see that."

"I saw it," Phoebe answered. Jason was bewildered.

"OK, so I fell off. My back's messed up, but I can still walk. Is there anyplace where we can get some bottled water and food, and maybe some sort of pain reliever?" Jason looked from Phoebe to Bootstrap, and realized that he had missed something.

"OK, what happened? You both are staring at me like…" his voice trailed off as he glanced down and noticed his twin shadows again. Bootstrap spat on the roadbed and looked searchingly at him.

"I ain't never seen *nothin'* like that. Yeh were 'bout t' go right unner that wheel, an' yer damn *shadow* jumped up an' yanked yeh back. I wouldn've believed it if I han't seen it." Bootstrap's voice was a tremulous amalgam of fear, accusation, and wonder. Phoebe didn't speak, but when he looked to her, she nodded.

"I just don't understand how this is happening. I mean, we've all heard of ghost stories, but none of them are replicable, and none of them were anything like – like *this*," he said, pointing to his lighter shadow. "First I hear voices, then I get a migraine, and now…" he shook his head helplessly, wincing as he did so.

Phoebe was still watching him, not speaking, and after a moment Jason realized that she wanted to tell him something, but couldn't with Bootstrap present. He shook his head, kicking at the ballast and then wincing in pain. "I'm ready for it to stop."

Bootstrap nodded. Phoebe had retrieved their food and water, and she handed Jason the half-empty jug. The hobo asked, "yeh need me t' carry this box?"

Jason took a deep, painful breath and let it out slowly. "I think I can get it. For now, anyway. I hope I don't have to impose on you to take it."

"Thass awright," Bootstrap answered, handing him the box with an odd grin. "Y' think yeh've seen everthing in this life, an' then somethin' jumps up outta nowhere an' hollers, 'yew don' know shit!' atcha." He began trudging along the line, angling away as they approached an underpass. A few minutes later, they lowered themselves down a low stone retaining wall onto a sidewalk paralleling a four-lane road. The bridge and the girders supporting it through the underpass were heavily rusted, so much so that even the usual plating of graffiti was absent.

They followed Bootstrap under the bridge. Ahead, the road stretched straight for some distance through a decaying, listless-looking industrial area. Traffic was sparse, which was a relief to the two fugitives.

"There's a gas station 'bout halfway t' th' catchout spot," Bootstrap said. "Yeh kin git whatcha need there, an' take a leak if yeh need to." He grinned at Phoebe. "Can't blame yeh fer not wantin' t' go on th' train, but now's prob'ly the best time."

Jason thought about that. "I don't like going in someplace where I know they've got cameras, but I guess if there's anyplace they won't find me right away, it's somewhere like this." He looked at Phoebe. "You OK with that?"

"I think so. And he's right... I – have – to – *pee*." Phoebe answered. "How far is it?

"Two miles, I reckon," Bootstrap answered.

"Well, let's get there as fast as we can," she said, "before anyone recognizes us."

They continued on for several blocks, with Jason urging them in a low voice to moderate their pace – not only because of the pain in his back, but also to avoid notice by walking unusually fast. Their appearance was incongruous enough without drawing attention. They encountered no pedestrians, and though it was getting close to rush hour, there was only a light flow of traffic on the road beside them.

They had traveled about a mile, and had gone under another bridge, when the street bent hard to their left, away from the tracks they had been following, and went east for a quarter of a mile. This area looked slightly less run down, and Jason looked worriedly at Phoebe, but no one spoke, and before long the road bent south again. Jason could still see the railyard between the buildings on their right, and not too much farther ahead on their left lay the gas station Bootstrap had mentioned. Jason breathed a sigh of relief; the late afternoon was cooling, but the exercise had been more than either of them had done since leaving Atlanta. He was thankful to see that Phoebe was bearing up under the physical strain better than he was.

There were several cars gassing up at the station. Jason was acutely aware of how grimy they all looked, and how incongruous, but he followed Bootstrap into the store without making eye contact with anyone. The moment they entered, Phoebe made a beeline for the restrooms, while the men picked out food that would keep for two or three days without refrigerating. Bootstrap also pointed out a display with several duffel bags.

"Yeh'd best git somethin' like that, keep all yer shit together," he said. Jason agreed, and also picked out a small bottle of ibuprofen and a large, garishly-painted can of an alcoholic beverage called Tsunami, whose main selling point – at least according to the can – was its eleven-percent alcohol content.

"Yeh might not want t' be drinkin' that shit, not if yer gonna be jumpin' on 'nother train," Bootstrap cautioned. "Lot of hobos git to drinkin' that swill. Makes 'em useless."

"I wouldn't ordinarily get this," Jason answered, "but we've got a long ride ahead, and once we're on, I might need this to rest if the ibuprofen doesn't dull the pain."

"Fair 'nuff, but don't make no habit of it," Bootstrap said seriously. He glanced over his shoulder to see Phoebe emerging from the restroom and walking toward him. "Awright, I'm gonna take a piss, and yeh two kin pay fer yer shit. If yeh gotta go, do it while I'm payin fer mine, and we can git movin' again. We still got two-three more miles t' go."

Bootstrap shambled off toward the restrooms as Phoebe returned. Jason looked meaningfully at her, and whispered, "what did you want to tell me?"

"I couldn't say it in front of him," Phoebe replied in a low voice. "If he knew the whole story of how you got here, he'd run like hell."

Jason chuckled slightly despite himself. "You're probably not wrong."

"But Jason, we both saw what happened. The thing is, I think I know what it was. Remember what they said about how when you die, you – you sort of merge with another version of yourself, in another reality?"

Jason looked at her again, more warily. "I think I know where you're going with this."

Phoebe sighed. "What if the 'you' that – that your other you, the one you killed – what if he merged with you, right when you came back? What if he was still alive when you came through the – the thing you came through, and he died right as you went through the lab?"

Jason nodded, and then his eyebrows raised. "If he didn't pass into another parallel existence and merged into mine instead, but was still on his origin plane… oh man, who knows what that might have done?" he asked.

"It might explain why you have two shadows… well, sort of, maybe. I don't know." Phoebe looked worried, and more than a little fearful. "If – if the other you shares your body, he might have been able to make you fly backward from the train. It's –" Phoebe looked helplessly at him. "It's *weird*."

"Can't agree with you more." Jason glanced behind her and saw the restroom door opening. Handing her his wallet, he said, "here, go pay for our stuff."

He headed back to the restroom as Bootstrap emerged. Looking up at the register, then at Jason, the hobo asked, "she OK?"

Jason studied the man for the briefest moment. Then he nodded. "She'll be all right, I think. I don't think she ever thought train-hopping would be something she would have to do one day, but she's handling it."

Bootstrap nodded in reply. "Awright, go take yer piss and doubletime it if you kin. We still got a ways t' go."

AFTER A FEW MINUTES spent repacking their supplies, they were back on the road going south. The afternoon traffic was picking up, but was not heavy enough to slow down. As he waited for his pain medicine to take effect, Jason noted that no one seemed to be paying them much attention, and tried to lessen his worrying.

After a slight southerly bend in the road, they were paralleling the interstate; they walked under an interchange that led across the railyard to their right and the creek beyond. Their sidewalk was bordered by the highway fence and a narrow line of trees as they approached a large intersection. Jason and Phoebe tried not to seem anxious as they waited to cross at the light. Bootstrap pointed toward their right.

"Ov'r there's th' intermodal depot," he said. "Shame we can't git one of them out, 'cause they's th' hottest trains that run. Th' one we'll want's not so high a priority, but it runs a reg'lar schedule, an' it leaves at night, so we kin git on without nobody seein' us."

"I don't think I'd want to try to get on there anyway," Jason answered. "Looks kind of crowded."

Bootstrap laughed. "It is."

They all laughed at that, through the strain and worry, as they continued south toward the end of the railyard. Bootstrap began to tell stories of past adventures on the rails, interspersed with bits of the hobo knowledge gleaned over a lifetime, as they walked down the gradually emptying street in the fading daylight. Jason's respect for their companion grew steadily as he talked, slowly unfolding the stored wisdom of his unique life, and he realized that they had somehow met the best possible fellow traveler that they could have found.

At length they arrived at Cincinnati's Union Station. Ahead, their street tunneled under the station plaza for about two hundred yards; they would have to cross the street to remain on the sidewalk. Bootstrap looked over to Jason.

"After that tunnel, it's 'bout a half mile or so. Yer back holdin' up?" he asked.

"I've felt better," Jason answered. I just hope it doesn't hold me up when it's time to get on the train."

"From where we're gittin' on, that could be a problem," Bootstrap replied. "It'll be dark, 'r close 'nuff to it, an' the train'll prob'ly be movin' faster this time."

There was nothing he could say to that, so they crossed the street and entered the tunnel in a silence that was soon enforced by the noise of the sparse traffic within. It was poorly lit and the sidewalk was too narrow for them to walk abreast; Jason walked behind the others, trying not to betray the pain he felt through his expression. The medication had barely eased it.

The tunnel seemed to take longer to traverse than it actually did. About halfway through, it had occurred to Jason that if they had been spotted, they had walked into the perfect trap. He had a few ugly moments of fear before he realized that if in fact someone had recognized them, they likely would already have been captured. He repeated that to himself several times, keeping his mind steady as they eventually reemerged from the tunnel.

The area south of the station was in better condition than the neighborhood they left, but it was still an industrial area, and was mostly quiet. "I guess most of the night life in Cincinnati is over on the riverfront," Jason said aloud. Phoebe looked back at him, alarmed at the pain in his voice, but Bootstrap guffawed.

"Night life in Cincinnati's mos'ly sittin' home watchin' TV," he said. "I read somewhere that th' swankiest restaurants in Cincy're th' ones where they pick yer tray up from th' table after y' eat." Despite his discomfort, Jason laughed at this, but Phoebe still looked worried.

They walked for another half mile, crossing two more large intersections before the road bent again to their left. The daylight was failing by that time, and the traffic had slackened to the occasional eighteen-wheelers going to and from the intermodal depot. To their right, an empty trailer lot bordered twin rail lines that paralleled their street; a last few sidings from the Queensgate yard petered out beside it. Jason noted an old, rusted Chessie System caboose, left beside an unused concrete platform, and pointed it out to Bootstrap.

"Ayup, that ol' caboose's been there awhile," Bootstrap said. "Think it was here last time I came through, 'bout three years ago."

"It looks like it's been there thirty years," Phoebe said, with an odd note of pity in her voice. Jason looked at her questioningly.

"It's just that – well, it was made to do something, and now no one wants it anymore," she said. "It's just left here to rot. We've passed a lot of things here that were left to rot, just on this walk, and it's really sad."

"Cincinnati ain't so big or rich as it used t' be," Bootstrap said. "But it ain't as bad here as on th' other side of th' creek. 'Bout everthing that side's boarded up or closed, an' th' neighborhood ain't good. Be a long time before it gits better."

"It makes me think of that arena in Dayton," Jason said quietly. "It was used up and left standing, too."

They crossed the street at the bend in the road and followed it a little way further, until they drew near an underpass. The rail lines were less than fifty yards to their right, and trees bordered their far side. Beyond the bridge, they could see the nearest tall buildings of the downtown skyline.

"Unner there," Bootstrap said, and they left the sidewalk and began to walk toward the last clump of trees before the underpass. Jason saw that a little way beyond the twin main lines lay a third track, nearly overgrown, paralleling theirs. He pointed it out, gingerly, trying not to reinjure himself.

"That track there's a spur," Bootstrap said. "It used t' run over t' some of th' businesses near th' river, but ain't nobody used it in ferever. I remember as a young feller, them tracks went all the way to th' old stadium, but even then wadn't nobody usin' 'em. Won't nothin' be comin' up that line."

They reached the last little patch of growth, and Bootstrap immediately plowed into it, getting out of sight from the road. Jason and Phoebe followed him.

"Now we sit an' wait," Bootstrap said. "The train we're lookin' fer's not due fer a few hours, so yeh kin rest an' maybe eat somethin'. Just be ready. The train'll be goin' a little faster through here, but not too much. It can't really open up 'n go till it gits 'cross the river."

"It'll be dark by then," Phoebe said.

"Ayup, an' better fer us," he answered. "Lot safer fer us, if we don' wanna git caught."

Jason had lain back in the brush, his head resting on the duffel bag, trying to ease the pain. He had already retrieved two more pills and taken them; he did not dare take more. Phoebe glanced over at him.

"Jes' let him rest," Bootstrap said. "He took a hell of a fall, back there. Guess it could've been worse, if that gray angel hadn't caught him."

Phoebe nodded, unable to answer him, and they lapsed into a waiting silence as the evening deepened into night.

Chapter Twenty-Six

THE THREE TRAINHOPPERS sat uncomfortably in an empty, trash-strewn gondola, listening in vain for anything other than the train's crashing, thudding passage through the deep Appalachian night. They were traveling through mountainous country, so that every so often, the haunting echo of the engine's distant tritone horn would drift back to them. Occasionally they would pass through some tiny hamlet or other alongside the tracks; none of them looked very large or very well-off, from what they could see through the small gaps cut into the gondola's sides.

The train wound sinuously along the line, which had been built long before to parallel the river routes through the mountains. Usually there would be a road running alongside as well, except when the train would enter the occasional tunnel; then there would be blackness for a minute or two, followed by the train's re-emergence beside a different stream or road.

Shortly after they had crossed the Ohio River, Jason had drunk as much of the horrible beverage he had bought at the gas station as he could stomach, and had slept on the dirty gondola floor beside Phoebe for the first half of the night; he had awakened with a mild hangover and a slight easing of the pain in his back. Bootstrap had laughed when Jason groaned on awakening.

"Now yeh see why mos' of th' old hobos us'ly don't drink that shit," he chuckled. "I won't say I didn't when I was younger, but not no more. At my age, it's tricky 'nuff gittin' on without tryin' t' do it drunk."

"I don't doubt it," Jason replied. "I couldn't have gotten on here at all if it had been moving any faster, and that was without that crap."

"How's it feeling now?" Phoebe asked.

"Not great, but a little better," he answered. "I'll need to stretch some and try to loosen it up some before morning."

"I'll be off th' train by then," Bootstrap said. "This train goes into Kingsport, Tennessee, an' then turns south into Johnson City. My stop's there, 'bout two miles from a town called Austin Springs. Yeh'll stay on this train 'til y' git t' Spart'nburg.

"It's tricky there, 'cuz there's a couple smaller yards 'fore y' get t' th' big NS yard – the Hang Yard, they call it. Yeh go unner I-85, and hit th' first yard, an' then yeh go unner 'nother highway, an' yeh hit th' second one – that 'un's where yeh git off, right at th' end. Th' train'll be goin' slow through there, 'cause th' big yard's th' third one, where th' wye switch is. This train we're on'll be goin' on t' Columbia, straight through th' Hang Yard. Yeh'll need t'walk west along th' wye an' wait for th' stack train goin' into Atlanta."

Jason was nonplussed. "Won't it be daylight by then?" he asked.

Bootstrap was silent for a minute. The train continued to sway and crash under them.

"It'll be near sunrise when I git off," he finally answered. "This train'll take 'bout another eight or nine hours t' git t' Spartanburg, so it'll be gittin' on inter th' afternoon. Git out on th' right side of th' train, an' hide in th' woods, an' foller th' tracks till y' see one line split off t' th' right. Yeh'll want t' git down to the far end, down near where th' other switch is, an' git under cover there. If yer lucky, yeh won't have t' wait long, but if yeh get there late, yeh might have t' hide in them trees fer a while."

Jason and Phoebe absorbed all this, looking slightly confused. Jason finally asked, "so it'll be day after tomorrow morning when we get to Atlanta?"

"Thass right," Bootstrap replied.

"I hope they don't figure out where we went," Phoebe said.

Bootstrap laughed. "Even 'f they knew yeh hopped a train back in Dayton, they'd still have t' figger out where yeh went from there."

Jason groaned aloud. Phoebe looked worriedly toward him.

"I'm ok," he said. "My back's not that bad. It's just that I have a bad feeling… Phoebe, do you trust Jensen and Greene? I mean, do you think they told us everything?"

"I don't think they lied to us," Phoebe answered, after thinking for a few seconds. "But I don't think they told us everything, either."

"That's what worries me," Jason said. "Tinsworth knows that I know about Bryant's lab, and that means that the DARPA guys know that, too. I think that means Jensen and Greene probably knew as well. Even if they don't know any more than that, they'll probably guess that I'm making for Atlanta. I just hope they don't have Nesmith Hall surrounded by the time we get there."

"I'm hoping they think we went back into hiding again," Phoebe said.

Bootstrap had been watching them, and interjected, "wait a minnit. DARPA's follerin' yeh? Ain't they the guv'mint folks who do defense projects?"

Phoebe and Jason both stared at him in surprise. Bootstrap laughed.

"Even yeh two unnerest'mate me. I know what DARPA is. They're prob'ly the ones as funded yer bridge project, weren't they?" he asked.

"They were," Jason answered guardedly.

"That box yer carryin' wouldn't have somethin' t' do with all that, would it?" he asked shrewdly.

"Not exactly," Jason answered. "I only got this the same day I left Dayton. If they're following me, it's because I know some things people aren't supposed to know."

Bootstrap squinted. "Tain't what yeh *know* that's dang'rous, it's what yeh'll *do* about it," he said. "Y'awl ain't plannin' on blowin' up somethin' else, are yeh?"

"Not if we can help it," Jason answered. "The blowup that happened before wasn't anyone's fault – well, not when it happened to me – and it wasn't political. It was a side effect of something that happened in the lab."

Bootstrap nodded. "So – what're yeh *tryin'* to do?"

For a heartbeat, Jason hesitated. The hobo surely was no more than he appeared, but the question was just probing enough to raise his guard. He thought for a few seconds before answering, choosing his words carefully when at last he slowly responded: "I know that our future is in serious jeopardy because of climactic issues. I know that there is a possibility of averting the crisis before it becomes inevitable, and I know one specific – one particular piece of information about the type of world we will have to have. So I have to ensure that our world, our present time, is shaped to match that type of world."

Even in the dark night, they were looking directly at each other, and for a long time only the noise of the train, slowing as it neared a junction, was heard.

Bootstrap finally replied, "That sounds like th' kind o' shit yeh hear 'bout the Illuminati, or th' Knights Templars, or somethin'. Yeh ain't had no truck with any o' them types, have yeh?" Even in the dark, his eyes glinted.

"Not as such, no," Jason answered. "But with everyone else that's after us, I wouldn't be surprised if they were, too."

Bootstrap suddenly guffawed, even as the train neared a stop, the brakes squealing so loudly that Phoebe covered her ears. "Thass funny," the old hobo chuckled. "I don' believe them Templars're still around, or them Masons're any more'n a bunch o' feed store owners with a damn secret handshake. But some o' them guv'mint types, thass a whole diff'runt ball o' wax." He paused, still chuckling, as the train ground to a halt.

"Crew change?" Jason asked, after a few seconds.

"Yup," Bootstrap replied. "We're almost in Tennessee now, jus' outside Kingsport. They switch out th' crew at th' junction up ahead, an' then head on through. 'Nother twenty miles or so, train'll hit a slow order goin' through Johnson City, and I'll git off there an' head home."

"You think they'll walk the train?" Jason persisted.

Bootstrap laughed again. "Shit, yeh think some railroad bull's gonna walk a mile-long freight train in th' mountains in th' middle o' th' night? Them bastards're lazier'n th' hobos are." He chuckled some more, then added, "besides, yeh see how dark it is? They start walkin' th' train, we'll see 'em long before they kin see us, an' we kin hide in th' woods 'til they're gone. Th' train can't leave if they're walkin' it." He shook his head. "We'll be goin' again in 'bout twenty minutes, and in about another hour, it'll be time fer me t' hop off."

"OK, then," Jason said, and then added, "so we just wait for the one horn blast, and then we start moving?"

"Prob'ly won't hear th' horn," Bootstrap answered. "But th' train'll drift back a hair, like it always does, and then it'll jerk th' shit outta yeh when it gets goin.' Yeh'll hear it comin' before it happens."

They lapsed into silence, listening to the dead quiet of the mountain night, waiting as the minutes dragged by. Jason was just about to speak again when they heard creaks and groans coming from the cars in front of them, and felt their own car inch backwards as a series of crashing noises came toward them, growing steadily louder.

"Awwww, shit," Bootstrap breathed, right before the deafening BANG that accompanied their own car's sudden lurch forward. Even though they were all seated, they were still nearly knocked over by the momentum shift in their car, and Phoebe and Jason heard Bootstrap growl, "Son-of-a-bitch!" as they adjusted themselves, and their began moving slowly, steadily faster.

IT WAS CLOSE TO SUNRISE when Bootstrap donned his pack and carried his can to the end of the gondola. Phoebe had fallen asleep again, leaning against Jason; he had dozed briefly, but awakened when he saw Bootstrap preparing to disembark, and carefully leaning Phoebe back against the wall of the car, he got up and walked over to him.

The train was slowing again, and the predawn light was sufficient for the two men to see each other clearly. Jason extended a hand, and the hobo took it, and they shook gravely.

"Thanks again for your help. We wouldn't ever have gotten past Cincinnati without you," Jason said.

"Glad t' help," Bootstrap said. "But I want yeh t' promise me one thing before y' go." He looked very serious.

"If I can possibly promise it, I will. What is it you need?" Jason answered.

Bootstrap sighed heavily. "I done time in th' Army, and served m' country. I'm proud o' that. These folks comin' t' find yeh, they may not be good people, but they're servin' jus' as I did. This thing yeh got to do – can yeh do it without hurtin' nobody?"

Jason thought. "Depends. What time does the stack train get to Atlanta, usually? Do you know?"

"That train's an overnighter, gits there 'bout this time tomorrow, most often," came the answer. "Thass if it ain't runnin' late, but unless there's some problem with th' line, it's us'ly on time."

Jason thought. "If it hits the yard early enough, we can get from there to campus long before classes start. It's only about a mile, if I remember right. That'd make it easier to do what we have to do, because the classrooms will be empty. They usually don't even open the buildings until seven or so."

"Awright, then. Try to git it done without hurtin' no one. I don' want t' have t' live with knowin' I helped git someone killed, just 'cause I helped yeh on th' way." Bootstrap spoke earnestly, and more quickly as he went along, as they both felt the train slowing to near walking speed.

"I can promise I'll do my best," Jason answered. "If I have to, I'll pull a fire alarm or something and get everyone out, but if I can get there before they open, it'll be a lot easier."

"You do that. Thanks… Argo." He smiled one last time as he hefted the can and started climbing up the gaps at the end of the car's inner wall. "Take care o' yer girl. Today could git hairy if yeh have any run-ins."

"That's definitely a promise," Jason smiled back; following the hobo's eyes, he glanced back behind himself to see that Phoebe had awakened, and watching them. Bootstrap waved, and she waved back, calling, "Thank you!"

"Stay pretty, Moongirl!" he called back to her, and a few seconds later, he had reached the top of the car, swung over, dropped over the edge, and was gone. Jason scrambled up the wall behind him, wincing at a momentary twinge from his back, and saw that he had landed safely beside the rails, and was already almost two car lengths behind. They waved one last time to each other, and then Jason climbed back down out of sight.

Phoebe had moved over to where he stood, dragging their supplies with her. They had enough food and water to last one more day, he thought.

"Next time this train stops in the woods, I'm going to climb out and have a pee," she said. Jason laughed, but grew serious again.

"We'll have to keep an eye out for ourselves from here on out," he said. "I hope it's not too hot today, or this ride will get bad really fast."

TWO HOURS LATER, the train had stopped on a siding, apparently waiting for a northbound train to pass it on the main line. Jason and Phoebe climbed out of the gondola, taking their supplies with them. They were still well up in the mountains, and there were no signs of human habitation around.

Phoebe disappeared into the underbrush to take care of her needs while Jason walked a little way along the train, looking for a better, more shaded place they could ride. He wound up nearly twenty cars down before he found one that was suitable – a grainer that was similar to the one they had taken out of Dayton. This one was older, and its extremely grimy platform was surrounded by a somewhat lower lip, but it was still easily deep enough for them to ride relatively comfortably. He looked back toward Phoebe, who had just emerged from the trees, and waved to her.

At that same moment, Jason realized that he could hear the rumble of an approaching northbound on the main line, on the other side of the train from them. Frantically, he motioned for Phoebe to get down, then dropped to the ground himself, trying to stay out of the front engine's line of sight. Most of the rail cars between their gondola and the grainer were lower than a locomotive's window – enough so that a person walking next to the train on the siding would be visible.

Fortunately, Phoebe saw and heard what was happening, and shrank up against the car next to her, ducking low; within fifteen seconds, the locomotives had reached them, and roared past, pulling their cargo at a higher speed than their own train had reached at any point since leaving Cincinnati. Phoebe started running toward Jason as soon as the engines had passed, joining him as the end of the fast train went by.

"I'd hate to be caught in front of that one," she panted, as Jason took her share of the supplies and tossed them into the end of the grainer. She breathed heavily a few more times, then began to climb aboard, just as their train began to lurch forward. Jason followed after, and they were both safely out of sight by the time the train had accelerated past walking speed.

"This is better," Phoebe said over the noise of the wheels. "It's filthy, but it's still better. I was worried someone could look into that other car and see us."

"Well, the good thing is that the only big town we'll go through between here and Spartanburg is Asheville," Jason answered. "We'll have to stay out of sight when we go through there, and I hope they won't cut any cars from the train then. Once we're past Asheville, I think we'll get there all right."

Phoebe sighed. "I hope so," she said, and lay down on the platform with her head in Jason's lap as he leaned against the grainer wall. Within a few minutes, even with the noise of the train, they were both asleep.

THEY AWOKE SOME HOURS later, near midday. Jason felt a brief moment of panic when he realized how much time had passed, but with the train running at full speed, he relaxed, realizing that if they had been seen and reported, the train would have stopped, and they would have had to get off and hide.

Not that they could do that now, Jason thought to himself. They had reached the outskirts of Asheville. Fortunately, the rail line ran beside the river that flowed through the town, and most of the development they had passed was across the water from them. He hoped that that meant that there would be no cut made on the train there, and that it would go through to their destination without slowing.

Every minute mattered, he was beginning to realize. If their train reached Spartanburg late, they might miss the stack train Bootstrap had told them about, and then they would be stuck – trying to stay out of sight, with their pursuit given an extra day to find them.

The train was turning slightly to their left, and leaning out, Jason could see that they would soon cross a bridge over the river, and pass through the center of the small city. Behind him, he could hear Phoebe's groan as she awakened, followed by a minor exclamation of dismay as she realized how filthy they both had become.

The note of the wheels on the track changed slightly as their car reached the near end of the bridge. The land around them dropped away, leaving only the water running much farther below them.   Jason noticed Phoebe looking out of the car's other side.

"It's kind of like flying, a little," she said over the din.

"Yeah," Jason responded, "if you're riding in the world's shittiest airplane."

Phoebe laughed at that, and he smiled at her; then he remembered that they would be visible to anyone who happened to be looking, and motioned for her to lie down, doing likewise just as the train left the bridge. They remained flat on the platform, watching as the buildings passed through their respective fields of view, each dreading the moment when they would see someone looking back at them.

Fifteen slow minutes passed, and they began to see trees on either side of their car. They did not seem to have slowed. Jason risked a look out and saw that they were out of the city, passing through neighborhoods bordered by the tracks on one side, and paralleling a highway on the other. He breathed a quick sigh of relief as they both sat up.

Their relief was short-lived, as the train began to slow only a few minutes later. Phoebe looked worriedly at Jason, who could only look back at her with the same expression.

"Why do you think we're stopping?" she asked.

"I'm hoping that that it'll be a crew change," Jason answered. "That, or we may have to wait for another train to pass."

"Do you think they saw us?" Phoebe was trying not to be too afraid, but her voice shook even at the volume she had to use to be heard.

"I hope not," he replied. "I can't imagine they'd change the crew out again this soon, so I'm just hoping it's stopping to let a northbound go by."

The train continued to slow, and Jason was alarmed to realize that they were entering another, smaller town; as they approached a rail crossing along a slight incline, Jason saw a city limits sign. He groaned as he lay back down on the platform, motioning for Phoebe to stay down as well.

The train ground to a halt a few minutes later. Jason risked another peek over the platform's low skirting wall and groaned again. Phoebe looked terrified. "What is it?" she whispered.

"We're stopped in Hendersonville," Jason whispered back. "It's not a huge town or anything, but it's big enough that someone will see us if we get off, and there's a road running along the track, about thirty yards away, and there's no cover. If we move, we'll probably get caught."

"But what if someone already saw us and they stopped the train?" Phoebe looked close to panic.

"We're on a double line," Jason answered. It was true; they had gone through the switch not long past the crossing. "If we're letting another train pass, this would be where the train would stop. We just have to hope that's what it is." He thought for a moment. "We could probably fit between those two flanges in the center, along with our stuff. It'll be cramped, but if another train comes by, they'll have less chance of seeing us."

Phoebe nodded, and after two minutes of careful maneuvering, they had managed to hole up in the V-shaped gap between the two flanges. Phoebe perched herself carefully astride their duffel bag, and Jason managed to contort himself in such a way that his feet were at least underneath him, though he was precariously balanced. His back sent complaining twinges around his ribcage and up to his shoulders as he strove to maintain his equilibrium.

The minutes dragged by, as slow as the train itself as it had ground to a halt. Jason's back began to protest more vigorously, and his leg muscles quickly grew tired; he knew they would not be able to hide much longer. Just as he was about to lean back out and try to see whether anyone was looking for them, he heard a train horn sound for several seconds, well ahead of them.

"Was that our train?" Phoebe asked. Jason shushed her as the horn sounded again with another long blast, followed by a short one, a pause, and then another long one. Jason's face broke into a grin.

"That's another train, and it's heading for a crossing ahead of us. Ours is letting it by," he said, and felt a rush of relief as some of the tension drained from him. "We just need to stay in here until the locomotives pass, and then we can lie back down on the platform and wait until the train leaves town. Shouldn't be too long, I hope," he added.

Phoebe groaned. "I thought that platform was bad, but this is worse," she grumbled. "I hope that other train is coming fast. Hiding in here sucks."

Jason didn't need to affirm agreement, and they lapsed into silence, listening. The locomotives for the bypassing train grew slowly louder, but it took nearly three minutes for the first engine to pass by them, going barely faster than running speed. As soon as all of the engines were past, Jason half-fell out of their hiding place, stretching back out on the platform as Phoebe crawled out behind him.

"Good thing we hid in there," Jason called to her above the din of the other train. "That thing's going so slow that they would have been able to see us, if they were looking."

"How long before we get moving again?" Phoebe asked.

"Fifteen or twenty minutes at most." Jason watched the train pass them; it appeared to be gaining speed. "I think it has to clear this area of track before our train can move, but it's speeding up, and we won't have any other reason to wait."

"I hope we don't have to do that again. That really sucked," Phoebe said.

They waited as the train ran past them; by the time the last cars went by, Jason guessed it was going nearly forty miles an hour. He tried to remember where Hendersonville was relative to Spartanburg, but drew a blank.

"I think we have about sixty more miles to go," Jason said in the relative quiet that followed the last car's passing."

"I hope we don't stop again. It's getting on towards the middle of the afternoon, and we still have to get off and hide, and wait for the other train, and get on it, and do all this again." Phoebe covered her ears as they both felt their car drift backward, anticipating the crash of the couplers pulling taut and the scream of steel wheels on steel rails. The noise was not long in coming, and in a few more minutes, they were leaving Hendersonville.

"You'd have to be insane to want to do this all the time," Phoebe shouted, venting her frustration and worry. Jason looked at her, nodding agreement as best he could as they both remained flat, waiting until they could safely sit up.

Chapter Twenty-Seven

JENSEN AND GREENE WERE both surprised to have been released early.

"Gesture of good faith," Haverhill had called it. Jensen thought that even the General should have known better than to think either of them believed that, but regardless of his motives, the two KOPO agents found themselves on a downtown Atlanta sidewalk. Greene had fetched them some roast beef sandwiches from a nearby diner, and they sat on a low concrete wall beside a midtown park, wolfing their food down and trying to determine their next move.

"We have to report in," Greene mumbled through a particularly large bite.

"Not until we know what Anderson's up to," Jensen answered. She glared at Greene, who looked questioningly back at her, still chewing. "We can't report that we let him get away *and* that IUD got us. We'd both be reassigned to Sewage Falls, South Dakota.

"We still don't know where he went. For all we know, he's still in Dayton," Jensen continued. "He could have gone to ground, like he did before."

Greene swallowed, visibly uncomfortably, before answering her. "But that doesn't make sense. We knew where he was last time because Reyes' brother was helping them. Last we heard, the FBI had detained him, so if Anderson's gotten help, it's from someone we don't know about."

"He might have been told where to go while he was in that – that thing," Jensen said.

Greene smiled. Jensen carefully concealed her annoyance.

"If someone from our future gave him a job to do, shouldn't we let him do it?" Greene asked. "It seems to me that our future selves knew what mistakes we were going to make. They told us what we have to do, but they never told us to do anything with Mr. Anderson."

"Do you trust them?" Jensen asked.

"Why wouldn't I?" Greene seemed genuinely puzzled.

"I wouldn't trust me, and I don't think you would, either." Jensen was emphatic. "You know we both would put the mission first."

"Exactly," Greene answered. "*The mission comes first.* So whatever they told us was designed to ensure we do what is required *for the mission.*" He took another bite, smaller this time, and chewed, visibly enjoying Jensen's irritation. "You're trying to outthink someone who knows what your thoughts are. We probably should just report in, and start working on establishing a liaison with IUD, if that's what the brass wants."

"But that's not what we need," Jensen protested. "We're trying to break free of our – our other selves' timeline. So we have to do something other than what they did."

"But we already have," Greene answered. "We didn't know IUD was outside the arena until *he* told us. If we had tried to leave before we knew that, or if we hadn't let Anderson go, they'd have gotten us all. No way *they* would have turned Anderson loose. So we've already broken loose from their timestream."

"Fine. But Anderson still had to get clear. We know he was heading to the railroad. Do you think he was going to try to hop a train?"

"Maybe," Greene answered. "Or maybe he just wanted a path out of Dayton that didn't have cameras all over it."

"Where do *you* think he's going?" Jensen asked.

"No idea. He could be going to D.C., maybe take out someone who's a threat. Or New York, to sabotage a financial institution that'll profit from whatever disaster's going to happen. I just don't know." Greene shook his head, his smile fading. "What I *do* know is that we probably should leave him alone and let him get on with it."

Before Jensen could reply to that, her phone buzzed. Her momentary annoyance at the interruption dissolved from her face as she read the message.

"We got a hit. A convenience store in Cincinnati." She looked meaningfully at her partner. "It's right up the street from the railyard there."

Greene laughed. "So they really did hop a train. That's awesome. If we see him again, I want to hear *that* story."

Jensen rolled her eyes in annoyance. "There was someone else with them. Analysis is running facial recognition to see if they can identify who it was."

"So we know he was heading south, at least as far as Cincinnati," Greene said. "That might rule out a lot of places."

"It doesn't rule out D.C.," Jensen objected. "Cincinnati's a bigger transportation hub than Dayton, and he could go a lot of places from there."

"True. But it does rule out Chicago out, along with Detroit or anyplace else north or northwest," he answered. "We'll probably know more once we have an ID on whoever it was that's with them."

"That shouldn't take long," Jensen replied, and held up her phone, showing Greene a picture of their man. "I'd bet a lot of money that this guy has a criminal record – if nothing else, he's obviously a railroad bum, so there's probably some trespassing citations out there."

"It's strange, though," Greene mused. "Anderson and his girl were – *are* – on the run. I would have thought they wouldn't trust anyone, let alone an obvious hobo."

Jensen thought about that. "Maybe. But he trusted us, once we talked with him a bit. If they met this guy on the way, maybe they decided to trust him, too."

"Well, once we have more on this guy, we can figure out what to do. Until then –" he took another big bite of his sandwich, which muffled the rest of his sentence – "we can eat while we wait."

"WHY DID WE STOP here?" Phoebe asked. Jason shrugged.

They were a short distance past the second bridge Bootstrap had mentioned. The train had stopped alongside a series of sidings that ran past a scrap yard. Jason could just make out a track turning off ahead, half a mile away in the late afternoon light. A seedy-looking neighborhood of trailers lay off to their right.

Their train had stopped twice more en route, but neither stop had been in any place nearly so precarious as Hendersonville had been. On the first stop, they had actually been able to get off of the train for a few minutes, both to stretch their legs and to attend to other physical needs. The delays, however, had worried them both.

Jason had been watching the trailer park for several minutes, and he finally said, "I think we'd better get off here."

"Are you sure? Do you think it's safe?" Phoebe asked.

"The trailer park looks ok," Jason answered, "and there's a line of trees after that. They go all the way to the switch up ahead, so we can stay along there and be out of sight." He looked out again. "And I think we'd better get going. Now."

"Why? Is someone coming?" Phoebe's expression darkened with worry.

"No. I'm worried some*thing's* coming," he answered. "I think this train might be stopped to let the train we want go through the switch up ahead. If we wait too long, we might miss it."

"Oh. Then we'd better hurry," she answered, and with that, she grabbed the duffel bag and swung it over the side onto the roadbed below, and began to climb down. Jason followed, more slowly, still wincing at the pain in his back, and a few seconds later, they were walking beside the tracks toward the front of their train.

"I don't like this," Jason said quietly. "Even if we get up to where we have to catch the Atlanta train, the crew on our train might see us. This is bad."

"We can't stay here," Phoebe said. "We have to figure something out."

They began walking faster as they reached the trees, moving into their shade against the long, slanting beams of sunlight. They had covered half the distance to the switch, and Jason could see the engines farther ahead, alongside a building that sent a sudden chill through him.

"Shit!" he hissed. Phoebe looked over at him. "The train's stopped at the fucking yard office. We've got to keep going down the line after we get to the switch, or we'll be too close. It's fifty yards from there to where we thought we could get on."

"But if we go down too far, won't the train be going too fast for us to get on?" Phoebe asked. "I thought it would speed up once it left the yard."

"It will." Jason thought desperately, even as they drew even with the switch and began following the side track, curving away from the yard and their train. "We have to get across the tracks and catch it from the other side. That way they won't see us get on from the office."

"Won't they see us from the office if we cross the tracks?" she asked.

"Not if we cross right now," he answered. "The sun's shining right along the track there. They'll probably have the shades drawn. If we're going to cross, we need to do it now, and hurry."

They continued on for another minute before he looked back. They had come about two hundred yards down the wye track, and ahead, squinting and shading his eyes against the sun, he could see the series of switches where multiple tracks from the other line merged with the line beside them, until only two tracks led away from the junction. One more yard building lay ahead of them, but it looked unoccupied; no vehicles were parked near it and the windows were all dark.

"We'll have to risk someone in there seeing us," Jason said resignedly, and then looked beyond. "There's a spot we can hide from the other side. The Atlanta train'll have to slow down to go through here, so we can wait to get on at least until it gets through those switches ahead. I think."

"You *think*?" Phoebe said warily. Jason shrugged again.

"I'm no railroad expert. I liked trains as a kid, but it's not like I was a railroad geek or anything. I'm having to guess." He scanned the yard buildings again, looking for any watching eyes. He saw none. "OK, let's go across. Fast, while the sun's still hitting the buildings."

They jogged along the last stretch of track, passing an unused warehouse to their right, and then cut across the multiple westbound lines some two hundred feet beyond the last yard facility. It was another hundred feet to cross all of the tracks; the last two looked extremely well maintained and were clearly the main lines leading out. As they crossed, Jason looked east down the tracks, and whispered, "Shit!" again before following Phoebe into the trees bordering the right-of-way's far side.

They barely had enough cover to hide, as it turned out. Just beyond the trees were two sheds, which belonged to businesses whose properties bordered the rail line. Jason scanned the area as best he could while remaining out of sight; he saw nothing untoward.

"What was that about?" Phoebe asked.

"There's a train coming up the line," he answered. "It's about a mile away. Depending on how fast it's going, it'll be here in two or three minutes. If it's a stack train, we'll need to get on it if we can."

"My God. Did we cut it that close?" The surprise in her query was tinged with horror.

"Yeah," Jason said. "I think so. Otherwise I think our train would be going through and the train that's coming would have had to stop. Maybe." He sighed. "If we ever see Bootstrap again, I'm going to ask him how he knew all the different rail schedules. I wouldn't even have known which way to go out of this yard."

He looked down at the duffel bag, which Phoebe had set between them. "I'll take this. When we get on, we'll have to figure out how to stay hidden. It'll be dark soon, and that'll help a lot, but until then we can't risk being seen."

"Do you know what kind of car to ride on?" she asked.

He didn't reply, but listened for a moment; underlying the ambient noises from the yard and a nearby road was the low, thrumming bass of the approaching locomotives. He frowned.

"It's almost here," he said, and then added, "I'm not sure. I asked Bootstrap about this last night. I'm hoping to find a car with a container that's shorter than the car is, so that maybe there will be a gap at the end. But that'll also depend on what kind of flatcar it is. There might not be anyplace for us to ride on a train like this."

"What do we do if there's no place to ride?" Phoebe asked, panic rising in her voice. The noise of the train was growing loud enough that she had to talk over it. Jason pointed.

The train was coming up the other leg of the wye, and had closed to within two hundred yards of where they crouched. Jason breathed a sigh of relief when he saw that it had slowed just enough that they could get on.

"We can do it. Now we just have to hope we can find a car we can ride on," Jason shouted, as the roar of the engine locomotives as they passed subsided into the thudding, creaking, squealing and occasional crashing that they had almost grown used to on their way there.

"Wait a little longer," he added, as Phoebe was about to stand up. "Look down the train."

She looked, and well down the length of the train, another column of thin, gray smoke rose into the air. "A lot of these trains have engines in the middle – like the DPU, back in Dayton," he said. "It makes it easier for them to slow down – remember how the brakes work?"

She nodded, and together they watched as the train moved slowly by, each car laden with at least one shipping container, and most with two. Just as the middle engine passed them, they both heard a change in the note of the engine's growl, and rose at the same time.

"It's speeding up. Come on," Jason said, already running toward the tracks. Several quick glances confirmed what he needed to know: the train blocked the view from the yard offices, and no one else had seen them. The train already appeared to be picking up speed, even as they closed to within a few paces of it.

Jason turned as he jogged, looking up; the train was faster than he was running, but not by much. He looked back and almost fell when he didn't see Phoebe behind him; then he remembered, and looked over his other shoulder. She was right beside him; if anything, she was running faster than he was.

The car beside them had slid by. The next car held two containers, with a longer one stacked on a shorter one, creating a short overhang on each end.

Jason looked ahead, saw a pair of flashing red lights, and realized with horror that there was a rail crossing only about five hundred feet away.

"Now!" he shouted, and turning to his right as he ran, he grasped the ladder at the flatcar's back end and began hauling himself up; as he reached the top and looked back, he saw Phoebe, running harder, reaching to climb on as well, just as she lost her footing and sprawled forward.

At that moment, his back screamed in pain, and even though Phoebe was being left behind, he could only close his eyes in agony, screaming. He felt a wind that threatened to pull his hands free of the flatcar's railing, but he held on, and after a moment, the pull subsided. Panicking, he opened his eyes and was about to climb down when he saw Phoebe below him, climbing up, her face almost blank with dreamy wonder.

It was as though the sound of the train had ceased the moment she fell, and resumed the moment he saw that she was still with him. The loud bangs and crashes of the train's acceleration reasserted themselves in his ears, and he helped her up, and then down into the six-foot gap between the end of the container and the end of the flatcar. There was a metal walkway at the car's end, about eighteen inches wide, under which they could hide from anyone watching above. The rest of the car's floor was low enough so that they could lie hidden without having to be completely flat.

"Thank God!" Jason shouted above the noise of the train. "I was scared there'd be no floor in this thing!"

"How would they put the containers in without a floor?" Phoebe shouted back.

"Some cars just have a metal ridge on each side that the containers rest on," Jason answered, crawling closer to her. "They also have a spine in the middle to stabilize the load, but that's it. I was afraid we'd have to ride on a spine like that – they're only about two feet wide."

"That's dangerous!" Phoebe cried.

"Yes, it is," Jason replied. "I don't know what we would have done. We might have had to climb across all these containers until we got to one we could ride on. As it is, we're lucky we didn't."

The Hang Yard and the crossing beyond receded behind them as the train drove west and south, accelerating into the sunset.

"I think we'll have one more crew change on the way, and that'll be it," he said. "These stack trains are usually priority trains, and they go pretty fast. We're three hours by car from Atlanta, so I think we have five or six hours to go. We'll get back in the middle of the night, and can do what we need to do in Nesmith Hall long before anyone gets there. We can be out before sunrise."

"And what then?" Phoebe asked.

Jason looked at her for a long time. "We'll have to see what happens from there. But you saw what's going to happen to the world, Phoebe. This is a big step towards preventing it, but I'd bet there's going to be a lot more to do."

"Are those two agents going to help us?" she asked.

"I don't know," Jason answered. "I just hope someone will. We may have to call Al again."

Phoebe stared at him for several seconds with an expression Jason wasn't sure he could read, and wasn't sure he wanted to interpret even if he could. Then she nodded, a little curtly, and they settled back on the floor of the flatcar, watching the sky dimming to twilight as the train moved them ever closer to home – if, in fact, it was their home anymore.

Chapter Twenty-Eight

Pax in Tempore Nostrum

2048

ARGO STUDIED THE BANK of tubes before him, waiting, as the Threebirds and Allison watched.

The ebb and flow of the multiverse, of its myriad planes merging, splitting and reforming, were captured in the velocities and hues of the datastreams that flowed and glowed within them. He had tuned these toward a single event, isolated to a specific timestream in a specific place, and now he waited for the multiple planes to converge, warping and flattening as events spiraled across four-dimensional spaces. The colors of the data were becoming homogeneous, and their speeds were matching each other. A resonant note, at first too low to be heard, but growing in volume and rising in pitch as the convergence loomed, vibrated everything in the Station office.

Jensen and Greene had been discussing something with Tinsworth, but all three of them looked up when the sound grew loud and invasive enough to reach their ears. All of the data streams glowed brightly as their shades matched, becoming brilliantly verdant, and in the center tube, a bright line of gold flowed down its middle.

"What is that?" Jensen cried out.

"Remain where you are!" Argo's voice, which was normally blandly mild, had grown in volume with the note from his instrument bank, and had become commanding. Jensen blinked, almost stupidly, and glanced toward Greene, who was staring at the spectacle before them in fascination.

"It's time," Argo said, and walking over to a small cabinet next to his instrumentation, he drew out a box identical to the one he had given another iteration of himself, just minutes before.

He opened the box and set what looked like a small world globe onto the top of the cabinet, and adjusted a single dial on the globe's base; he then turned the sphere on its axis, and rotated its housing carefully, until he stepped back, apparently satisfied. The pitch from the instrumentation became a set of notes, a perfect C-major chord, and all at once, the entire instrumentation apparatus turned the same golden color as that one center thread.

"Allison!" he called, with the same commanding tone as before, but with an odd, tremulous undercurrent to it. She had been waiting only a few steps away from him, and was at his side almost at once.

Argo looked over toward Jensen, Greene and Tinsworth, and his voice, though still commanding, had softened.

"For you, I do not know what will happen next. Either you will merge with later iterations of yourselves, or you will learn where your final iterations will take you. If that proves to be oblivion, then I am truly sorry, but this is what must happen in the end, for better or worse, for us all."

Tinsworth looked fascinated by this, and Greene seemed confused as he tried to work it all out – but Jensen's expression suddenly widened in panicked terror, and she took a few staggering, labored steps toward Argo. He held up his hand, and almost numbly, she halted, still staring at him as he pointed toward her.

"You failed because you allowed Jason Anderson to be captured. All your life you have lived with this failure, the one that cost everything. By doing what I am about to do, you may yet experience an existence where you never made this mistake." He paused. "I hope that that is where I am sending you, but for good or ill, this timestream will merge within seconds. Farewell, and be at peace." He turned, and took Allison by her hand, and together they reached toward the globe, which now glowed with the same white brilliance that the portal had before.

"*NOOOOOOOOOOO!!!*" Jensen shrieked, and staggered forward again, but it was too late; there was a blinding flash of golden-white light, followed by a shockwave that knocked all of them flat. By the time Jensen had recovered enough to look for them, they had gone, and the instrument bank had gone dark.

Jensen looked up, and saw that the Station's foundations had destabilized; the building was crumbling around them, even as it, along with everything around them, had begun to disintegrate. Terrified, she looked back toward Tinsworth and Greene. Both of them had been knocked flat, as she had been. They were both unconscious.

She lifted her hand before her face, seeing particles flying off of it, and shrieked again, but even as she did, she felt an airy touch on her shoulder. Grasping the hand with both of hers, she half-turned to see Lisa gazing serenely toward her. Julia and Rosamind were beside her, and all three looked unafraid.

Jensen tried to form words, but found she could barely draw air; even as her external body was coming apart, her internal organs were failing. Her vision dimmed, and she barely heard Lisa speak as she faded out:

"Jason Anderson has kept his promise to us all, and will bring us to a world where we will never be what we are."

Amor Semper Vincet

2023

THE TRAIN GROUND TO A halt only a little while after midnight. Multiple tracks surrounded them on either side, and ahead, Jason and Phoebe could look around the container on their flatcar and see a vast railyard stretching out in front of them.

"It's time to get off," Jason said, picking up the duffel bag. He checked it to ensure that everything was still in it, and then zipped it closed. "I'm beat. I'm glad this is almost over."

"Yes. I don't think we want to go in there," Phoebe said, pointing unnecessarily at the yard.

A little way behind them, a bridge arched over the seven or eight tracks that led into the main complex; Jason and Phoebe made for it, climbing up the embankment of the wide cut where the lines ran and emerging on a sidewalk paralleling a four-lane road.

Jason's face broke into a wide grin. "Wow. I didn't realize it would drop us this close. Look where we are!"

Phoebe was looking around in wonder. "I was beginning to think we would never be able to come back here again," she whispered.

The road leading over the tracks ran through the university campus, less than four blocks from Nesmith Hall, and a little more than twice that far from Williams and Hampton. The street was deserted; the only visible vehicle was a half-mile away, moving away from them.

"Come on. There's all kinds of cameras here, and if any of them are hooked up to facial recognition, they'll be on to us right away. We're just lucky that we only have to get there, hook up whatever this thing is, and let Argo handle it from there." Taking her hand, he led her east along the thoroughfare, making for Nesmith Hall.

JENSEN AND GREENE WERE both awakened by pings from their respective phones.

Jensen was awake first, pouncing on her phone within a second; Greene was slower, but within moments, both were reading the message sent to them both. They looked up at each other.

"Shit. He's here. He's on campus." Jensen's face wrinkled in disgust. "I should have known."

They had taken a room at a university hotel intended for parental stays, but also used occasionally by various government and academic types. After waiting the entire day for more word on the mysterious stranger who had joined the fugitives, and learning nothing further, they had retreated to their hotel room to await more information. They still had not received any.

Greene's face was puzzled. "How could he have gotten here? We had a watch on every southbound train going into and out of Cincinnati. All of them."

"That's not what worries me," Jensen almost snarled in reply. "I want to know why we've literally gotten *nothing* on that clown they were with. If he's IUD, that'd be a hell of a trick to pull on us, but *we'd know about him.* They'd have ID'd him right away. Our people couldn't pin down *anything* on him, and that means someone has been hiding him – and we don't know who."

"Well, never mind that," Greene said. "What's his next move? Where's he going?"

"Where else would he go?" Jensen was already putting her shoes on, preparing to leave. "He has to be going to the lab. So – that's where we're going. I'll take Williams Hall, and you take Hampton. I'll call for backup on the way. We'll need eyes on the place, if only to make sure he doesn't sneak out of there."

IN LESS THAN TWENTY minutes, Jason and Phoebe had arrived at the side door to Nesmith Hall. To their best knowledge, no one on the road had seen them.

Jason opened the door using the key Tinsworth had given him, and tucked it back into his pocket with a grin. "Just in case I one day work here again, I'll need this little guy," he said, pulling the door open for Phoebe, and following her inside.

A flight of stairs led down into Bryant's project lab. The lights were out in the hallway, and the check-in station was deserted, with only an emergency light and an exit sign illuminating the area. Jason pulled the box from the duffel bag, set it on the desk at the check in, and was just about to open it when he paused, and whispered, "oh, *fuck.*"

"What is it?" Phoebe whispered back.

"There's someone still in here. We can't pull the fire alarm until we deal with him, and… *shiiiiiiiit.*" Jason's frustration might have looked comical had the situation not been so fraught. "There's probably someone covering the night shift here, and if it's who I think it is, he's a *big* dude, and if he knows I'm supposed to be dead, he'll *really* freak out if he sees me."

"Who?" Phoebe looked completely flabbergasted. "Jason, what are you talking about?"

"Remember how I told you about waking up in the morgue? The guy who got me out of the freezer. His name's Mikey." Jason shook his head, and then turned to go up the hall. "We can't leave him in here. I promised Bootstrap, and even if I hadn't, I owe Mikey this even if he doesn't know it."

"Jason —" Phoebe started after him, but he held up his hand to stop her.

"If Mikey gets freaked out, he may attack me, and if he does, I'll need you to unbox whatever that is and power it up, and then *run*. I don't want him to get hurt, but we *have* to put an end to this project. None of the rest of what has to happen can take place unless *we do this first*. Now *move*." Jason turned and jogged up the darkened hallway, leaving his very nonplussed girlfriend at the desk.

As he went up the hall, he tried to remember exactly how he had left that morgue, what seemed an eternity ago, in a world to which he could never return. He remembered the door, and that there were two – or was it three? – more between the morgue and the desk. Then he remembered Tinsworth, warning him in this same place in a different existence, and in spite of himself, he chuckled.

"Sorry, Doc," he whispered to himself, "but I'm *really* going to fuck with Bryant now."

He reached what he was fairly certain was the correct door – a blank, unlabeled, windowless portal – and knocked on it twice. As he did, he called out, in a voice just below a shout, "Mikey Leroux! Are you in there?"

In less than five seconds, the door opened, and a hulking G.A. peered out. It was Mikey.

"What the hell, man? You know what time it is? Hey —" his eyes widened as he realized who was knocking. Jason just managed to get his foot in the door before Mikey tried to slam it; it was a move he regretted.

"FUCK!" he shouted, certain that every bone in his foot had been broken by the heavy, solid door, but he pushed it open again nonetheless, limping into the morgue. Mikey was backing away from him, a wide-eyed expression of fear on his face.

"You're dead, man! I remember when they brought you in! You're that Anderson dude, the G.A. from the astrophysics department!" Even as he backed away, Mikey looked like he might be gathering himself for an attack. Jason talked as fast as he could in response.

"I know. You're not seeing things. I'm real, and so is the body in this lab. I'm not going to hurt you, and I *really* don't want you to hurt me, so just calm down a bit and hear me out. OK?" Jason held his hands up, palms out to show that they were empty. Mikey's fear was draining, slowly, but his distrust wasn't. Jason could almost read the different thoughts passing through his mind as they registered on his expression, so that he was unsurprised when Mikey finally asked, in a loud but shaken voice, "what the *hell* were they doing in that lab that blew up?"

"Nothing like in here, I promise you," Jason said. "Someone else – sabotaged it, I guess, but yeah, I know it's weird." He tried to smile in a way that wouldn't look like a crazed grin. "I've lived it, so I know how fucked up it is. I'm trying to help fix it, but to do that, I need you to get out of here, *as fast as you can*. We don't have much time."

Mikey's expression of distrust deepened, further colored by obvious disbelief. "You want me to leave, in the middle of my shift? You ever meet Dr. Bryant? If anything happens here, I'll be teaching fourth grade science in some asshole elementary school in Bumfuck, Idaho. I'm staying."

"Mikey." Jason looked squarely at him, waiting until their eyes locked. "One way or another, this lab is going to be gone tomorrow. Permanently. This is your last shift here, no matter what happens. I came to tell you because I don't want you to get hurt when everything in here gets wiped out. I need you to run out of here, *now*, and on your way out, pull the fire alarm in case anyone else is in the building."

Mikey didn't answer. They continued to stare at each other.

"Please," Jason said quietly.

Five seconds ticked by. Ten. Fifteen.

And Mikey brushed past him, breaking into a run as he charged down the hallway, back toward the stairs. A few seconds after he disappeared, he heard the alarm klaxons that told him the fire alarm had been pulled. He ran back down the hall to the desk, where Phoebe had crouched in hiding, and was covering her ears against the noise of the alarms.

"All right. We're almost done." He opened the box and found what resembled a world globe, except that it was much smaller – the sphere was perhaps six inches in diameter – and it was housed within two metal circles, one vertical and one horizontal, each of which divided the ball within into hemispheres. A small dial was set into its round base, and a note was attached to it. Jason read aloud:

"Jason, Phoebe, when you have reached the laboratory where the Cybwomen are being manufactured, place this globe in the same building – preferably, on the same floor. It will need to be plugged into a standard outlet. Once that is done, set the dial to 'beacon,' and stand back at least ten feet. We will arrive within sixty seconds. Be sure to destroy this note at your earliest opportunity. Thank you for your assistance. – ARGO."

There was an outlet in the station wall, set just above the desktop. Jason yanked out one of the plugs in it and plugged in the globe; leaning close, he found the dial setting Argo had requested and matched it. As soon as he was done, Phoebe pulled him by his arm away from the desk until they stood about fifteen feet from the globe, which had already begun to glow whitish-gold, brightly enough to illuminate the room around it.

Jason looked at Phoebe, and she returned his look for a second, before their gazes returned to Argo's sphere. All at once, it became too bright to look at, and was enveloped in an equally bright halo some eight feet in diameter; they both shielded their eyes as a very gentle tremor shook the building.

In moments, the alarms cut off, and the glow lessened, though it did not fade entirely, and looking up, Jason and Phoebe could see why.

The second shadow that had followed Jason from Dayton had become detached from his body, and hovered between him and Argo, who stood hand in hand with Allison near where the globe had been. The shadow dimmed some of the light from the portal, and it was drifting toward Argo, who held a similar globe in his free hand.

Jason looked at Allison; her eyes shone joyfully as she watched the shade drawing nearer to them. Phoebe grasped Jason's hand with both of hers, staring in sheer amazement as the shadow enveloped, and then was absorbed into Argo's body. His expression barely changed, except that his eyes closed briefly, and when it was done, he blinked several times, looking from Phoebe to Jason, and then to Allison. Then, for the first time since they had met him, Argo's face widened into a true smile, and taking a deep breath, he murmured, "she was right, after all."

Jason came closer to them, and said quietly, "Your globe isn't plugged in. I know how much power that must be using. Did you build a fusion reactor, too?"

Argo raised an eyebrow. "Of course. But with the ability to collapse bridges already becoming a viable technology in this timeframe, I'm not about to risk the possibility that some lunatic professor might try to power a larger bridge with a small atomic bomb." He smiled again, and nodded toward Allison. "I've just discovered that I have much too much to lose."

"Why didn't the shadow come to you when we first met you?" Phoebe asked. Jason silently thought that that was an excellent question, and listened carefully for Argo's response.

"Two reasons, I think," Argo said. "One is that Phoebe's safety had to be ensured until this timeline could merge into the target frame. That was a personal consideration, I believe.

"The second is that my analysis of the KOPO and Ius Divinum agencies required the presence of a third entity in order for their configuration to remain stable. Without that steadying force, internecine attrition would have felled this country's government decades before now. It was my intention that you would flush out that third agency, and I am confident that you have done so, though it is not clear to me how. Perhaps someday we will meet again, and we can tell each other the remainder of each of our stories." Argo looked kindly at each of them, and then added, "but we are out of time now. In about three minutes, Allison and I will leave for our next temporal destination, and once we depart, this building will implode. From the alarms we heard at our arrival, I assume that everyone else in the building has left?"

"That's right," Jason answered.

"Then let us say farewell, for now. I believe that we will meet again – soon, for us, but rather later for you, I'm afraid. Live well, my friends." Argo turned to leave, but before Jason or Phoebe could react, Allison ran to Jason and threw her arms around him.

The gesture was affectionate, but Allison was still a Cybwoman, and her affection was physically somewhat overwhelming for him. He managed to keep his feet, steadying himself and grimacing, slightly because of the pain in his back, but in large part for Phoebe's benefit, as she observed the scene with an expression that lay a considerable distance from approval. She rolled her eyes at him, looking away for a moment, as Allison broke away from him, mouthed the words "thank you," and returned to Argo's side.

"Three minutes," Argo repeated. Jason and Phoebe both lifted their hands in a quick farewell wave, before turning of one accord and pelting back up the stairs where they had entered. They reached the side door and ran out, just as the sounds of multiple sirens reached their ears. An armada of emergency vehicles was coming down the main road toward them, and was less than two blocks away.

"Shit!" Jason exclaimed, and together he and Phoebe dashed away from Nesmith Hall, crossing the street in front of it and entering a small commons. They were almost to its far side, and the sirens had closed to a block away, when a terrible rumble shook the ground under their feet.

Both of them knew what that meant. A low brick wall ran along one of the commons paths, built as a retention wall for an ancient live oak that dominated that side of the commons. They dived for shelter behind it at the same time that the exterior walls of Nesmith Hall collapsed inward, and the entire edifice crumbled into a massive pile of broken concrete and twisted steel, completely filling its basement footprint, and burying Bryant's lab beneath it.

Jason and Phoebe, lying on the damp, dewy grass behind the wall, looked out at the giant dust cloud that had formed over the wreckage, and began to laugh almost hysterically. Then they cried, with nearly equal hysteria as they held each other, each reassuring the other that maybe – just maybe – it was finally over.

Postlude

Jensen, Greene, a handful of KOPO agents, and an army of police officers from several nearby precincts had surrounded Williams and Hampton Halls, waiting for Jason Anderson and Phoebe Reyes to show themselves. The mobilization had been the fastest Jensen had ever ordered, and she had been absolutely sure that they would be one step ahead of him.

And the bastard hadn't been there. The buildings were dark, both labs were empty, and there was no sign of either of the fugitives. Jensen had thought that perhaps Anderson might be nearby, and had fanned out several of her people in teams to search the surrounding blocks for any sign of him. Right up until that point, she had felt like she was in control of the situation.

Then she had gotten the word that a fire alarm had been set off in Nesmith Hall, and instantly, she knew she had been outsmarted. Anderson had been targeting a different research project – one that was under IUD control.

Desperate to contain the damage, she and Greene, followed by two carloads of their associates, had driven at truly felonious speeds across the campus, pulling onto the main road passing Nesmith just ahead of the emergency vehicles dispatched to the scene. As a result, they were the closest individuals to the building when it collapsed.

Though the building crumpled almost entirely in on itself, small random chunks shot away from it in all directions, peppering their vehicle; unfortunately for them, this SUV was not armored, and all of its windows were smashed. A rock the size of a nickel struck Jensen in the temple as she sat behind the wheel; instead of hurting her, it seemed to double her fury. She climbed out of their car, trying futilely to wave the dust cloud away from her face, and looked about herself even though she knew it was no good. Either Anderson had gotten clear, and was already away, or they would find his body in the wreckage.

Again.

"GOD-*dammit!*" she shouted again.

After another minute of waving the dust from her face and trying to breathe through the collar of her blouse, she decided that she was better off farther away from the building, and stalked across the rubble-strewn street to the edge of the commons. Instantly, she regretted the decision.

"And what brings you out here on a night like this, Agent Jensen?" a familiar, and distinctly unwelcome, voice asked from behind her.

She whirled, and would have laughed, if she had not been so monumentally pissed off. General Haverhill had somehow decided that it would be appropriate for him to wear sunglasses at the scene. At one-thirty in the morning.

"I released you and Agent Greene in the hope that you would lead me to Jason Anderson," he intoned, his voice deliberately conveying pompous contempt. "Instead, you embarked upon a wild goose chase, which has ended in a significant setback for one of our research programs."

The menacing note that accompanied those last words was unmistakable, and for the first time, she was genuinely afraid. She had acted without consulting her superiors first, and now, to all appearances, she had bamboozled Ius Divinum into looking the other way while one of their major projects was blown to hell.

"General –" she began.

"An action like this runs counter to all of the agreements between our agencies, dating back at least sixty years," he cut her off smoothly. "Since you have – apparently – opted to dispense with standard conventions, you can hardly expect that we will not do likewise with you and your partner."

A chill ran down Jensen's spine. "Greene isn't responsible for this. I am the senior agent."

"Indeed you are," Haverhill's voice was flat, and promised evil. "And if not for one consideration, you would already have been removed from this place."

Jensen held her breath for five seconds, willing herself to remain calm, before answering, "And what would that consideration be, General?"

The sunglasses made his stare seem buglike, and even more menacing. Jensen no longer found them even remotely humorous. His scrutiny lasted almost thirty seconds before he replied, "We know that you got a hit on Anderson in Cincinnati, and that he was with an unidentified male at least twenty years older than he or his girlfriend. Our sources have turned up absolutely nothing on this man. What have you learned of him?"

"Shit," Jensen mumbled, concealing her barely-stirring hope. Haverhill had nothing on the man, either. "I'm sorry, General. If I had anything, this is the time I would give it up, but we hit the same dead end on this man that you did. He's obviously connected, but he isn't one of ours."

"Fascinating," Haverhill replied, sounding much less enthusiastic than the word he had selected, as he looked out at the wrecked building. An uncomfortable silence fell. Jensen longed to walk away, but knew she would be apprehended if she did, and forced herself to remain still and silent.

"Very well, Agent Jensen. You may depart, for now." The General was studying her again from behind those sunglasses.

"Thank you, General." Jensen nodded, and turned to depart.

"Oh, you don't need to thank *me* for this one," he called after her, as she walked away. "That call came from on *high*."

Almost completely unnerved at this point, Jensen returned to her car without looking back again. Agent Greene started to speak, but Jensen silenced him with a glare, and they drove away from the scene, weaving around the emergency vehicles that had fanned out around the building.

JASON AND PHOEBE WATCHED the confusion around Nesmith Hall for a few more minutes, growing increasingly uncomfortable as the damp grass of the common soaked their already-filthy clothing, until Phoebe could stand it no more.

"Let's get out of here," she said, and Jason nodded in agreement. They rose to their feet, brushing off the dew and the underbrush as best they could, and followed the path leading away from Nesmith Hall, out of the commons onto the next street over.

The huge oak tree would have shaded their path in daytime; at night, it made their path almost impossible to see, and even nearby objects were obscured. As a result, they failed to notice the bench set a few feet back from their path, and were startled almost out of their wits when a vaguely familiar voice said, "Where do you two think you're going?"

Phoebe had clutched at Jason when she heard the voice; Jason had turned quickly toward it, but had tweaked his back in the process, and was breathing heavily in pain as he looked toward the shadowy area where the speaker sat.

"I was wondering whether someone was going to turn up and answer that for us," he replied, guardedly. "I was expecting it to be your friend."

"Bootstrap?" the voice laughed, and a small penlight in the man's hand lit up, revealing his blond hair and a not unpleasant smile. "He's a good man, actually. Tells me a lot about things that aren't easy to find out, and smart enough to figure out on his own what I need to know and what I don't. Very useful, and no one ever suspects he's gathering intelligence."

Jason nodded. "So what do you want with us? I take it you're not working for either of these two nutball organizations I've heard about." He couldn't completely stifle a chuckle. "You don't look like you're Illuminati, and anyway, Bootstrap doesn't believe those kinds of institutions really exist."

J.T. laughed. "Not as such, no. At least not the old ones. They come and go over the decades now. Used to be centuries, but that pretty much ended with feudalism, and after a while, every one of these kinds of agencies eventually falls behind the times, and can't compete, and a new one replaces them." He tilted his head, studying them. "Our present outfit is still pretty new, by intelligence standards. You might find it – interesting, to say the least."

"I don't know," Jason answered, trying to keep his tone even. "I think I've had as much of 'interesting' as I care to deal with for a while."

"If you're worried that we're going to have you doing any more time travel, you can relax," J.T. answered reassuringly. "I think you two will probably want to just be home and rest for a while before you even think about anything new."

They considered that, and Jason glanced toward Phoebe. "It's not like I can go back to my old job anymore," he said. "Even if I could, it's too dangerous. Einstein-Rosen bridges are probably something we should stay away from until we can figure out how to prevent the endpoints from being altered."

"We know about that," J.T. replied. "Our tech would definitely interest you. We also know how to detect bridge signatures indirectly."

In spite of himself, Jason was surprised. "You're ahead of where we were."

"Well, we don't have to provide clarity to government agencies, for one thing," J.T. answered. "We're more of a worldwide organization."

Jason looked at Phoebe again. "This might be what we need."

She looked doubtful, and addressed the blond man. "Why didn't you just tell us who you were when you met us in Dayton? You had to know who we were then," she asked.

"We knew you had something you needed to do, and we had a pretty good idea why, but we didn't know what it was," J.T. answered. "And we needed to find out whether we could trust you to act ethically.

"You made sure that building was cleared out before it came down. Not everybody would have done that, but that's the sort of thing we expect. When you leave a trail of bodies, sooner or later, you'll leave one on that trail that someone will be pissed off about, and they'll follow it back to you, and then you got a problem."

"Makes sense to me," Jason said.

Abruptly, J.T. shone the penlight directly at them, strobing it slightly by shaking his hand. Both Jason and Phoebe shielded their eyes, and Jason said, almost too loudly, "hey!"

"Keep it down," J.T. cautioned them. "And I see you lost your extra shadow."

"Yeah." Jason smiled in spite of himself. "I'll kind of miss having it. Did Bootstrap tell you anything about it?"

"Did he ever." The blond man chuckled. "Scared the hell out of him, that did. He kept worrying that shadow would jump up and throttle him."

"It wouldn't have. And it told us we could trust you," Jason added. "If you can give us a few weeks to rest and get our feet back under ourselves, I think this might be our best option."

"That's great. I think you'll be a great fit," J.T. said, standing up and extending a hand to Jason, who shook it, and then to Phoebe, who still looked uncertain.

"Everyone thinks I'm a terrorist. Or a lot of people do, anyway. How are you going to deal with that?" she asked.

"Do you know how many times Bootstrap's been caught riding freight trains?" J.T. asked her in return. When she was silent, he continued, "probably hundreds. And every time the police try to pull his record, he comes up totally clean, so they let him off with a warning or a ticket." J.T. scratched an ear, grinning a little. "In a week or two, the records disappear for those, too. We can do that for you two as well."

Jason and J.T. both watched her as she considered for almost a full minute, before she finally said, "all right. So where do we go for tonight?"

"Jason's apartment's still intact," J.T. said. "He's been on our radar for a while now. Phoebe, when your apartment was cleared out, we sent someone to retrieve your things. They're in storage. We can have them at Jason's place tomorrow, and you two can stay there for now."

"OK. But one last thing," Phoebe said, and she was almost pleading.

"What's that?" came the response.

"Can someone please, please give us a ride home?" she asked, and Jason realized that she was near tears. He put his arms around her as she leaned against him, and nodded to J.T. "Please. We had a rough trip down here. We're both wiped out."

"You got it. I'll drive you myself," he answered. "Anything else you'll need before tomorrow?"

"I think that's it," Jason answered.

J.T. studied them both for a moment, nodding, and turned. "My car's parked on the next block," he said. "You'll be home in ten minutes. You got your apartment key?"

"Shit," Jason said, in a voice too tired to be truly annoyed. His shoulders sagged.

"No worries," J.T. answered, grinning, and producing a key from his shirt pocket, handed it to Jason. "Hang on to this until you can get a duplicate made."

Jason took the key, and together the couple followed J.T. out of the commons, looking forward to their first night at home together in a very long time.

Epilogue

Perhaps when I am all of me
And you are all of you –
When all that we are meant to be
We are, and all we do
Has been completed, you and I
Upon some starlit shore
Might meet, in the great by-and-by
Of our forevermore.
I hope to see your smile again –
So like the dawning sun,
That smile that long is gone.
Perhaps we'll not be two, but then,
Perhaps in worlds that might have been,
Perhaps we two were one.

> *"Perhaps"*
> *4 January 2020*
> *13 September 2021*

Author's Note

THE YEAR OF COVID proved to be monstrous, as my daytime job put me nearly a year behind on writing this companion to Phoebe. I'm not sure what I did to merit having to deal with all of the joys of the pandemic in my final year in Corporate America, but I probably deserved it. At any rate, I won't complain too much. I'm finally retired, and can focus on my true passion – online poker. Wait – no, this. Writing.

Creating *Angel* proved to be both problematic and fascinating, as both the concept of the Gray Angel as a being/thing and its role in the story started as one thing, and evolved into something totally different, dragging me along from what was originally a dystopian Robin Hood tale into a treatise on the infinite multiverse, and how its denizens interact with it. This was not expected, but was not unwelcome, and proved to be both very challenging and great fun to write.

If you've gotten this far, dear reader, then of course you're probably asking – will we see more of Jason and Phoebe, Jensen and Greene, Argo and Allison, or J.T. and Bootstrap? What happens to Mikey, now that Jason's left him unemployed twice? Are the Cybwomen gone forever? What happens to their souls, the essential spiritual component of their composite being? Argo's experience opens a lot of bait cans that I'm not sure yet that I'm ready to use for fishing.

At any rate, this series is not the only one I'm writing, and it isn't even my first one; that would be the *Legends of Starreach Realm*, which has been on hiatus following the release of Monolith (Book One) concurrently with *Phoebe* at the end of 2019. Unfortunately, the original edition of *Phoebe* was rushed into print, and contained a horde of errors that went uncorrected until mid-2021. If you attended CONJuration 2019 in Atlanta and purchased a copy of Phoebe at that time, that's the original. There are only about fifty or sixty copies in existence, so hang on to yours. It could be worth tens of dollars someday.

So – once this book is drawn from its birth waters in late 2021, I will resume work on the second volume of *Starreach*, which will be titled *Sanctum*. This series is weightier than the *Phoebe* series, and takes longer to write (*Monolith* took six years). Thankfully, with retirement, greater experience and fewer commitments to manage, I hope to write *Sanctum* much more quickly than the volume for which it serves as prequel. I also have a concept in play for a series of novellas, based upon a character called Simon the Redsnake (whose descendant made a cameo appearance in *Monolith*) which will be loosely allied with the Starreach universe. We'll see how that goes.

I know – I haven't answered the question. Will there be another Phoebe novel? Sigh. I'd like to write at least one more; they're fun, and I love hiding references to things I've seen or enjoyed in my work. *Phoebe,* of course, has a monster easter egg in it which is fairly obscure – it's unlikely anyone under the age of fifty will recognize it – and Angel has characters who are not people I know, but whose bases are in people I've seen and in things that interest me. I'm not sure where I would draw the material for a third book, but unlike Argo or Allison, I can't see through time – so, for the time being, my answer is a hard "maybe."

Most of the locations in both *Phoebe* and this story are real. The Drome/Station is adapted from the present-day Avondale MARTA station east of Atlanta. The unnamed university where most of the Atlanta characters work is an amalgam of Georgia State University and the Georgia Institute of Technology; by the way, the GSU police department really is one of the best accredited departments in the US.

Hara Arena, sadly, was in the process of disintegrating as this story was written; it was severely damaged by a tornado in May 2019, and could not be salvaged. It was slated to be demolished as of 2021. Having visited it only a few years before the end of its life, I felt rather sad for the place, as it had become run-down and neglected. By the time this story was begun, it looked in reality rather like it did by the end of these pages, and it's a shame it couldn't have been saved.

The casino beside the Dayton railyard, and the Queensgate Yard environs, are relatively accurate in the descriptions. Bootstrap, Jason and Phoebe followed Spring Grove Avenue (which becomes Dalton Avenue) to bypass Queensgate. The abandoned caboose that caught Phoebe's attention is still visible in the street view from Google Earth on Dalton Avenue, right where the road – and the tracks paralleling it – turn east near the Ohio River. I don't know for sure how long it has been there, but my guess is over a decade.

To learn more of a character who might remind you of Bootstrap, check out Hobo Shoestring's channel on YouTube; he is an American original and very entertaining – and informative – to watch.   Another excellent train rider channel is Hobestobe, named for James "Stobe the Hobo" Stobie. Sadly, Jim's no longer with us; riding freight trains or even walking railroad tracks can be terribly dangerous and is definitely illegal, and Stobie lost his life on a rail bridge in Baltimore in 2017. For this reason, I deliberately obscured some details involving catchout locations, schedules and train routes – I don't want anyone trying to ride after reading this story. Having heard the scream of a girl who'd just realized her leg had been cut off by a train wheel, I cannot emphasize enough how much I *don't* want to have that happen because someone thought I made it look fun. It's not. It's a tough life for tough people, and Jason and Phoebe's experience with it, while harrowing enough, was still miles from the even grimmer reality. If you doubt me, look up the F.T.R.A.; while perhaps not as maleficent as portrayed by law enforcement or the media, they are still not people to be trifled with, or taken lightly. It's dangerous out there.

For railfanning from the non-rider's perspective, Jaw Tooth's channel contains wonderful material presented as only he can. He's quirky, but a genuinely pleasant guy – and he and Shoestring are actually good friends.

Thank you for reading. Be well and stay safe. I hope to have something more for you soon!

- MCV   9/13/2021

About the Author

M.C. VAUGHN IS A retired logistics engineering generalist and native Atlantan. He is the author of three novels – *Monolith, Phoebe* and *The Gray Angel.* He currently resides south of Atlanta with his family. When not writing, he is an avid poker player and baseball fan/historian.

M.C. is currently working on the next novel in the Legends of Starreach Realm series, *Sanctum.* It will be the prequel to *Monolith.* Currently there is no projected date for its completion, but he hopes to finish it in 2022.